YOU'VE BEEN SUMMONED

AN INTERACTIVE MYSTERY

LINDSEY LAMAR

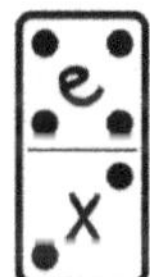

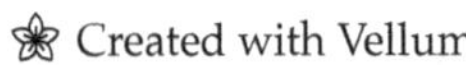 Created with Vellum

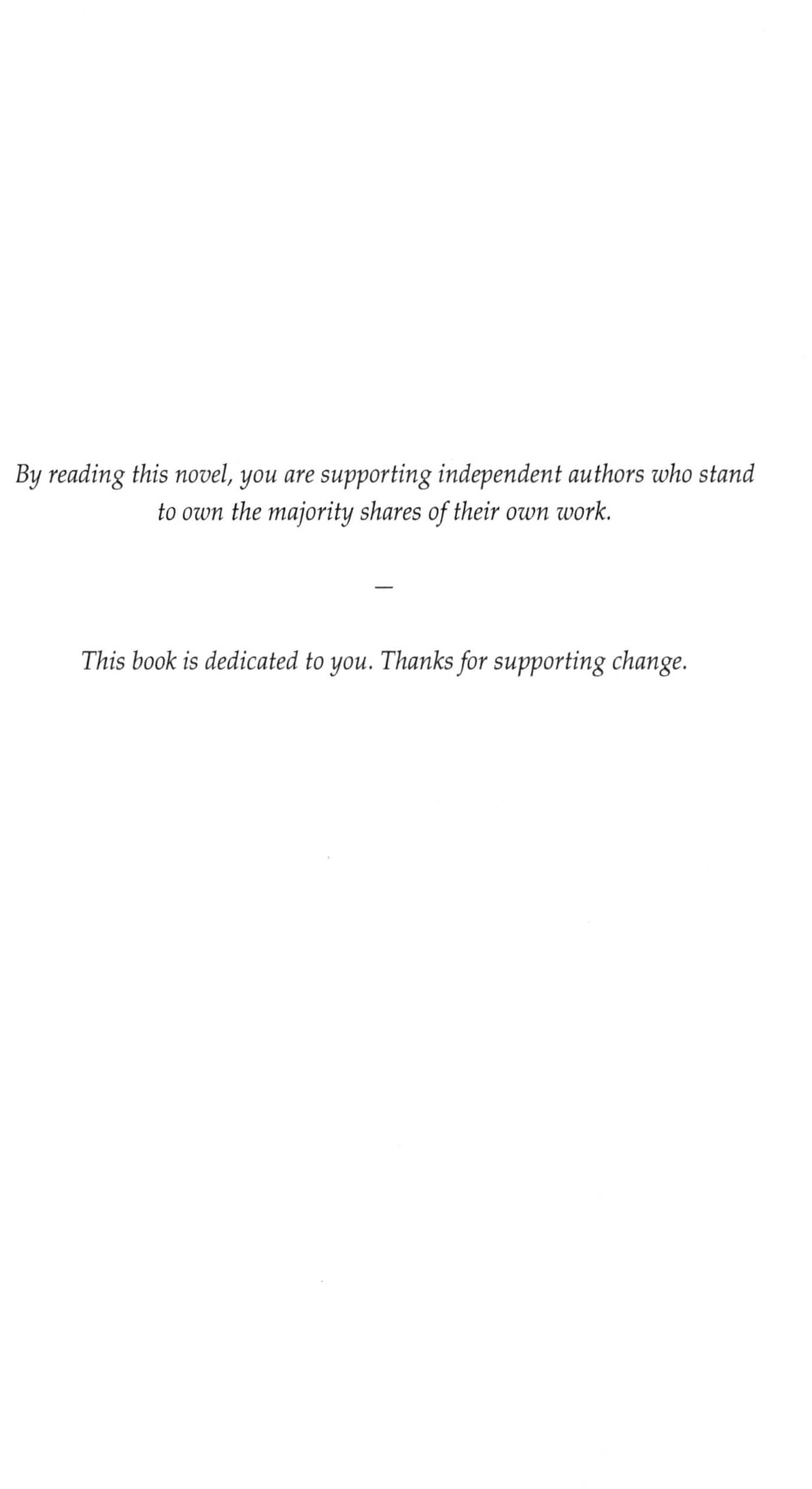

By reading this novel, you are supporting independent authors who stand to own the majority shares of their own work.

—

This book is dedicated to you. Thanks for supporting change.

WEAR YOUR BEST COSTUME
& TELL YOUR WORST SECRET...

YOU'VE

BEEN

SUMMONED

MARCH 4 2023

TO AN OVERNIGHT EVENT
AT THE SOPHOMORE MANOR

HOSTED BY SILLIAN

A LIST OF LIARS

Elle: "The amount of erotically charged jealousy in this situation is astronomical. You should start with the boys. Their frontal lobes aren't fully developed yet, along with their self-control."

Robin: "She was acting so...*weird* leading up to the party. Sill was hiding something. And I think it was something very, very big. Someone spotted the target on her back and *poof!* She disappears. And did you hear about the man with the axe?"

Michael: "We're close-knit. I'd like to call us a friend group. Alcohol is partly to blame here. I mean, it was a party after all, and I know none of us were completely sober. I know that Sill would agree with me right now. If she could."

Alex: "Nobody even likes coming to these parties. A lot of people just smoke weed and hope the time flies by. Not me, of course, considering that would be illegal. But most. Considering everyone who attended was a quote-unquote *'regular,'* I'd be surprised if this was some inside job. It's obviously not. None of us wanted to do away with Sillian."

Cameron: "No. Sillian wasn't upset with any of us... If she was, would she have invited us to her party? Come on now, we're her *best* friends."

SOPHOMORE MANOR'S REVIEWED STAYS

STEPHANIE: *"Pretty cool that they rent out this piece of history as a vacation home. I've always loved old jazz bands. The manor was huge. However, the structure was extremely…odd. The builder seemed unable to keep a straight line going, especially in that garage. Rooms were also shaped oddly. Wood floors were extra whiny. But, gorgeous overall."*

PAUL: *"Every history buff's dream. This place is incredible. Especially if you like postwar celebrities. One night, my wife swore she heard women whispering in our bedroom. Probably the ghosts of Macie and Mary Sophomore. What a riot! We will be back for more."*

AARON: *"No cell service. No wifi. Barely any insulation. I get that this place is older, but seriously?"*

DETECTIVE'S DESK

CASE FILE EIGHT

CASE FILE NINE

CASE FILE TEN

TIME'S UP, DETECTIVE!

CASE FILE ONE

<u>**Case file one contains nine items to be inspected.**</u>
Files should be reviewed in numerical order

- **0.0 Dear Detective** *Urgent Procedural Notice*
- **1.1 Jane's Recount** | March 2023
- **1.2 Jane's Recount** | March 2023
- **1.3 Jane's Recount** | March 2023
- **1.4 Jane's Recount** | March 2023
- **1.5 Mary Sophomore's Diary** | 1944
- **1.6 Police Questioning**
- **1.7 Recovered Newspaper**
- **1.8 Mary Sophomore's Diary** | 1944

0.0: DEAR DETECTIVE

Welcome to PI Inc. Investigations!

It's wonderful you've decided to join our team. We haven't perfected the onboarding process here at PI Inc., so I hope you're eager to get started on an assignment. My plate is full and I need you to take charge.

There's been a weekend full of trouble at a local rental site called Sophomore Manor, and the Richmond police station has contacted our company for outside investigative help. Jane Parks, a twenty-five-year-old local journalist, recently called the police from a costume event to report her twin sister, Sillian Parks, missing. A mixed group in their twenties had been partying inside the rented manor the night before. Upon light police questioning, the attendees appeared to be heavily drinking and very focused on the social dynamics of the setting. Everyone but Jane Parks seemed to believe that Sillian was in no danger and likely stepped out that night to break away from the pressures of hosting a party.

After taking a look around the grounds, the police issued a standard forty-eight-hour waiting period before filing a missing persons report. The cause for concern was, as the police put it, "weak at best."

That was until Jane Parks found the victim's comatose body the following evening. Foul play was immediately suspected.

Your job is to help the police with mountains of recently recovered evidence, from detective interviews to recovered letters. Jane has recounted her story to help with the case. Additionally, we've recovered several historical items from the crime scene, including a diary from Mary Sophomore—the 1940s movie star wife of the manor's original owner. It is worth noting that Mary Sophomore and her sister went missing nearly eighty years ago, last seen at Sophomore Manor.

The police are starting to believe that the historical elements of the location could be at play here and want you to scrutinize the details further. Plenty of historical research and present-day evidence has been put together to investigate before you make a recommendation. Ten files worth, to be exact.

Our intern at PI Inc. has organized the case files in a chronological sequence. I'd suggest you don't skip ahead and stick to the designated order. You can follow the story from there. Don't forget to analyze each suspect's motives and their opportunity. Hopefully, you can find a valid culprit to turn in to the police station. After your first six files, I will check in with any new information I've received.

Good luck then,

Phillip Beacons | CEO of PI Inc.

1.1: JANE'S RECOUNT

HE WAS SITTING across the dining table. *His* dining table. At my studio apartment, you ate your microwaved meal at the countertop. At Dakota's place, there's a dining nook with a Sputnik chandelier hanging over you and your rigatoni like a bad omen.

He thumbed through his phone when the private chef set the plate in front of him. Noodles again. We used to have meats together. Steak, chicken, occasionally veal. But lately, it was like he was scared to lay a knife out on the table between us. As if I'd have his throat before he tucked the napkin into his collar.

"Camping?" I finally broke the silence. It was my turn to speak, after all. "I'm surprised."

Dakota liked to try on hardship like a pair of vintage pants. With flint and paracord in the back seat of the Bronco, he casually tested his scoutcraft against the rugged elements of Mother Earth every other month. Not because he particularly like camping. I don't think that was the case. Thanks to his kin, Dakota had enjoyed nearly every privilege since birth. I liked to think pitching tents in the middle of nowhere, Virginia was his own silent and semi-frequent rebellion.

"Surprised? Why's that, love?" He sat his cell phone down to meet my gaze across the long glass table. I nodded a *thank you* to the cook as he placed a plate in front of me. Dakota only had Chef Lenny on Tuesdays and Thursdays. So, that was approximately when we had dinner together—no more, no less.

"Well, you usually only camp in the summer. Won't it be too chilly this time of year?"

It was particularly cold for late March. I'd noticed that on the mile over there. Usually, I didn't walk to Dakota's, but that night he hadn't sent the cab out for me. And calling one myself wasn't an expense I could've stomached at that moment.

"Work has just been *so* stressful, Jane. The cold is the least of my worries."

"Yeah…I understand." I stared ahead at my untouched plate.

Dakota's ambition had been one of the first things about him I'd fallen in love with. He'd started his own digital journalism company three years before. Never mind that his father had been the only seed round investor, and the company had a six million dollar valuation. That would be beside the point. Or at least it was at the time.

"Here's an idea: why don't you come with me?"

"Camping?" My heart skipped a beat. That could be the recharge Dakota and I needed. But, my sister's event… "Sill is having one of those parties. And I already committed…"

Even I knew it was a weak excuse. My twin had a million parties a year. Always overrun with pissed-off, early-career people.

While I fostered a deep sense of love for Sill, I genuinely *hated* her soirees. She'd held a party the month before because her 23andMe kit had come in. She spat in a test tube and then had a few too many shots. The whole night had been a wasted effort.

My boyfriend waved his fork in the air at me. "You hate those parties. *And* you've had writer's block for a month. Is drinking your weekend away really going to help?"

Ironically, that was what Dakota had been doing for the past four.

"Well…is camping?" Even though the conversation had nothing

to do with my sister, I couldn't help but theoretically defend her festive habits.

"I think it might help. Cold air. Snuggling up with me in the rugged woods. Hell, you can journal longhand. Write a think piece."

I wasn't the uppity type. Even after eleven months of sleepovers at Dakota's place, I still felt like the foreign object in every room. The vaulted ceilings belittled me as I walked underneath. Egyptian silk sheets slithered across my body like a snake at night. And sometimes the chandelier would flash when I entered the living room; a threatening wink that the condo itself knew I didn't belong amongst such wealth. I'd told Dakota about it once after a glass of wine.

"Ridiculous," he'd said that night. "You're being utterly *ridiculous*."

Dakota and I had spent almost all of our time together in a variety of upscale spaces. It would be nice to strip it all down and equalize the playing field for a change. Trade the Egyptian silk for a sleeping bag and the chandelier for some moonlight. My heart skipped a beat at the camping daydream.

"I'll have to see. With my sister's party and all." I shrugged off my uncertainty. "But I think I can manage it."

Dakota stared at his plate blankly, avoiding any eye contact. "So you'll come with me? Yes or no, darling."

I picked up my fork for the first time that night and pushed it across my plate.

"Yes," I said, deciding forthright, feeling somewhat proud of my decisiveness. I reached for my glass of wine in a moment of sophistication. Except, I missed a drop, and it fell to the center of my blouse, as red as a bloodstain.

Dakota winked at me across the table with a serpentine look. Refrigerated chills crawled through my spine, right up to the center of my head. My eyes started to water as I held his stare.

"Is it cold in here to you?" I asked across the table, dismissing the witnessed creation of my new stain. Nice shirt, too. One of my only satin blouses. I couldn't afford to replace it.

"I suppose it is a bit chilly. We can't have that." Dakota craned his neck around the room. "Chef Lenny! Chef? Could'ya crank up the heat? Jane's got visible goosebumps."

I echoed a *please* and a *thank you* to Lenny on Dakota's behalf. Sometimes, he forgot to extend niceties to his staff. He'd say, *"They get paid either way."*

Nearing the end of the dinner, Dakota's cell phone started ringing across the table. He made a big deal of it, shuffling the phone out of his pants pocket with an exaggerated eye roll as he checked the screen.

He silenced the ringer before standing up and walking the length of the table toward me, still chewing the food in his mouth.

"Babe," he said, "I've got to take this work call. It's my breaking news guy in Canada. You know their political unrest situation?"

I didn't, but I nodded anyway. I was in journalism, too; I should've known.

He swallowed the food down before kissing my forehead dismissively.

"Stay as long as you like. I'll call you tomorrow?"

He barely smiled before returning to his phone, not waiting for my response. I watched him as he made his way up the winding staircase with his phone between his shoulder and ear.

Chef Lenny magically appeared to take away Dakota's abandoned plates on the other side of the table. I wasn't done eating, but I stood up from my seat anyway. I liked to take my own plates to the kitchen. Despite the fact that Lenny's job was to cook and clear dinner, I felt a pang of guilt at the idea of leaving another human responsible for the messes I made. Like entitlement had a price tag.

Chef Lenny nodded with a genuine smile as he took the plates from my hands, a subtle rejection of help. "Thanks anyway."

"Of course."

"Will you be back for dinner tomorrow?" he asked, walking toward the kitchen. "I'm making steak frites."

A pang of anxiety reached my chest.

"Tomorrow's Wednesday." Chef Lenny didn't work for Dakota on Wednesdays.

"Oh, that's right. Tomorrow is *Wednesday*," he said over the run of the sink. "Apologies, Miss Jane."

I managed a smile as I turned for my coat and the door. When I stepped outside into the windy chill, a single tear streamed down my face.

1.2: JANE'S RECOUNT

MY SISTER HAD a key to my apartment. Originally, it had been in case of emergencies. If I was out on a work trip or taking a vacation—which I never was—she'd be able to get in and water a lazy money tree or trim the holy basil. Never mind that I had never owned a single houseplant; that had just the thought behind it when I'd given her the spare.

The idea of discretion went over Sillian's head. So coming out of my bedroom that morning to see her sitting on my kitchen barstool, reading a newspaper with bare feet up on my countertop, wasn't a surprise.

"Jesus, Sill. I was in the shower. You couldn't have announced that you came in? I could've been naked." I stood across from her and wrung my wet hair out in the kitchen sink so it wouldn't leave damp marks on my bathrobe.

"We have the same body. I can basically see you naked whenever I want." She didn't look up from the newspaper.

Sill and I were almost identical twins. Her smile was in every photograph I took. When I was window shopping and I caught my reflection, it was her legs I saw, not mine. We laughed the same and cried the same. Except she was better at most of it. All of it. Like she was some upgraded version of who I was supposed to be, leaving me forever stuck as the offspring beta test.

"You in this one?" Sillian finally looked up, pointing at the newspaper.

"No. Work at the paper has been slow."

"I'd say." Sillian waved her hand. "They're not giving you enough at that paper. You need to go work for The Times or something. You'd be good on an advice column, you know."

"Wish I could take my own."

The only thing I had that Sillian didn't was a writing job.

We shared the passion for writing the way we shared everything else in life. In grade school, we'd write stories together in sparkly notebooks about dogs and witches. When we were teenagers, we'd make up pen names, print all the neighborhood gossip out on our father's Xerox, and deliver it to every mailbox within a two-mile vicinity. We'd written thousands of things together; it was how we kept our union.

But when I'd gotten a job as a reporter two years before and she hadn't, our relationship had spun in a different direction. Sill had moved out of town for a sales job and had stopped looking at a career in writing altogether. She'd started pretending that writing was my thing. And while she still showed an unwavering support for me, I could tell it killed some part of her to do so.

I took the empty barstool next to her at the counter. "Any good stories today?"

"Not in the paper." Sill took her feet off the counter and turned to face me, putting some distance between us with her posture. "You know I'd never come over without a good story, though."

"Let's hear it."

Sillian smirked at me from her side profile. The green in her shirt made her eyes sparkle.

"But, business first. Listen, sis, you've *got* to be at my party this weekend. It's truly so important that you're there. Crucial."

"Actually, I've—"

Sillian put a hand up to me. It was trembling. "I know. You don't always love my parties. But this one is going to be different." She furrowed her brows together and continued. "Trust me, trust me, trust me. I've got a surprise for you. And it's big. *Please*. Please-please-please."

"Seriously, Sill?" I groaned. "I went to last month's."

"This one's different. I swear on my Nicolas Cage dining set. You won't regret it."

"You've never even seen National Treasure. I don't know why you bought that dining set."

"The theme for the event is Halloween in March, so you'll need a costume. It's an overnight party—full weekend kind of ordeal. You'll want to bring a bag. And some holy water 'cause the place might be haunted."

I didn't respond.

Since my sister took the sales job, she was always throwing a party or planning the next. Her dual states of existence. She'd have a party for just about anything. The year before, when she'd bought a new car, she'd thrown a farewell jamboree for the old one and forced all attendees to take a shot of vodka inside the parked minivan before it had been hauled away. Those ridiculous parties had become the norm for seeing Sill.

Sometimes, Sill threw a fun gathering, but most of the time, she didn't. They weren't hard to get an invite to, but they were incredibly hard to leave. Sill would spend the majority of the night walking around like Aunt Lydia, chest out and ready to force a good time into you. Eventually, she would get too drunk herself, and that was when you could Irish goodbye out the back door wearing a full-size bear costume or whatever kind of shit Sill had forced your hand at that particular evening.

Except *this* weekend, it seemed there would be no back door.

"It's really that important to you?" I said with a sigh, tugging at my wet hair.

"Really, Jane. It is. You don't have to come to another party ever again. I just need you at this one." Behind a smile, her voice cracked a little.

"You don't mean that."

"I do."

Sill stood up, gathering the items from her purse she'd left all over my counter: ChapStick, hand sanitizer, and mint wrappers.

"That's all you came over for?" Usually, she at least stayed over through a few reruns of NCIS and a press of coffee.

"That's it."

She had a tremble in her voice. One that worried me.

She was almost to the front hall when I asked her if everything was alright.

Without hesitation, she threw an award-winning smile over her shoulder at me, one foot already out the door.

"Just peachy, sis."

She left without telling me that story. I had a feeling I'd have to find it myself.

1.3: JANE'S RECOUNT

A SINKING, churning feeling came over me as I pulled on the sweatshirt. Chef Lenny was a man who didn't talk much. When he did, it almost felt like a confessional.

I played the memory over in my head again.

"Will you be joining tomorrow?"

There was still time to be reasonable about all this. To call Dakota and ask him what he was up to that night. He'd be at the office. It was *"Work-late-Wednesday."* I'd hear his click-clacking on the keyboard and my anxiety would have the opportunity to reverse.

I pulled up our texts on my cell. Three hours since he'd last replied. Not uncommon for a run-of-the-mill workday. He was a busy guy working in a small office. Being on his phone too much would set a bad example. For whom, I didn't actually know. Between him and his two early-thirties male coworkers, I had a hunch that office was practically a boys' club. God forbid Dakota texted back his ol' ball and chain.

The call rang three times before pushing me to voicemail. Call declined, girlfriend rejected. My gut twisted. No follow-up text either.

I placed the phone back on the bathroom counter and stared at the mirror. I'd picked up a black sweatsuit from Walmart that morning. This aesthetic was going around like the plague: matching oversized sweatpants to a sweatshirt, then calling that a completed outfit. I was all for comfortable and practical, but I would've been better off holding onto the high school track joggers I'd frequented years ago.

I hadn't had the cash on me to buy a nicer set. The Walmart sweats were close enough. I'd gotten all black. Black was slimming. And black blended well into the darkened alleyway on the side of Dakota's low-rise condo. At checkout, I'd promised myself it was strictly for loungewear. If it fit right enough, I'd even bring it camping. But, deep down, I knew I'd be wearing it out tonight.

After I tried on the premeditated outfit, I did my best to tidy up my bedroom. If I came home broken-hearted later, the least I could do was prime the apartment for a hermit on a Hallmark bender.

I plugged in the string lights draped over my bed and rechecked my phone. Nothing.

Another ten minutes passed, and the anxiety had been replaced by a punishing daydream of Dakota sitting across from the most beautiful woman I could dream up, steak frites hanging like a dying tulip from the tip of her fork.

She'd be wearing an orange satin dress. One that matched her curly hair. And God, she'd be stunning. Her hands would be manicured to perfection around her glass of chilled vodka.

The idea that there wasn't a diamond ring clinging to one of her fingers would be unnerving. How many half-wits in America had fumbled this woman? She would smile across the table at my boyfriend. Dakota wouldn't stand a chance.

She would twirl her hair between two fingers, raising a frosted glass to her lips. I wanted to die.

The image of this woman had become so visceral and unforgiving that I hadn't even realized I'd already walked halfway to his condo in my bedroom slippers. Drool started to wet my chin from the sleepwalking, which was the closest word for me to describe the happenstance that had just occurred. I finally exited the daydream as my feet turned blue with the cold.

That rarely happened to me anymore. How long had I been out of it?

A man passing by looked me up and down before twisting his face into an expression of disgust. My hair was tied back, tears had strung out my makeup, and I was wearing a Walmart sweatsuit with the tags on. Once you caught sight of my soggy slippers and matching salivation, your judgment had already been fully formed.

I couldn't show up to Dakota's in this state. If he saw me like this, he'd never shake it. But the daydream was so loud between my ears. The idea of leaving him alone any longer with this beautiful human was tormenting me into a literal delusion. I needed to get there. Faster.

Her hair color had changed three times by the time I turned the block. Yet, her beauty remained just as disturbing. Of course he had steak with her now, leaving me the pasta. The cold stung my eyes as I pressed forward.

"'Scuse me, lady." A strung-out boy no older than nineteen stepped into my path and knocked me out of the delusion. He looked like he was on something, eyes darker than oblivion. "Can I bum a joint?"

"Do I look like I have a joint of anything?" I barked back with as much condescendence as I could muster. I didn't want to talk to him too long. Keeping my focus on the daydream gave me some comfort of faux surveillance.

The boy laughed. "You sure do, ma'am."

In disbelief, I pressed on, wringing my fingers together. A remark like that damaged a woman's esteem and surely would catch up to me later. But I was on a mission.

Another tear streamed down my face in the wind. The Virginia weather was relentless this time of year. The smell of wet kept me grounded, reminding me that I wasn't sleepwalking.

I turned the corner to look Dakota's building in the eye. It glared back at me through grandeur windows framed in linen curtains. I even heard the condo laugh as I got closer. Finally, it had evidence for what it had known all along: I didn't belong inside. *How can its dweller be deceived by a woman so lowly?* In my own drool, I'd been caught.

"You're being ridiculous," I whispered to myself.

The lights inside flickered as I got closer. Feeling resilient and damn near insane, I winked back.

My stomach turned with every approaching step. I tucked my hands in my sweatpants pockets and kept my eyes down as I came up on the alleyway. Moment of truth.

Ducking low, I maneuvered my way up toward the window frame. My breath was on pause. The world had stopped turning around me. *What color will her hair be? Will it match her silk dress? How long has Dakota been cheating on me?*

But, she wasn't inside. Of course she wasn't. She didn't exist.

Dakota was at his designated head of the dinner table, a half-eaten steak frites platter in front of him. My breathing felt uneven. Chef Lenny *did* work on Wednesdays.

Next to Dakota were two guys in cable-knit sweaters, similarly aged. I deduced they were wealthy from the sharp edges of their groomed hair and shaven jaws. They had silver laptops sitting next to their dinner plates, but they were instead focused on conversation with each other. Knee-slapping, laughing, and rattling around in their chairs like pirates at sea.

Dakota's coworkers. *This* was work-late-Wednesday.

I swallowed the cold relief in with the air, not realizing I'd been holding my breath since I'd arrived at the window. To think that I'd been worried about *this.* Wow. Hilarious.

As if to double-check, I looked in once more.

Dakota's friends had gathered around his side of the table, analytically moving their hands about as they talked, a serious look plastered on each face. *This,* I realized, *is what businessmen do.* In the driver's seat on the electronic highway, they were all consumed in their blue-light brilliance. They were the architects of their fate. The captains of their own world. Hadn't they been taught that since Lincoln Logs and Legos?

It was natural for Dakota to get caught up in his work. Of course I'd thought something was being hidden from me when Chef Lenny commented on today's menu. From my perspective, Dakota had seemingly forgotten about his cell phone and the girl on the other side of it. From his, he was *just* working.

Silly, silly girl. I nodded to myself. Girls grow up with dolls and houses. We were taught early on to stage-manage our relationships through the windows like God. My reaction was simply hardwired and inevitable.

Of course I trust him. I was acting on instinct. That's all. Nothing more to it than that.

We were okay. Our relationship was *fine*.

The night would've turned around from there had I not seen it.

Forget it, Jane. It's nothing.

But I couldn't do that. Because just beyond the dining table, I caught sight of Dakota's mahogany coat rack. Hanging from the last hook was a pink, furry woman's coat.

And it wasn't mine.

1.4: JANE'S RECOUNT

DAKOTA HAD CALLED me and told me how excited he was to take me camping that weekend. I wasn't even sure what I replied with. I couldn't stop thinking about that pink coat.

It was too small to fit any of the men at the dining table, not that it was likely to their taste. Maybe it belonged to Dakota's house cleaner—a fifty-year-old woman. She would be paid well enough to afford a dyed fur. But no, it was much too juvenile, with its pink and metallic fringe threads peeking out on the seams. That's actually what worried me most about the piece: its excitability. A young and unripened wardrobe choice that screamed: *I'm young, and I'm female, and I'm full of libido.*

Maybe it amounted to nothing at all. Chef Lenny could've brought his daughter in—if he had one. Or an art commissioner might've stopped by to sell a painting. Dakota did buy a lot of art.

I forced the endless possibilities out of my head and returned to my computer screen. I found a footbridge on a hiking path online. A bridge that allowed me to cross into both worlds and attend both the party and the camping trip. It was eight minutes by foot from the manor my sister had rented out. Eleven minutes from Dakota's campsite.

Online, I'd researched the trail that the bridge sat on. The hiking reviews stared back at me:

"Thought I was going to get axe murdered in these woods in broad daylight. Eerie and abandoned."

"Someone needs to come cut down the trail brush. Two out of five stars."

"Cottonmouth snakes. Beware! Trail underwhelming otherwise."

Safety was a luxury that wasn't afforded to girls like me. Girls who can't say *no*. We settle for the trails less traveled. Ask me if I enjoy running into an axe murderer or a cottonmouth. Truly, I can't say otherwise! I'm a car salesman's walking dream.

I sighed audibly in a moment of self-pity before walking over to my coat closet.

I'd divided my suitcase in half. One side for my sister's off-beat costume party. Another for the camping trip with my boyfriend. I made it down to the shoes before my phone rang.

"Hello?"

"*Jane.* How ya doing, kid? Haven't seen ya around the office much. Just that damned Zoom screen. I know we got that *remote* option now, but you know we're a pretty small team. I like to look at my reporters in the eye once in a while. That lease on our office ain't cheap, you know."

Chief Simmons—my boss at the paper. I'd been trying my best to avoid him, given I'd been out of new material for nearly two months. My journalism career had been in a rut for almost a year, but my boss had only started noticing recently. And worse, making comments about it.

I was hoping to get a transfer out to the Pacific Coast branch, where I assumed there'd be more newsworthy action. An upward trajectory of news in Virginia was slim at best. My record lacked a heavy-hitter story that could swing me into a promotion and trans-fer. My outlook on finding one here in Virginia was more than grim. The idea of moving away and starting over was beginning to feel like a teenage dream I was getting too old to recall.

Surely, things would be better in California. But the longer I dated Dakota, the less effort I put into the goal. We wouldn't survive the long distance. We'd snap in two before I even loaded the U-Haul.

"Jane? You there, kid?"

My boss on the line. Right.

"Hi, Chief. God, I thought I sent an email! I caught a stomach bug and teleworked last week. Didn't want to get any of the crew sick. I thought I mentioned it."

I'd helped edit the other journalist's pieces all week, but I didn't have the heart to look my boss in the eye and tell him I hadn't written one of my own.

"Huh. Maybe I wasn't CC'd."

"Any big news up this week?"

My boss grunted. I could barely hear him through the static and that thick beard of his.

"Nothing to write home about. The normal government spending on this. School district drama on that. No headlines on the surface, but you never know what's looming in the waters. Hopefully, a fucking whale."

"That's right. You never know."

"Well, hey. I'll let you rest up and recover from your sickness. Are you feeling better now?"

"So much better. Probably a virus. Just that time of year, I think."

"Well…glad you're feeling better. Wanted to remind you that you're scheduled to be on call this weekend for any local breaking news. I know it's rare around here, but I expect you to be on the scene if we get a breaking call. And fast. The Gazette has been beating us to it the past few months. That's no good. We need to be ready."

This can't be happening. Not now. The campsite and manor were over half an hour from downtown Richmond.

"Thanks for the reminder, Chief."

I went to pack my phone charger immediately to ensure I'd at least be equipped with one tool. If news broke, I'd have to put the gas pedal into the floor to get back into town.

"Good. And I'm serious. I don't care if you show up to the scene in your goddamn pajama pants. As long as we get there first. That Gazette needs to remember who's broken this town's news for *twenty-six* years."

I swallowed hard as he continued.

"Maybe God will throw ya a bone this week. A big story is just what you and I need. Sit tight. And pray for news in that forecast, kid. We need it like rain in a drought."

The phone clicked. I laughed in disbelief.

"What could go wrong this weekend?"

1.5: MARY'S DIARY

1944

IN NEW YORK, on the opening night of my last picture, I thought of my mother.

My star had risen. Sister and I had climbed the ranks of Hollywood playing the dumb blondes, the hopeless romantics, and finally, the femme in *femme fatale*. And when the curtain had closed, we got to wipe the soot off our skirts and walk home. Draw a hot bath. Our names remained in lights.

But my mother would always be dead. Dinner on the dining table in front of her with a butcher's knife in her throat. She was frozen bloody in her onetime headline.

It was no secret that filming *Violent Queens* had messed with my head. I hadn't played a murderer before. Getting cast as one had put my name at the top of the marquee. But it had also dangled my mother's mysterious existence in front of my nose like a carrot. A woman who had known what it was like to kill. A woman with a romance for violence, who would've prided her gory death in a trophy case. I had studied her existence as much as I could to be fit for the role. I let her ghost occupy my body.

My twin sister, Macie, had started to notice.

"Mary...we ought to take a break from these kinds of movies.

You're not acting right ever since they put you in this role. We can tell Sandy that we want romance scripts."

We were in the drawing room smoking cigarettes before the picture. Macie was sitting in the velvet armchair. I sat by the fireplace on the floor.

"I haven't played a mad-woman, but I don't think it's supposed to…" Macie let her voice trail away. She'd been cast as my sister in the movie. As usual. We were the only identical twins in film. The writers got a kick out of the possible storylines that could come from twins. Double this and twofold that.

In *Violent Queens*, my character killed Macie's character's husband because I was unmarried and jealous. I wanted her all to myself. Comical on the surface, but it was the most potent role I'd ever played.

"What was that now?" I asked seconds later, finally catching up to the question.

Macie shot me those concerned doe-eyes of hers. She always got the part of the dumber girl. The sweeter girl. The more agreeable girl. I'd usually get the role as her opposite.

Even with eyes the same size, the same color, the same shape—it was never mistaken that there was something darker in mine.

"You're just not acting normal. Something's different this time," she said. "I need you to have your head about yourself."

"I'm alright, Macie."

Our manager, the only female manager in the States, had put us in matching dresses and heels for the movie premiere. She'd stuffed our breasts with papery cones and fitted tight belts around our waists. Hollywood was good at doing that sort of thing, turning the little girl next door into a bosomy and sultry sensation. Macie and I had succumbed to Studio Four's powers at age fifteen. At the time, it felt like a bestowed magic. Eventually the magic transformed into a stolen identity.

Sandy came to shoo us out of the drawing room and onto the stage for the New York premiere of our picture. I preferred the studio's Hollywood theater, but the war was picking up and New

York dominated the manufacturing industry. The city had trans-formed into a headquarters for servicemen and three-piece suits alike.

After the premiere, Macie and I returned to California on a Star-toliner.

"I told Sandy," Macie whispered in my ear.

We had to talk in hushed tones when we traveled. The plane was filled with businessmen traveling from New York. We didn't trust the high-end industrialists. Gossip was a bartering chip in their biz. They were well connected enough to put a dent in our reputations.

"Told her what?" I asked, lighting a cigarette between my teeth.

"That we want more romance scripts. Noir might not be for us."

"And how'd Sandy reply?"

"She said she'd never heard such cock-eyed crap in her life."

I exhaled a mouthful of smoke. That was something Sandy would say. As one of the few female talent managers in the country, she had less flexibility than the men. Sandy had to ride along with the trends to survive. And noir was only going up in film's popularity.

"She did say there was one thing we could do, though. To take a break from the acting scene."

I pushed my sunglasses up on my nose and looked around for snooping ears before I responded.

"You stop with all that now. I don't need a break."

Macie shook her head. "You do, Mary. The job is making you dizzy. I can feel it."

"It was *Violent Queens*. Made me wonder about mom."

Macie slapped my knee in dismay. "Don't you dare go wondering about our mother out loud. It's dangerous."

"We need to keep Sandy happy, sister." I ignored her and took another drag. "She's managing our cash well enough right now. Her husband's an honest guy. We're not having to dance around in our unmentionables for a paycheck."

Sandy's husband held our money in his bank account since we

couldn't do it for ourselves and didn't have husbands to do it for us. He paid us honestly and on time. The arrangement was about as good as they came. We'd had worse in the past.

Macie stopped responding and went back to her book. Our conversation wasn't over yet. I knew she'd bring it up again.

"What's the one thing?" I finally asked her.

"How do you mean?"

"Sandy said there was one thing we might be able to do. What is it now?"

Macie closed her book and looked straight at me. By the look in her eyes, I knew I wasn't going to like what she had to say.

"The studio might like it for us to linger around with some other famous men. Both of us at the same time. Fans would like it. The papers would love it. We'd get some paid press. Sandy said we'd likely grab enough cash to take a long vacation."

I gritted my teeth. Macie and I hadn't dated much. And what I meant was that she'd dated some and I'd dated none. We were far too close as sisters for a man to have room to breathe in a real relationship with either of us.

But I liked the proposition of a vacation. And I knew it was a good career move.

"Maybe," I whispered back.

But when Sandy introduced us to The Sophomore Brothers, two siblings turned famous musicians; I failed to recall why I would've ever disliked the idea in the first place.

1.6: POLICE QUESTIONING

DB: "It's presently 18:53 hours on March 5th, 2023. I'm Detective Bruno, here to interview Jane Parks at the Richmond Police Department. This is for Case number 2023-555. Also present in the room is Doctor Eli Dunn of the Richmond Emergency Hospital. Jane, I want to go ahead and get some basic info down that we want to get ironed out for the report. Your first name is spelled J-A-N-E and Parks is spelled P-A-R-K-S, correct?"

JP: "That's correct, sir."

DB: "And you are the sister of the victim, Sillian Parks?

JP: "Yes. We're twins."

DB: "Alright. Thank you for meeting me here today, Jane. We have a lot to cover, considering you were the one who called us to report Sillian missing and the one who found her body."

Sniffling sounds

DB: "A little bit of background on yours and Sillian's upbringing, if you will?"

JP: "We grew up in a loving home. We're the only children. Our parents were much older when they had us. I think that made them a little clueless about our whereabouts and choices growing up. Mom passed when we turned eighteen. And Dad's, *gosh*...in his seventies already? He's the epitome of a nice old man. Always has been."

DB: "Any recent trouble at home?"

JP: "No. Not at all. Mom was a hero to us. And we love our dad. I mean, just adore him."

DB: "How is your relationship with your sister?"

JP: "We're best friends. Always been like that. The only reason I don't see her every day is because we work in different towns now. Otherwise, we're practically inseparable."

DB: "And you're a local reporter? Is that your only job?"

JP: "Yes, sir. It's my only job."

DB: "What do you know about The Sophomore Manor—the party's location?"

JP: "I know that it belonged to that jazz duo, James and Josh Sophomore, back in the, uhm...1940s? Fifties? And their movie star wives—Macie and Mary. I think that's what they were called. To be honest, I didn't know much else about it until, uhm...well, until I found my sister."

DB: "Do you have any reason to suspect, or any prior calls or conversations, that might suggest your sister knew more than meets the eye about Sophomore Manor?"

JP: "No prior conversations, no. But there was a lot of tension and weirdness about her leading up to the party. She was acting odd. And after I found her, I knew she was looking for something in that house. Something dangerous."

1.7: RECOVERED NEWSPAPER CLIPPING

| AUGUST 2022 |

GHOST LOVERS AND HISTORY HUNTERS WILL FLOCK TO RICHMOND FOR TOURISM

Vol 13-15   August 2022

AFTER 81 YEARS OF PRIVATE OWNERSHIP, THE HOME OF THE LEGENDARY 1930S & 40S MUSICIANS: *THE SOPHOMORE BROTHERS* IS NOW OPEN TO THE PUBLIC AS AN VACATION RENTAL.

After 81 years, The Sophomore Manor is open to the public as a vacation home. Hit 1930s musicians and brothers James and Josh Sophomore lived in the family-owned manor at the peak duration of their career. They wrote several hits such as '*Airbus to 7th Ave*' inside of the Victorian home.

The brothers lived there until they mysteriously vanished after speculation followed them around their wives possible murders, a famous case that remains unsolved. Heirs of the famous family finally decided to sell the home. There are several rumors around haunting findings inside of the manor, all with no evidence. But...who knows? Now its visitors can explore the secrets themselves in Richmond, Virginia!

Image by: [Jeffer Berrire x Pexels] via Canva.com
Image is not intended for standalone use.

1.8: MARY'S DIARY

1944

THE NEXT MONTH, Sandy arranged for James and Josh Sophomore to take us to *The Rhythm Room* in Los Angeles. The jazz club was a downtown hotspot where we were all likely to be recognized, but James and Josh didn't seem to care. They'd flown in to play a gig there the following night and wanted to stop by beforehand and *'survey the acoustics.'* Mine and Macie's invitation to join seemed more of an afterthought than a prospect.

James and Josh arrived at our building in different cars at the same time. In retrospect, this was *the* defining moment for both of the relationships. Since we hadn't met and two pairs were involved, there was no precedent over who would date whom.

Macie and I had shrugged at one another as we stood in the apartment's lobby. The boys stood outside their respective vehicles near the road, each with a bouquet of white flowers. Their suits were both gray, sunglasses both black. Each brother had a tall build and blonde hair. From afar, they even looked the same age. In a game of spot-the-difference, the only obvious variation was that one of their convertibles was red while the one behind it was baby blue.

The fact that I went for the car at the top of the driveway rather than the car parked behind it meant I'd selected to be Josh's love interest for the evening. And then for the rest of my life. Sometimes, even the most calculating women left their fate to be plucked out of a hat.

"For you…"

"Mary," I said politely. There was no way he could've known.

"For you, *Mary*. I'm Josh."

Josh held out the flowers as I walked up to his car. It was almost boring how gorgeous Josh was. Detached cool eyes. Strong jaw. I'd come to find out that I'd undoubtedly selected the looker out of the pair.

"Will there be a vase for me at The Rhythm Room, or will these die on the drive?" I asked as I received the flowers, a tease in my tone. It was summer in Los Angeles. Much too hot to leave them in the car for the evening and expect them to survive. I could've run them upstairs into a vase if I wanted to, but I didn't want to ask Josh to wait. It would've felt girlish to be so eager to preserve a bouquet from a man I didn't know. A man who'd been offered up to me as nothing more than a business deal.

"Those flowers will certainly die on the drive." Josh opened my door, and I stepped inside. Then he quickly hopped over the other side of the car without opening the door and plopped right into the driver's seat.

Once the car started moving, I dropped the bouquet out of the window and onto the road.

"Now, darling, why'd you go and do that?"

"Shouldn't they be spared from a slow and miserable death?"

Josh Sophomore chuckled at me but kept his eyes on the road. I took a peek in his rearview mirror to see Macie in the car behind us, smelling the flowers in her hands with a stupid grin across her face. Her driver, James, had already run his tires over the bouquet I'd thrown out the window. A quick and respectable ending.

"How old are you, Mary?"

"Twenty-four."

"Twenty-four where?"

I laughed. "You like your ladies younger than twenty-four?"

"Older. My last girl was thirty-one. It was dynamite."

"And how old are you?"

"Twenty-six."

"Then you're not looking for a dame. You're looking for a mother," I said with a smile in my voice.

He didn't respond.

When we got to *The Rhythm Room*, the four of us took a corner booth. Josh sat opposite me, with Macie on my side and James beside her.

Macie's new companion was twenty-two, and up close, he looked it. Macie had brought her flowers into the club from the car, and when James fetched the waitress for a vase and some water, Josh gave me a smug look across the table.

After ordering a round of Manhattans, Josh and James stood up from the table to survey the stage they'd be playing the following night. Macie and I watched them step in between dancing couples, looking up and down the room. We let them get a safe distance before turning to each other.

"So…" Macie tucked her hair behind her ear and turned to me. "What's Josh like?"

"I don't really know. He seems a bit withdrawn."

"Right. They must be worried about the show tomorrow."

I took a sip from my drink and nodded without saying anything further. She was blushing, fidgeting with her hands on the table. I could tell she wanted me to ask her what she thought of his younger brother. While I found it pitiful, I went on to ask her.

"Oh, Mary. He's so polite. He's got a real nice demeanor. An innocence, maybe? You'd think it'd be emasculating, but it isn't."

"He's twenty-two. He hasn't grown into his drawers yet."

Macie frowned hard. "Yeah. Maybe that's it."

When James and Josh came back to the table, we ordered another round of drinks. Somewhere in between the cocktails, we eventually had dinner and desserts. And as much as I wanted to hate them, I couldn't. They were nice and respectful men. Neither of them probed us with personal questions or brought up our bawdier pictures—the way most men did. We simply talked the night away as if we were all just ordinary people. And that was everything.

James was looking around the room awkwardly after they'd paid the bill. Like a yarn ball of nerves. Eventually, he turned to my sister.

"Macie, would you like to take a walk outside with me?"

My eyes went narrow at her. She gave me an understated wink before she looked up at him with those willful doe eyes. He took her flowers with them, cradling them like a baby.

As they walked out the bar's front doors, I realized I had no idea what that wink meant.

"So, Mary." Josh leaned back in the booth across from me. "You think you and your sister might come see us play tomorrow?"

"Maybe we would."

"You seem like the type of woman I can be honest with. I like that. So, I'm going to be honest with you."

He leaned forward over the table and loosened his tie. I didn't know if he was making a pass at me or an avow.

"Dottie broke my heart." He took out a cigarette after he said it, creating a long pause. The way he had said *'Dottie,'* as if she was some common denominator in our social circles, led me to believe the tabloids had gotten ahold of the relationship he was referencing. Like the story should be common knowledge to me. But it wasn't. Before our date, I'd never read a thing about him.

I decided to play along.

"Did she now?"

"She was older. She'd seen the world. I met her in New York after she'd spent a year in Peking...doing God knows what. Dottie was—*is* a big socialite in New York. The parties she threw. Hell, I think they put James and I on the map. We played for the president in our own backyard. The woman knew everyone who was anyone."

Josh chuckled, reminiscing his good times alone.

"That's nice of her." Despite my lack of lust over the man, I still found it to be quite rude. Out on a date and bringing up old beaus. I was growing annoyed.

"What I'm saying is, I proposed to Dottie twice. And I'm a single man." He lifted his left hand to me, showing his bare ring finger. "She got married last month to one of them royal elites. A Brit. Not even three months after I'd proposed the second time."

His blue eyes shined a bit brighter. A glass coated over them. *This grown man might be about to cry right here in the booth.*

"The way she left me… I wouldn't be good enough for a woman like you. Not yet," he finally said. "I'm sorry. One look at you and I wish that I was."

"Ahh." I nodded, impressed by his honesty. "You know, I'm not searching for a sweetheart, either."

The truth came easily. I wasn't at a place in my life where I could fall in love with anyone. I never had been. Survival capitalized every square inch of my brain. Even though we had money now, I wasn't naïve enough to think Macie and I could care for ourselves forever. We couldn't even hold our own cash. Acting was a great endeavor. But our prime couldn't last forever. And all I wanted was a vacation with my sister. Some time to start feeling like myself again.

And maybe, just maybe, a friend to trust as my own.

"Really? The most beautiful woman on this side of The Colorado isn't looking to settle?" Josh raised his eyebrows at me in surprise before putting his lips to his cigarette.

He was charming. He really was. And he wasn't hiding anything. I think I already adored him a bit just for that.

"My agent says if I want an acting break, I need more box office."

He offered me a cigarette, and I accepted.

"So…" He lit my smoke. "You need a man to hold? For the cameras."

"For the cameras." I nodded.

"My manager says mine and James's ratings are down since the

Dottie split. Fewer parties, less press. Nobody's as tuned in as they were before. And we're about to put out a new single in a few months."

"That's no good," I said.

"No good at all."

"Tell me, then, if it's beneath you," he said. "A relationship for the cameras."

I laughed genuinely. "Oh Josh, you should know there's little beneath me."

"And Macie and James?"

"She's in on the plan. If he is."

He put out his smoke on the tray between us. "It's fantastic."

And the idea of it really was.

He held my coat for me and opened my car door. Nothing short of a gentleman, even with our parameters on the table. The honesty between us felt so sudden and sacred. I couldn't help but respect him, despite how manipulative the nature of our deal might've been. We were a team then. Us against the world.

"So we'd never be just a little more than business partners? Behind closed doors, that is," he said as he walked me to my apartment building.

"Never say never." I chuckled as he kissed my cheek goodbye.

"I'll take it." He gave me a wink and then turned back toward his car.

I was so wrapped up in the coolness of Josh Sophomore, the honesty that no man had ever regarded for me, that I'd failed to notice that Macie had never come home from that walk.

END OF FILE ONE

Well done, detective! You completed your first file. Below are checkpoints to keep you on track to uncovering the right suspect:

- **HINT:** When reviewing Mary's Diary and Jane's accounts, keeping a list of people's career paths might be a good idea. Even people who might not be the main characters in the story.

- **CONSIDER:** Jane reflects on her twin's past events throughout the entire case. Perhaps Sill has a pattern when it comes to hosting?

- **TIP:** Read to enjoy first, then proceed with analysis. Memory recall is maximized if you're having fun.

- **FUN FACT:** *The Rhythm Room* was a popular WW2 Jazz Club that shut down in 1972. It has since been restored and is open to the Los Angeles public under the same name.

Be sure to take notes or annotate your book when you come across noteworthy information. Staying organized will help you place the right suspect behind bars.

CASE FILE TWO

Case file two contains nine items to be inspected.

Files should be reviewed in numerical order

- **2.1 Overheard Conversations**
- **2.2 Suspect Profiling**
- **2.3 Jane's Recount** | March 2023
- **2.4 A Left Behind Letter**
- **2.5 Mary Sophomore's Diary** | 1944
- **2.6 Jane's Recount** | March 2023
- **2.7 Mary Sophomore's Diary** | 1944
- **2.8 Jane's Recount** | March 2023
- **2.9 Rental Brochure**

2.1: OVERHEARD CONVERSATIONS

Michael: "So we know that my girlfriend isn't here. We know there's blood on the floor. And we also found out that *she's* the liar. She might have gotten into something terrible. But even if she did, how are we supposed to know? Sill's been lying to us. Or me, at least."

Elle: "Is she the only one who's lying, Michael? Maybe you've not been honest with her either... Just a hunch."

Michael: "Oh, shut up, you. Please. A little speculation from you guys and Jane will be framing me for the murder of my very-much-alive girlfriend. I get that Sill's her sister, but she's acting downright crazy."

Alex: "Probably because she found a pool of fresh blood on the ground and her sister went missing. Seems like a cause for concern to me."

Michael: "*Missing* is such a strong word. Look, I want to find her. But after finding out she's been lying to me... I'm not in the most mournful mood. We're going to find her. She will be fine. And I'm sure she'll run straight past me into Alex's arms when we do."

Alex: "I'll start doing pushups to prepare for the big moment."

Michael: "I'm gonna beat your ass, you…"

2.2: SUSPECT PROFILING

OFFICIAL GUEST LIST

IMPORTANT PARTY GUESTS

JANE PARKS

- Sister of Victim
- Costume: None

ROBIN REED

- Roommate of Victim
- Costume: Gypsy Witch

CAMERON CORTEZ

- Friend of Victim
- Costume: Waldo

MICHAEL MULLINS

- Love Interest of Victim
- Costume: Gatsby

ALEX ANSLEY

- Victim's Ex Partner
- Costume: Indiana Jones

ELLE EWING

- Roommate of Victim
- Costume: Carmen Sandiego

2.3: JANE'S RECOUNT

THE DRIVEWAY WAS like something out of a whodunnit. A dirt road mix-matched with ornate white fencing embellishing acres of overgrown, weedy pastures. A few bored cows scattered the land alongside the road. Typical of rural Virginia, but somewhat odd for the area, which was seemingly deserted. *How did my sister find this place?*

The manor gave quite the impression. Two-story windows were framed in washed red brick, while gray wooden shingles on the roof had weathered and faded in abnormal places. There was a dead fountain in the middle of the asphalted walkway and leafy green trees lined up like soldiers guarding the entrance. The sight of it made me think Professor Plum and Colonel Mustard just might be inside, killing each other with candlesticks. The building itself had to be over a hundred years old. Contrasted by rain clouds scattering the sky, an eerie feeling came over me as my cab driver put the car in park.

A group of Sillian's friends were sitting outside around the old fountain. Michael (my sister's on-and-off boyfriend) was perched at the top of the group, with Sillian's roommates (Elle and Robin) on either side of him.

"Jane!" Michael walked over and greeted me at the pitch of a southern sorority girl as I approached the giant home. "You're making this weather look good."

"Hi, Michael." I forced a smile. Sill started dating him last year, and he quickly became a repellent of all things good in Sill's life. They'd broken up too many times to count. Yet, there he was. Still around.

He pulled me into an embrace. His Polo golf shoes were soaked with water; it had been raining on and off all day. Everything was dreary out, yet he still wore sunglasses. He was very suspicious, but it was hard to find an exact reason, given how tactful he usually remained.

I quickly pulled away from him. "I wasn't expecting to see you, Michael! You and Sillian are good, I take it?"

Michael took an over-exaggerated drag from an e-cigarette before letting out the smoke with a friendly smile. "She's keeping me around."

"I must be behind because last I'd heard, she dumped you."

"Oh Jane…we had an argument. What couple doesn't argue?" he replied in a comical tone. "It's not all fun and games, you know."

"Right. Well. I'm glad you worked it out then."

There was a long-lasting awkwardness in the air—a forced friendliness that you could often find between the semi-acquainted barista or grocery bagger at your local store. Like that, but worse.

"Work still going good?" he said, offering a subject change.

I shuddered. "Great."

"You know my mom's a big executive in publishing. Hard job. You writers are obsessed with your work. Have to be."

I laughed to fill the silence, unable to fend off the career panic I was experiencing. Michael seemed to notice.

"Go along now. Say hi to the others. I won't hog you." He gracefully tapped me on the back, as if we were old soccer buddies. "I've got to go and get something out of my car."

Michael stepped aside to clear a path toward Sillian's roommates, who were sitting cross-legged and leaning into one another.

It looked like they were knee-deep in a puddle of good gossip. On a reporter's instinct, I carefully inserted myself into the conversation.

"Michael's back already? How many breakups is this?" I walked up to Elle and Robin, ready to perform. When digging for information, it is good to build camaraderie with the other party. Offering these girls a statement would show I was prepared to team up. That I could already confide in them. Chief Simmons had taught me the tactic on my first field interview. It worked well on women who had an inkling for socialite drama. Opened them up like a can of worms.

"Oh, Jane!" The pitch pierced my eardrum, sharp as a knife. "Jane, it just feels like it's been forever since we've seen you." Robin pulled me by the elbow to sit next to her and Elle. "We have so much to catch up on. I want to know how you've been. What new frontier have you been conquering lately? By the way, I love the new hair. Brown? Great!"

It wouldn't have been Robin if she hadn't tacked on a thirty-second intro. I smiled and casually greeted Elle, the quieter of the two.

"Yes. Brown hair. I went back to my roots." It was the first time Sillian and I hadn't had the same hair color. We'd been dyeing our hair platinum since high school.

Robin herself had light red hair. Nobody knew if it was natural or not, as it seemed to change hues with the season. And while she probably wouldn't care if we did, no one ever asked.

"You are just too funny, Jane! A free spirit. You know, I thought about dying mine black when I got the news I was *fun-employed*." Robin went on, ready to hear herself talk. Elle was twiddling her thumbs awkwardly on the other side of her. A smog stench stuck to them, which was odd because I knew neither of them smoked.

"Holding a job in this economy is not easy," Robin said. "Honey, it was a total drag. I almost went on one of those sugar daddy sites until I got hired on as an office girl at the dealership. Working with those men—those dirty, greasy men—well, it might even be worse than being unemployed. I'm *so* much happier as a jewelry dealer."

"Yeah. Wow. I'm so sorry about that, really. God, this economy. Everything's been going to shit. Rent is through the roof. Money is worrying us all." I swallowed hard at the reality that I could be the next in line for *'fun-employment.'* The urge to check my phone heightened. I was supposed to be working this weekend.

"Hey, Robin. Uhm…sorry to change the subject, but do you know where Sill is? I haven't seen her yet."

Robin's soft face hardened at the question. Her eyebrow arched into an expression I didn't understand but felt perhaps I was supposed to. Robin looked to Elle for some confirmation to continue. Elle nodded.

"Oh, honey." Robin took a big sigh before laughing out of the corner of her mouth. "You are so far behind."

Robin was a particularly odd person to be around in social settings. When you were next to her, she felt like your best mate. And when you weren't, you realized you'd stuck your nose in someone else's business. Netflix could probably sign her for any reality show under the sun, and she'd create enough drama to get it renewed.

Elle leaned over Robin's lap toward me, cupping the profile of her mouth like a schoolgirl, ready to pass along a secret.

"Your sister is on the back patio…with *Alex*."

"What? Alex?" My sister's ex-boyfriend.

"Yeah," Robin said. "I think she invited him half in pity and half because she still loves the guy. She didn't think he'd come. Poor baby. You know Sill. Everyone's always got to be invited. And if you're invited…you come."

It was true. Once you started coming to these parties, it was an unspoken rule that you had to *keep* coming.

I failed to understand why my sister would invite Alex and Michael to be in the same universe, much less the same house, for an entire weekend. Many times in my life, I'd wished for twin telepathy. Sillian wasn't the type of sister to pour every detail of her life out to you on a silver platter. At least, not purposefully. But at that moment, it would have been particularly helpful.

Robin, Elle, and I were all staring at our feet, unsure what to say next. It felt like they had more to tell, but an invisible boundary prevented them from going any further on the topic. They likely had something more to say about my sister.

To my good fortune, a roll of thunder echoed around us, so loud that it made all three of us jump. A shrill wind tunneled overhead as the sounds of a looming rainstorm shrieked through the air.

"Oh, my." Robin's eyebrows raised. "I think I left my Louis bag out back."

While Robin and Elle scattered away, I took out my phone, almost hoping to see a text from Dakota. Instead, I saw the 'no service' sign. *Great.*

Inside, the mansion held a delicate, goth feel. One that gave you a false sense of nostalgia. The architecture appeared so beautiful it was almost saddening: a dying art form withering away in age.

Red art déco paper was plastered against the hallway walls, the design on the paper barely visible under the light of a medieval chandelier that only held candles. As I walked across them, I knew the dark wooden floors would creak.

While jaw-dropping in its elegance, something felt off about the place. Walls randomly receded non-linearly just to pop back out again a few feet further. Structurally, the builder hadn't aimed for a seamless look. Odd choice given the century the house was built in.

"Sillian?" I called out as I stepped into the great room into an explorative state, hoping to link up with my twin. My voice echoed on each main room wall. "Sill? It's me, Jane."

I turned the corner to see my sister through Victorian windows, propped up delicately in a rusted bistro chair that faced Alex. His long body barely fit in the seat opposite her and his eyes were full of a classic Aries pout. The tall hedges encasing the patio made even a six-six Alex look small.

The wind was blowing through their hair dramatically. Dampness covered their faces like a serum as the storm continued to brew. They were screaming at one another, but I couldn't hear a thing.

Alex had made my sister dizzy with love since they'd first met four years before, enchanting her on page one. I'd loved him as a match for Sillian ever since. Much more than Michael. But I knew she couldn't handle the pressure of such a serious relationship. He was an engineer. He loved a puzzle. And he wanted Sillian to be his own solved riddle. The way my sister was, that just wasn't possible.

I took my bag and went for the wooden stairs, trying not to think of my sister's love affairs. I had my own. And I needed to be at Dakota's in precisely one hour, according to my self-enforced schedule. Unfortunately, I'd forgotten a raincoat.

The wind was pounding against the glass windows, and I heard wet footsteps begin to scatter inside. The stairs creaked as I ascended them, subtly enough to make me second-guess if that place might actually be haunted.

The manor's bedrooms appeared eerily, comprised of seven bedrooms with several beds scattered between them. I went on a treasure hunt for Sill's things. Since she had her boyfriend and I had mine just eight minutes away, we wouldn't sleep in the same bed, but we always shared a room. A headquarters for us to get ready, sneak away to, and retreat when we got tired of everyone else.

Growing up, our bunk beds had been chambers of secrets, commerce, and reflection. Sharing a room was like having a built-in therapy office where you could occasionally steal your shrink's clothes. But on the off day, you'd have to be prepared to go to battle 'cause sisters *fought*. Back then, she'd always gotten furious with me for my vivid sleepwalking and I had been annoyed by her awful snoring. Two habits we hadn't grown out of yet, but didn't bother us anymore since we'd moved out and lived separately.

I found her bag propped up inside of a corner en suite with updated purple bedding to match the walls.

On the double sink countertop was a notepad left wide open for all to see and an opened bag of blow-up party balloons. Their latex was red, blue, and green. Definitely not Halloween. My sister never ventured off-theme for a party—the girl was more on brand than Billy Mays. *So, what was with the birthday balloons?*

I moved closer, eying the notepad. Pages had been ripped out, and the writing had water drop splotches. Beside the notepad, there was a letter in my sister's penmanship. I didn't know anyone else who still wrote in cursive except Sill.

Uncertainty swarmed inside me. *Should I read it?* Of course, I shouldn't. My sister would never go through my things. This looked like a letter. And in our day and age, writing someone a letter carries a deadly tone. Nobody did it anymore, so if they did, you knew it was important. Even though I knew better, I picked it up.

A gasp escaped my lips as I scanned the torn page and the words settled in.

How dare she?

2.4: A LEFT BEHIND LETTER

FOUND BY JANE PARKS

I gave you the best years of your life and this is how you repay me?

You're nothing but a l-i-a-r and yes I had to spell it out for you A-l-e-x. You led me on and I'm upset. Just another girl on your roster. To think that I trusted you.

This letter might make you angry. Good. I wish you'd just stay away. From me. For life and then some.

But that will never happen, will it? Because I know what you did. You ___ on Together ___

Sillian

2.5: MARY'S DIARY

1944

"I HOPE YOU LIKE DUST." Macie unlocked the mansion doors ahead of me with a cough waiting at the bottom of her throat.

"Oh, my." I stepped inside the oak-paneled walls. It was as beautiful as I remember, but its allure was less obvious than the dirt that collected over its years of inactivity. "This is mom's furniture. Has no one ever changed it out?"

My mother, Lily Lake, had left behind the family manor in her name when she died. It had taken Sandy's husband several legal battles to get the Virginia countryside estate back under our thumbs. Three years' worth, to be exact.

Before we'd gotten the property back, politicians had purchased the manor as a rarely frequented countryside retreat. Reluctantly, they'd sold it back to us for damn near every penny we'd earned in our lifetime. All of our cash was tied up in the Lily Lake estate and the fees we'd paid Sandy's husband to acquire it.

Land surveyors had warned us it was a dying asset to hold. Especially given the dark history of the manor. But we had an inkling there was more there than what met the eye. We just had to find it.

Macie was dusting off the chairs with her handkerchief, her arm bent over to cover her mouth.

"I think it is her old furniture." We wouldn't remember it, though. Our mother had died before we were even a year old.

"We'll certainly need to sponsor a maid," I said.

"Or a fleet of them." Macie was running her fingers across a coffee table, picking up a line of dirt by her index. "Where should we sit?"

I looked down at my pastel dress. I'd ruin it by sitting down on the furniture. "How about we see the patio?"

The backyard of the Lily Lake estate was grandiose. Even without a housekeeper, it was unmistakably breathtaking. Trees went deep into the acreage. A few old sculptures scattered the grounds. There was an iron conversation set on the covered area near the back door that looked to carry less dust than the seats within. Macie and I both took a seat.

"I think they'll want new furniture." Macie laughed, tilting her head back. There was a light in her eyes that I hadn't seen outside the studio. She looked careless and *happy.* And she wasn't acting.

"New furnishings can be arranged." I managed a smile back at my sister's glowing face, taking a pen and paper out of my bag.

"So new fittings, a household staff— Oh! We'll need a plumber to come out and check the integrity of everything, and then a groundskeeper… What am I forgetting, Macie?"

"The drive up is dreadfully bumpy. And we'll need a home TV. A flagpole too."

"Expensive, but necessary, yes," I said, writing it down.

"Fresh paint?"

I nodded. "That's fine."

I put the pen down and looked up at the manor's backside. Despite its wicked past, it felt an accomplishment to own Lily Lake. To have some form of an heirloom from the mysterious woman we'd been born to.

"Do you think they'll go for it, Mary? James and Josh."

"Living here? Well, I don't see why not. New York's a hop and skip up the road. And the soldiers are coming back to Virginia now that the war is slowing. There's a new market of opportunity."

"James said wartime showbiz is different than regular showbiz," Macie said.

"So you've already spoken to him about it?"

Macie shifted in her seat. "Well, no. Not really."

"Well, surely it's different, but I think it makes sense to expand their showtime market. They'll still be on every radio in the country with that dad of theirs. Appealing to homecoming soldiers is the smartest strategy move for their career. As veterans themselves."

"I suppose that's true."

"Do you remember what years they served?" I asked my sister. "We need to know these things if we are to marry them. Come up with a love story that sells paper."

"Thirty-nine and forty. Company D, same battalion. Infantry, I believe."

I fought my look of surprise. I hadn't expected her to know so much about the Sophomores. Not yet.

"And they came home from battle because...?"

"Honorable discharge. James said their service ran its course. They were released in eleven months."

"Don't be foolish, Macie. The war hasn't yet run its course. Two able-bodied men like them... Their father was definitely pulling strings to get them back on stage while they've got their good looks. Even if the discharge was *honorable,* it'd likely be in their best interest to show some musical appreciation to the service. Patriotism is upstanding. And it sells records."

"I suppose you're right." Macie nodded. "People should know they paid their part."

"Did they now?" I asked, feeling defensive. While I truly fancied the Sophomore brothers, the idea of two men chasing fame while their fellow countrymen were bleeding... The thought irked me momentarily. Even if they had served their time. Or *some* time.

Macie lowered her brows at me. "Yes. They have. What's really the matter, sister?"

I dismissed the thought with the shake of a head. "Nothing personal. Just making sure we're prepared, is all. The papers will have a go at us from every angle, you know. We'll need to come up with a response for their shortened service."

"Well, James did say he occasionally gets devastating migraines."

I sighed heavily. "Well, I guess that's something."

We surveyed the rest of the grounds in an hour, adding a couple of items to the list. We needed to fix up the manor before we invited James and Josh. If we were going to take a career break, we wanted it to be away from the hustle and bustle of the city.

At that time, our agreement with Josh and James was solely verbal. The next actionable steps were to marry the siblings and merge our assets. The Sophomore brothers liked the idea and proved trustworthy enough to manage our money. We had a good thing going with Sandy's husband, but long term, it made sense to us to live with our account holders. Especially since we'd grown close friendships with them both over the past few months.

Macie and I would be able to take a career break in the Virginia countryside. They'd generate buzz for their new music while appealing to the wartime market. They could bed whoever they wanted, as long as they didn't get caught. Macie and I could try our hand at life as normal people with regular hobbies away from the glitterati. Something we hadn't ever had the luxury of experiencing in our entire lives. The plan was a stroke of genius.

Or so I thought.

2.6: JANE'S RECOUNT

"JESUS CHRIST, SILL," I mumbled as I heard mousey footsteps enter the room. My fingers rubbed over Sillian's dainty and killer cursive.

"Hey." My sister's white-flagged voice appeared before she did. "The party will start in an hour at six o'clock sharp...ish. 'Cause the gang is still rolling in. Like, twenty-eight people RSVP'd to Halloween in March. Only a few of us are staying overnight though. By the way, decorating is gravely behind schedule, as you might've noticed."

I ignored her and held up the notepad. "*This* is a nightmare waiting to happen."

Sill held her hands out in defense. She wore an innocent vulnerability inside her eyes that could be lovely at times, but also made you want to shake her into oblivion.

"Look, I never planned for Alex to see it."

"What does that mean?"

"I never *planned* to."

I took a deep breath and tried to ground myself. Reading that letter reminded me of my sister's audacity.

"Sill, I love you, but you have no right to say this stuff," I said, still holding the letter. "You have a boyfriend, and that boyfriend is not Alex."

Her eyes seemed to zig-zag the room for a logical response. She was dressed nicely despite the rain that covered her clothes. Her hands seemed to shake a bit at her sides.

"Trust me, I know. I wasn't going to show him." She sighed before plopping onto the bed. I continued to stare at her from the open arch in the bathroom while she star-fished her arms and legs across the old mattress. "I showed up at the manor two hours early. I was doing this *thing*. It sounds stupid out loud."

"A lot of stuff that you do sounds stupid out loud."

She nodded, wide-eyed, staring at the ceiling.

"This was different. I was writing all these letters that I wanted to put in the balloons and release into the air. I read it on this self-help website. This woman did it and she said it was so freeing. I thought writing could help me get my emotions...*organized*. I should've called bullshit on it because her next blog post was a recipe for vegan beef wellington. I mean, who has the stamina to make *vegan* beef wellington?"

"She sounds like a fun dinner party guest."

"Anywho, I was hung up on this idea of releasing letters in the sky to all these people in my life. Just letting go of all the hurt. You know we're almost twenty-five? I just wanted to do something to make it go away. Besides therapy, because that's fucking expensive."

She continued. I made a mental note to follow up on that statement. I didn't know what hurt she was talking about.

"So I came out here early with these balloons. It shouldn't have been a long ordeal, no more than twenty minutes, really. That's what I thought. But it took me an hour and a half."

"Vegan beef wellington lady didn't tell you about that part?"

"No. Quite the secret keeper, that one. The blunder of it all was that the balloons couldn't float away without *helium*. Blowing them up with *oxygen* was a total scam. Alex told me that when he showed."

She covered her face with her hands. All her nails were bitten down to the quick. I didn't comment.

"And when was that?"

"When I was on my last wasted breath. He didn't even let me know he was coming to the party, you know. My last balloon was going to hold that freaking letter. And when I turned around to grab it, Alex was standing over my shoulder, reading the damned thing."

"Oh, no." I sat beside Sill on the bed, putting an arm around her. She pulled away quickly, looking freshly mortified.

"So, we were having that conversation when you showed up."

I nodded without pressing on how the letter had gotten back up to the bedroom *before* they'd had a conversation on the patio. It was not the time for scrutiny. Not when she seemed so on edge.

"Did he understand?"

"Not exactly." Sill rolled onto her stomach and buried her neck like an ostrich into the comforter.

I tried a different question. "So, what did you do with all the balloons?"

"Tied them to trees in the forest," Sill mumbled. "All up in the branches. Hidden enough, I hope. We'll see with the storm."

I stood up from the bed and pulled my sister's palm in the air, who somehow still looked as beautiful as ever in the midst of all of her turmoil.

"C'mon. Get up. Sounds like we've got decorating to do."

After the first hour of decorating, I decided to slip out to Dakota's campsite. If all went according to plan, I could be back in time to get ready with my sister—our pre-party ritual.

I made it a few steps out of the yard before I had to lean against a tree and gasp for cold air. I ran because I didn't want anyone to know I was leaving. The manor was big enough that unless someone deliberately went looking for me, my absence would likely blend into the aloofness of the home itself.

The woods lined the back of the estate just behind the fence line. Lined like dominos, the tree line appeared organized until you caught sight of its never-ending depth. I pulled out my phone to find the picture I'd saved of the map, denoting which route I'd take.

I took a step inside the forest, hoping for the right footing, transfixed by the identical greenery that surrounded me in every direction. My backpack weighed me down as if to keep me from floating away into the maze. Luckily, the rain had stopped, but the mud was another challenge.

I kept the picture up on my phone as I picked up the pace. If I wanted to stick to the schedule, I needed to check for breaking news, meet with Dakota, and make it back to Sill's party in under two hours. The sun would start going down in about thirty minutes.

The daylight was crucial for me to recognize sights on the trail and note any danger head-on with my eyes before traveling in the dark later tonight.

First, I veered toward what AllTrails called *'Cell Mountain,'* which was nothing more than a small hill that apparently promised a bar or two for signal. It was easier to find than I'd thought. Despite the lack of markers, the trail looked as if it had been recently mowed down.

Once I got to Cell Mountain, there wasn't much to look at besides the sun making its way down and the two bars on my screen.

Within minutes, my phone was buzzing with the messages I'd missed since arriving at Sophomore Manor:

> DAKOTA | 2 HOURS AGO
>
> Hi, doll. Be at the campsite in 20 with the setup crew.
>
> CS BOSS | 3 HOURS AGO
>
> No news yet. But, I smell it kiddo… This is your weekend to get a story!

Neither message surprised me. Although, Dakota bringing a professional crew to pitch his tent for him so he could 'rough it' for a weekend…well, that should've surprised me. But alas, it did not.

I had taken the gamble that Chief Simmons would not phone me this weekend for a story. Likely not my most honorable decision. But not going camping this weekend could've ended me and Dakota. Dakota wasn't a prospect for forever just yet, but I wouldn't forgive myself if I didn't give the relationship a proper chance.

Sillian's party was another curveball. But the way she'd come to me a few days ago…it felt like she'd been on the verge of something cataclysmic. I was worried about her. More than that, I was curious about what she was hiding.

Luckily, the trail made it possible for me to semi-attend both events while keeping a side eye on work. I 'liked' both text messages with a thumbs-up before descending back into the dead zone of the trail. Fifteen minutes later, I'd almost made it. Danger hadn't found me. It had just been a typical, bug-ridden, and overgrown trail.

The campsite I approached was rather extreme. I could see Dakota's tent—or massive yurt, better yet—from a lowering in the bushes. The site itself wasn't a humpty-dumpty configuration. There were string lights, a movie projector, an outdoor grill, and a patio set. The whole scene looked like a Woodstock photographer was about to marry an upscale event planner in a secluded farm field, a vision primarily designed to go viral on Pinterest.

"Is that a popcorn machine?" I asked out loud, only to be heard by my own disbelief.

I powered over through a brush pile to create a makeshift exit. Once through, I cursed and pushed up the sleeve of my sweater to see the bloody scratches that decorated my arms.

Not attractive. At least I'd packed deodorant.

I made it to the front flap of the massive linen tent to hear the typing of a keyboard.

"Knock, knock," I called out with my ball in a fist, as if there was somewhere on the yurt to actually knock.

"Jane?" The typing at the keyboard halted with Dakota's voice.

"Who else?" I asked somewhat pointedly, still thinking of that pink coat I'd seen in Dakota's apartment. *Who else are you sleeping with? Who else are you lying to? Who else is leaving a coat in your apartment?*

Dakota appeared in a linen button-down and matching beach pants, not a drop of dirt on him. A scarf was placed around his neck; the whole look screamed ignorance.

"*Jeez*, Jane. Did you climb Mount Hua before you came over?"

"I thought I'd hike in. Since we're *roughing it* and all." I made sure to exaggerate the words as I stepped inside the tent. The first thing I noticed was the heater. The next was the massive percale bedding tucked neatly into its king frame. Without a wrinkle in sight, someone had definitely just steamed it straight.

"Yup, yup." Dakota opened his arms for a hug. He didn't seem to pick up on my sarcasm for a second. "Welcome to the badlands, doll. You need gauze? You're a hot mess."

I tossed my backpack carelessly on the pallet-made deck the tent rested on. Annoyance buzzed around me like a sting-ready wasp. It didn't matter how much I cared for Dakota; his wealth would always leave me with traces of resentment. My anxiety was not helping either. I should just ask him about the coat. But, telling him what I saw would be too hard to explain. Nobody wanted to date a stalker. Even one with good intentions.

"Just scuffs from the trail, but sure."

"Wi-Fi passcode is on the wet bar if you need it." Dakota nodded over to a bar cart placed next to a portable sink. On a looping cursive notecard was the word 'Wi-Fi,' as if we were staying in an Airbnb.

As pretentious as the whole scene was, I sighed relief at the thought of internet access. With it, I could get some work done and stay on call at the paper most of the weekend. God had indeed thrown me a bone.

As I pulled my electronics out of my bag I almost hadn't packed, Dakota went back to his seat on the bed with his own computer.

"Didn't you say you needed a break from work this weekend?" I asked as I logged into my iPad.

He chuckled dismissively. "We're journalists, aren't we? Aero-News is helping a bunch of smaller stations source stories. For a seller's fee. We're helping keep the little guys alive. The program launched this weekend. Genius idea. Bryan's, not mine."

Dakota was right. Most journalists didn't ever stop working. It was a masochistic career daydream for a writer. Never-ending stories meant steady opportunity. *AeroNews*, Dakota's company, was building up a reputation in the industry. He was busy in the big leagues. My lack of work and my ample availability reminded me that I was barely getting by at my paper.

"Are you saving them or draining them dry? These *little guys*." At this point, Dakota might have asked me what was wrong, my hostility coming out with my every breath. That pink coat was still at the back of my mind.

Dakota paused and looked at me long and hard. "Or...we're helping them break news before the big guys eat them alive. Aero-News is helping smaller stations get bigger news. Helping journalists like *my girlfriend* get more work. Chief Simmons is a client now, you know."

"My boss?"

"Your boss," Dakota repeated, still staring at me quizzically. "I thought you'd be excited. For me. For you. Symbiotic journalists."

I took a deep breath. Dakota might've done this as an act of kindness. Or maybe the act of kindness had even been an afterthought. But either way, he thought he was helping. He wanted to see me succeed. While it meant he might be my boss in some way, it also meant he was thinking of me. Trying to support my career. In his twisted brain, this had been intended as a positive step. I needed to remember that.

"I am excited, babe. Thank you for supporting local news. For supporting *me*."

He came over to hug me, his face beaming with satisfaction. Dakota loved being the one with the power in our relationship. He was never happier than when he was offering you advice at your bedside. He lived to be above you. To know more than you. To enable you to enjoy his blessings, but only when you were a *good girl*. His dating record steered clear of powerful women. It was no surprise that he'd picked a girl working at the struggling paper to spend his time with.

"Where'd you hike in from anyways?" he asked, releasing me from the embrace. "Your sweater has mud all over it."

"My sister's party. I helped with setup. I'm gonna go back later tonight for a cocktail. Then I'll spend the rest of the weekend here with you. There's a trail that connects the properties, actually. No service in that house, though."

He replied with a *'hmm'*. Definitely annoyed at the thought of me not staying put for the entirety of the weekend. Not when he could've potentially invited the pink-coat dream girl.

"The venue Sill booked is that old Sophomore Manor. Some famous jazz musicians and their wives died there in the forties. Or they think so. Case never got solved."

The typing at the computer resumed, like a subtle tell for me to shut up. Verbally, he didn't respond.

In the yurt's far corner, I played with my iPad on a leather bean bag chair tucked under a faux palm frond. I checked the headlines, then went to chess. I needed to be back at my sister's soon. Then I'd come back to Dakota's for the night.

"Hey, why don't you clean up outside? Farmhouse shower outback. Hot water. Totally exposed. Perfect view from the yurt." Dakota winked at me as he broke the silence. He seemed ready to blow off some steam. It was like he could sense I was about to take off again and needed to make sure I smelled of his scent before that happened.

"I wouldn't mind a shower."

He shot me that serpentine smile. The one that made me question everything.

"Good. I'll be watching."

2.7: MARY'S DIARY

1944

"YOU'RE NOT SERIOUS, ARE YOU?" I could hear the heat coming off Sandy's voice through the phone. I was alone in the sitting room of Lily Lake, phone cord wrapped around my fingers anxiously.

"It was your idea first, wasn't it, Sandy?"

I was filling in our talent manager, Sandy, about mine and Macie's plan to marry the Sophomore brothers. It was the first she'd heard of the relationship since the first date. The information also came with the plan to move our assets from her husband's account over to the Sophomore's. That one she wasn't thrilled with.

"My idea was for you to show your softer side, Mary. Kiss and tell a little bit. It wouldn't hurt you to fall in and out of love with the right kind of idiot. Have a big scandal with a stupid man who doesn't know how manipulative you are. Hell, I don't know. You're so stiff the papers think you might be gay!"

I chuckled under my breath. That was a particularly humorous headline that had come out several months before after Macie had been caught in the cameras on a first date with one of our co-stars. People then got curious as to why they'd never seen me out on a date and jumped to baseless conclusions.

"You are too much, Sandy."

"No, doll, *you* are too much. You and Macie just had your biggest picture ever. You can do whatever the hell you want. Sow your oats a bit, for Christ's sake. Get hot and messy for a change. This arranged-marriage-business-deal crap is not what I meant when I said a relationship might be good for your career."

"Well, the results are the same, aren't they? They're better. Because the boys don't want us as wives. They want buzz. We're one in our cause. And I think it could really work well. For both of us."

Sandy huffed on the other side of the line. "You know how hard I've worked to be in this business?"

"I do." Sandy had worked tremendously hard as our agent. As the female representation of her industry, when she showed up to work, it was with boxing gloves on. The woman put up a fight. Every single day.

"Now, Mary, I love you, kid. And not just because you keep my roof from leaking. But listen here, girl, you don't know a damn thing about business. If you did, you'd know a deal in showbiz ain't ever win-win. Someone is always willing to cut your throat in the name of a good bargain. Given you don't got agency over your own pockets, that bleeding neck is likely to be *yours*."

I paused to consider that for a moment. Sandy was pessimistic about almost everything I wanted to do, but rarely did she put her foot down like this.

"So you don't think we should get married?" I asked genuinely.

"No. I don't. But if you're going to get married, I think you at least ought to make a bloke believe he's not some puppet in a grand plan. Throw the word *'love'* around. Men don't like to be out-dealt, Mary. And they sure as hell don't settle for a tie."

"But Josh isn't looking for love. He told me that on our first date."

Sandy let out an angry chuckle. "Mary, if you and your sister want to marry these boys, then that's great. But don't hand them your bank account over as a wedding gift. Of course, I have selfish reasons, but I also know a thing or two, and I don't want your life's work in the hands of strangers. They're playing the same game you are, but they'll want to win."

"What's the alternative you're suggesting?" I asked.

"You should keep your holdings under my household. We've been good to you and your sister. Look, if it ain't broke, don't fix it."

"I have no intentions of firing you, Sandy. But if we get married, we'll need to move our money. You don't think bank tellers talk? They'll know your husband supports us more than our own do. We need to make the whole thing look real if we want to sell magazines."

"Oh, Mary, let 'em talk. If things go down south, you'll still be getting paid."

Sandy didn't want us to move our money. That much was obvious. And we did have a good thing going right now, but we knew it couldn't last forever. Sandy's husband was in his late sixties, to further the point. We needed to move toward something that could serve us more long-term.

Besides, Josh had never been anything short of honest with me. We were *friends*. And maybe we wouldn't be traditional lovers, but we could at least show one another respect. Something a man hadn't ever gifted me before Josh. If nothing else, I believed in that. Because what else was there to believe in?

"Sandy." I wrapped the phone cord around my shaking hand so hard that my circulation began to cut off. "Macie and I need you, but we also need you to let us do this."

Sandy took such a long pause that I thought she might've hung up. When her voice came back on the line, it was full of regret.

"Fine. I'll keep managing you two. But if these men rob you blind, there won't be much I can do. Once you set afoot a ship like this, you're there until it sinks. Don't come running to me to find ya a lifeboat when the waters get choppy."

"Come on now, Sandy. We've got your best interest at heart. We'll be back in film in a few months. If we're going to keep our careers going, we need to take this break. You know it as well as I do." There was a quiver in my voice. One I didn't usually have. Something about defying Sandy like this made me more uneasy than I'd thought it would.

"Alright then."

The line clicked, and I let the phone cord unravel from the twists around my fingers.

For the first time since I'd met the Sophomores, I was worried.

2.8: JANE'S RECOUNT

AN EERIE FEELING came over me as I made my way back onto the trail, hair still soaked. Mist from the earlier storm collected on the grass. I was going to be forty-five minutes late to my sister's party. I'd definitely missed the 'getting-ready' tradition we had. Nevertheless, I would still be at the event. That had to count for something.

Using my phone for a flashlight, I noticed shoe imprints in the dirt, fresh and much larger than mine. Someone else had been using this trail tonight.

I took a deep breath and tried to calm myself. This was a public trail, after all, with many outlet points. Many people love to hike at sunset. I convinced myself it was nothing.

Without bothering to stop at Cell Mountain, I kept moving. Dakota's had Wi-Fi. Nothing new had likely come up in the past eight minutes. Especially when nothing new had broken in the past eight months. I swallowed my career stagnancy down with the air as I approached the bramble I'd pushed aside earlier, leading myself back up to Sophomore Manor's backside.

There, I'd noticed a wimpish party balloon tied to a low tree branch. It darted back and forth with the wind. The yard was giant enough that there were probably several tied around, but I didn't have the luxury of time. I needed to get to my sister's party.

The enormity of the house overtook me as I stepped into the backyard. By the way the walls covered themselves with ivy and the stone wore its texture with time, you had to think something dark had happened here. The manor itself was hiding in plain sight. And unlike the feeling I got from Dakota's condo building, this building seemed to invite me inside. As if we were one and the same.

The moment I walked through the back door, a giant crash erupted. My eyes quickly swept the room. There were a few people scattered around downstairs in costume, already drinking in the great room, but the rest were still hidden away somewhere. Probably upstairs. Quickly, I turned toward the crash on instinct.

It was hard to see in such low lighting. The dark wood walls appeared even darker with the lack of natural UVs. A dizzying aroma that smelled strongly of a candle shop on fire made my head twirl. Sill had insisted the faux Halloween party only be lit by candles. Perhaps a poor choice amongst partiers.

The sound had come from the kitchen area, a small room with dated tile and cabinetry. It was stowed at the back of the house, as if it were built primarily for kitchen staff. This place must've been ancient.

As I approached, a tall silhouette appeared in the doorway. *Alex.*

"God, can you take this smell?" he said without turning around to see who had walked up behind him.

He was wearing a ridiculous canvas top hat complimented by a matching vest and a crossbody.

"I swear this table ran into *me*. I haven't even been drinking. Be careful with this glass on the floor..."

I looked below Alex's boots to see a sea of tequila and broken alcohol bottles pooling on the floor. The table in question looked like a kid's toy, a wooden miniature with keyholes pressed into each table leg. It looked like you could unlock each spot, but for what I did not know. More likely, it was someone's thrifting project gone wrong.

The keyhole frenzy of a table was sitting awkwardly in the path of the kitchen walkway. An odd spot for decoration. Especially one that only came up to my calf.

"At least the tequila will cover up the vanilla candle smell," I said to Alex.

"Watch your step, love."

Finally, Alex turned to face me. By the look of surprise in his eyes, he had certainly been expecting to see someone else.

"Oh. Jane. Wow! Haven't seen you in a minute. You look different."

"It's the brown hair."

He looked me up and down twice before nodding, shaking the canvas hat off his head, only to be caught by the strap around his neck.

"Yes. It is."

Alex held his hands out to offer a hug. Awkwardly, I complied.

Nearly immediately, he let go of the embrace and lunged toward the broken glass on the floor.

"Sorry, erhm. I need to get this wiped up before someone dressed as barefoot Jesus gets a bloody foot."

"There's a barefoot Jesus?"

"Isn't there always?" Alex said with a chuckle.

Alex had a way of doing that in conversation, making totally offhanded thoughts feel politely mainstream. Like you weren't educated in common knowledge if you weren't living under his brain.

"You got caught in the rain then?" He asked while opening random doors, looking for a supply closet.

I tugged at my wet hair. I hadn't had the time to dry it after the shower at Dakota's.

"Yeah," I lied. "On and off all day, according to the weather app."

Alex turned around with a broom. A sore sight for an almost

Indiana Jones. "You actually got cell service to check? I think that's considered a rare delicacy out here… Hey, would you mind if I log in to your cell to send an email?"

"Oh, well *no*. I mean, I don't have service either. I looked at the weather before I came."

Another lie. I didn't want Sill finding out I was splitting time between her and Dakota.

Alex didn't respond. He was too focused on sweeping up the floor.

"Not to be rude or anything, but why exactly are you here, Alex?"

Before he could answer, my sister scurried into the room.

"What happened, what happened? I heard a crash! We can't lose our deposit!" Sill trotted through the entry in a hot-pink sports bra and sweatpants, her makeup halfway done. I'd been gone for so long; how was she not dressed yet?

Sill and Alex glared at each other without a word as Sill rounded the kitchen island to check out the alcohol spillage herself. She bent down on her knees, looking more closely at the legs of the nearby table than the glass scattered around them.

"Not too bad of a casualty! Alex, do you mind opening another bottle for everyone? I have some upstairs. Jane and I will take care of the mess."

Without a word, Alex disappeared from the room.

"Thank you!" My sister clapped her hands and bent down on all fours despite the broken glass, pressing her knuckles into the small table's keyholes.

"Why don't we find a mop? It's dangerous to be down—"

"This table could've gotten a scratch. It's probably worth a fortune. Give me a minute."

I shook my head, confused. Since when was she so enamored by vintage furniture?

"Probably not if they were willing to rent out this place to a bunch of twenty-somethings for a party."

"Can you clean up that glass, Jane? I'm bringing this table

upstairs. I've got to protect it. Could be historic." Sill's dilated eyes were full of an urgency I'd rarely seen her wear. Normally, her half-done makeup would make her appear silly, but at that moment, she looked nothing short of terrifying.

"Sure." I shook my head, still confused. "Sorry I'm late, by the way. I had to check my cell service. I'm on call at the paper and—"

Sill nodded her head as she picked up the table, cutting me off in a state of hurry. "Don't worry. Everyone's behind. We've got all weekend to catch up."

Her voice cracked at the end of the sentence. Like she was scared to talk any further.

I shook my head, confused again. It wasn't like my twin not to get bent out of shape over a plan behind schedule. Something else was on her mind.

I went to the cabinets in mute disbelief as she carried the light-weight kids' table over her head toward the archway and up the stairs. Goosebumps covered my body as I searched for the broom Alex had just put away.

My sister was acting *strange*.

Amongst the partiers, I'd waited downstairs in the main room for my twin's return. Most of the guests were down there now. A good thirty-something people. But no sign of Sillian.

The more time that passed, the more anxiety came. I needed to get back to Dakota's at some point tonight. And I wanted to do so before another rainstorm. But something was telling me not to leave my sister tonight. That something might happen.

Elle eventually bounced over to me in her long-robed costume, holding two drinks.

"Want a drink, Jane?"

We'd been 'party friends' for years now, though I didn't know her well outside of my sister's events.

"Why not?" I replied, taking a solo cup from her ring-adorned hands graciously.

"Actually, can I tell you something?" Elle awkwardly picked at her nails after handing me the drink. "It's about Sill."

"Of course you can."

"It's just that—"

"Hello everyone! Thank you for coming!" My twin's voice boomed from the top of the banister. The scene was theatrical, all of us down here and her up there, as if she was some kind of celebrity. She was dressed up in a Nancy Drew costume. Except Nancy's skirt had gotten quite short and her shirt quite small. My sister waved with a theatrical smile down at the party attendees like some kind of monarch.

Elle and I exchanged an uncomfortable glance. Something was noticeably off about her. I tried to swallow the feeling with the drink Elle had brought me, but I couldn't. I crossed my arms and made myself smaller, wishing to disappear.

Sill twirled at the top of the stairs, bringing a toy spyglass up to her eye.

My sister let out a forced laugh and yelled, "Welcome to Sophomore Manor. Let the games begin!"

I swallowed hard. Everyone else cheered.

Elle slipped a piece of paper into my free hand and disappeared into the crowd.

2.9: RENTAL BROCHURE

| FOUND BY ELLE EWING |

RENT SAN FRANSISCO

Rent one of our gorgeous floor plans:

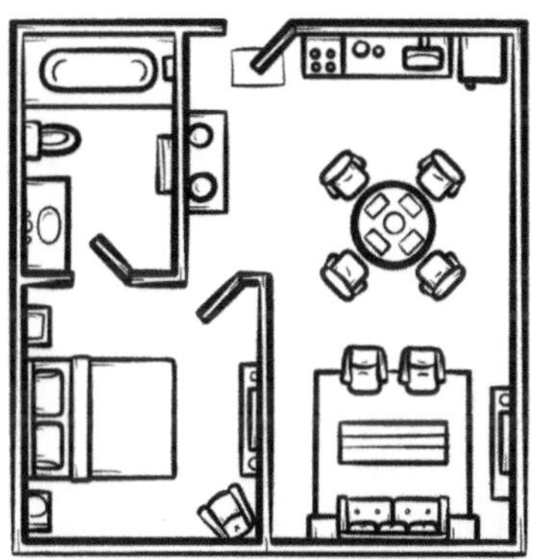

Our luxury community is fit with a parking garage, a gym, and a business center. You'll never want to leave!

Studios starting at $2900/month

1BR/1BA starting at $3200/month

2BR/1BA starting at $4050/month

3BR/2BA starting at $5100/month

Jesus Christ! Look at these prices...It is going to be way too expensive if Sill decides not to move in with me. Luckily she seems really serious. Time to bind her to a lease ASAP. I'll call tomorrow.

CALL NOW: 415-555-4252   Find us on   

Great work! You completed file two. Below are checkpoints to keep you on track to pinpointing the right suspect:

- **HINT:** *How* Jane comes across a clue can occasionally say more about a situation than the clue's contents. Think critically.

- **CONSIDER:** While it's essential to focus on a potential culprit's motive to harm Sillian, perhaps it is just as important to uncover Sillian's motive for hosting the party.

- **TIP:** Look up the definition of ad hominem. A good detective is aware of the fallacies they could be vulnerable to throughout a case.

- **FUN FACT:** Women couldn't legally own a bank account until the 1960s. Even then, most banks would not allow women to hold their own cash without their husbands' sign-off.

Good sleuths become great sleuths by narrowing down their mystery's objective while keeping all possibilities in scope.

CASE FILE THREE

<u>Case file three contains nine items to be inspected.</u>
Files should be reviewed in numerical order

- **3.1 Jane's Recount** | March 2023
- **3.2 The Balloon Letter**
- **3.3 Mary Sophomore's Diary** | 1944
- **3.4 Jane's Text Messages**
- **3.5 Wayne County Police Report**
- **3.6 Mary Sophomore's Diary** | 1944
- **3.7 Jane's Recount** | March 2023
- **3.8 Mary Sophomore's Diary** | 1944
- **3.9 Jane's Recount** | March 2023

3.1: JANE'S RECOUNT

 I grabbed one last drink and headed to Dakota's for the night. That was when I heard the high-pitched scream.

I dropped my cup in the backyard and ran full force back into the house. When I got back inside, I heard a stampede of footsteps running in different directions. I found myself getting caught in the rush with the other drunk partiers, moving with the crowd. Things were moving so fast that it was hard to understand anything other than widespread fear.

"Is the front door locked?" a male voice called out.

"Yes!" someone responded.

"Everyone in here. *Let's go, let's go!*" Elle took the lead, standing in a chair waving partygoers into a room off the corridor.

People pushed behind one another to squeeze into the room. I pressed my way inside what appeared to be a study. Towers of bookcases surrounded the crowd coming in. The red draped curtains were drawn and a series of candelabras were lit along the trim of the floors.

"Does anyone have cell service?" Robin whispered to the

packed bodies in the small room. That wasn't everyone, though. It couldn't have been.

"What just happened?" I grabbed Robin's arm as an anchor. My mind was swirling.

"Bad news. Very bad." Robin was frantically trying to call a number on her phone. Nothing was happening.

In the front of the study, Elle and another partygoer were closing the doors and checking the windows.

Robin's tone went hushed. "This guy came into the house. Kind of appeared out of nowhere. Huge. Like, could've been a professional basketball player."

Robin was hitting her phone with the side of her palm as if she could knock the cell service tower into range if she tried hard enough. She'd obviously had a few too many drinks.

"He was wearing this, like, Greek head mask thingy and walking through the house like a zombie. Sill has a lot of weird friends and it's fake Halloween. So, like, no big deal? Just another pity invite probably. Lord knows she does that, like, *all* the time."

"Okay…" I was hanging on Robin's every word, and I wanted her to *like* hurry up.

"Then the giant freak stood on the countertop and announced himself as Brutus? And that he came for revenge. He had this… machete with him? Or, like, an axe. It had to be solid iron. It looked quite heavy."

"Was he some actor for the party, or…?"

Robin raised a pointed finger at me. "See! That's what we thought too. No party stunt is too corny for Sillian. She's into all that theatrical shit."

My sister was into all things corny, but something underneath the idea that this was a party stunt bothered me. She'd been acting so strangely. There was something more to this gathering, and Sill was holding her cards close to her chest.

"So, Michael goes up to *Brutus* and hands him a fresh beer can. Tells him to simmer down or party on—whatever. Like, 'Okay, bro, we get it,' kind of thing. And the giant standing on the countertop apparently wasn't done. He swings his axe at Michael's face. Really awkward swing, also. It's so unattractive to see a man look like he's at a tee-ball practice. But, anywho. Michael must've caught the wooden handle with his cheek. He's not bleeding, but look at that swelling."

Robin turned over her shoulder toward Michael, who was sitting at the desk all alone in the crowded room. He could've passed as Gatsby himself if his right cheekbone wasn't the size of Texas.

"So that's why everyone ran then? Because of this masked Brutus guy?"

"Oh, honey, I wish. Everyone ran because the creepy fuck pulled two live snakes out of his pocket and threw them into the crowd."

I closed my eyes tight. Some part of me still thought this might be a party stunt orchestrated by my sister. But if it was, it was *harsh*. And Sillian was anything but.

Robin went back to tapping her phone screen excessively. "No signal. I had to switch to some cheap service provider when I was unemployed. Doesn't reach anywhere."

"Do you think it's serious enough to call the police?"

"Oh, please. Your sister lives for the theater of these things. It's annoying but definitely not out of character, is it? Maybe the Brutus face slam thing was to get back at Michael's cheating."

"Cheating?"

"Trust me, honey." Robin nodded.

"But...I don't know if Sillian would ever do that." And I really didn't. Before then, the possibility of her putting any of these people in harm's way was absurd. I needed to talk to my sister as soon as possible.

"I'm trying to call my boyfriend of the week." Robin hit her phone again. "I'm too intoxicated to drive home and I'm not trying to get snake bit or axed. I know they're probably, like, garden snakes or whatever, but I don't take my chances. Leaving my fate up to Sillian never works out for me."

"Well...I can maybe get a message out..."

As soon as the words left my mouth, the sound of glass shattering came from behind the barricaded study doors. Not long after, the whole house seemed to shake, like a miniature earthquake was in the making.

Robin threw her phone across the crowded room in horror. A sinking feeling came over me. I was starting to feel *very* concerned.

I wrung my hands together and looked around the room. Drunken costume characters were everywhere, all dialing on their phone screens with no success. Most of them were sitting on the floor by that point, some still drinking out of red solo cups that had survived the chaos.

Whether a crazy stunt or a violent party intruder, I needed to talk to my sister. And after a quick analysis, I noticed she wasn't in the room.

My heart pounded as I pushed my way over to the desk an injured Michael was perched at.

"We need to find Sillian."

Michael was staring intently at a boy in the front of the room, who returned his gaze like there was a secret message passing between their eyes.

Finally, he pulled his gaze away from him to meet mine. "Look at my face."

"Yes, someone hurt you, and I'm sorry. But maybe they did that because Sill's in some real trouble. If she is, don't you want to protect your girlfriend?"

Michael sighed, as if he was annoyed. "Alex isn't in here either, is he? Ever wonder why he was invited to the party in the first place?"

"Sillian said that Alex coming was just a misunderstanding."

"Ahh." He touched his hand to his swollen face, only to retract it immediately in pain.

"Michael, will you please help me find Sillian? You're dating her." My tone was pleading. The nature of tonight's events were rippling the waves of an oncoming anxiety attack.

My sister's boyfriend scoffed under his breath before standing up. "Fine…but I'm bringing backup."

My eyes followed Michael across the room as he walked toward another male dressed in a Waldo outfit. After whispering to him for some time, they waved me over to the study door. Elle was guarding it tightly.

The closer we got to Elle, the heavier her scent was—a thick gin smell over her breath.

"I'm locking the door back immediately when you leave. Can't risk the herd for lost sheep," she said matter-of-factly.

I rolled my eyes and stepped past her.

"The Parks girls have a death wish, I swear." Michael said with a sigh as he and 'Waldo' followed me back toward the great room. Not much urgency was obvious in their demeanors.

The great room was wholly emptied of guests now, only bottles and trash left in their wake. A grandfather clock stuck out to me, its ticking audible without the sounds of jamboree around it— 11:30 *PM*.

"Can you two search the house for Sill? Figure out what's going on? She's got to be around. I've got to get a call out."

It started to rain, but it wouldn't stop me from getting to Cell Mountain. First, the police needed to be notified. Then I'd have to let Dakota know I wasn't going to make it tonight. Whatever was happening with my sister demanded my attention.

"*We* don't get along with snakes." The guy dressed as Waldo shrugged casually with a smug look on his face. Michael gave him a look before nodding back to me.

"Alright, Jane. We'll look around. Or try to." They turned their backs to me hastily, without another word.

"Let's hope there's no more damage done to the nearest face," Waldo called out in a humorous tone. I felt a shot of resentment go up and down my spine. *Why is everyone taking this so lightly? Are they in on something I'm not?*

The backyard was thick with naked chestnut oaks, left eerie in their towering twists and turns. I worked my way around the maze of trunks. The space was at least a few acres with a haphazard organization that made my stomach churn. The man called Brutus could've been hidden back there for hours. *He could be hiding here now.*

With rentals like these, there were no security guards to post and no doormen to fetch. For all I knew, the rental host could be a sham. Some sick killer with an insatiable desire for murder. When a beautiful young woman like Sill submitted a booking request for a costume party, the temperature had been set for a perfect storm.

I was almost back to the trail when I saw a slight hint of yellow rippling between branches near the hedge fencing of the yard. That balloon.

I walked carefully toward the inflated elastic, knowing a secret of my sister's might be hidden inside. The ribboned balloon string had caught between branches and had wrapped itself on various stems a few times through. Rippling through the misted wind, I could faintly see a letter folded inside the stretched latex.

An itch came over my hands that begged me to pop it. Typically, it wouldn't be justified to read the private thoughts of my sister. But in that instance, right and wrong felt blurred. Danger was at the doorstep. And Sill had been acting so *strange*. She was hiding things from me. *San Fransisco? And what was up with that table?*

If there was ever a night to dig for some context, it was this one. My sister's secrets had always been safe with me. That wouldn't change, no matter what was in that letter.

I stole a bobby pin from my hair and pressed it into the balloon.

3.2: THE BALLOON LETTER

FOUND BY JANE PARKS

Dear

I know that you steal from me
frequently. Despite this fact, I
have still kept you around
because of the secret we share.
But I'm over it. I want all my
money back. I don't care who
knows anymore. To hell with
you. No one will side with you
anyways. Pay up by December.

                    Sillian

3.3: MARY'S DIARY

1944

WE'D PLANNED an extravagant dual wedding, leaving ample room in the budget to tip off the paparazzi and accidentally pass them through security. The ordeal was destined for *Sibling Marriage* double-take headliners. The clever ones still stood out to me: '*Whose Marrying Who?*' and '*Spot The Difference - Spouse Edition*'

Macie and I had a bachelorette party—just her and I. We'd invited another woman, our friend Corrine, but she'd declined. She was shooting a movie out west. Besides, it wasn't like we knew many other women, much less trusted them. Up to that point, both of us were in accordance with blowing off the whole marriage thing. At least, that was what I'd thought. We were at the manor we'd soon move into, just the two of us, celebrating.

We'd had sleepovers for years, but none as fun as that one. We swam in the creek, tossing ideas between breaths about the hilarity of married life. She said it would be sensational: a giant friendship between two sets of siblings. I believed her. I asked if she thought she ever wanted to be a wife—a real wife—someday. She said that if she did, that was when we could be on to the next scandal: *divorce.*

We swam for hours until it was dark and time to retreat back inside. I was filthy with creek water. I went to draw myself a bath, and when I was done, I noticed her outside, reading a letter.

"What's that, sis?" I drunkenly stepped outside in just a towel after soaking under the faucet and nearly two bottles of wine. Her body language shifted to stone immediately.

The back of her neck twitched under her short bob haircut when she heard my voice. Wasting no time, she crumpled the letter in a single fist.

"A letter from James." Macie's eyes twirled toward her skull theatrically. "He says he's excited to marry me."

"Ha!" The heartiest laugh escaped my throat as I made myself a seat on her lap, still in my towel. "Josh and I are friendly, but we've barely spoken once about the marriage without our lawyers! That's a hoot. Let me read."

Macie pushed me off her. "You're sopping wet. This dress is brand new."

Still laughing, I lunged forward in a swipe motion for the letter. "Sis, you've got to show me," I said, barely audible over the sound of my laughter.

Macie stiffened with the crumpled paper in her fist and shook her head. "It's not worth the read."

Sensing her discomfort through the wine, I felt the slightest tint of betrayal.

"Mace…you aren't soft on him, are you? You wouldn't…"

My sister raised her hands in genuine surrender; her left fist still closed around the balled paper. "God, Mary. No. I know the drill. Strictly business, take years off the acting scene, and finally, have *our* own life."

My eyes fell into a squint of scrutiny. "Then let me read the note."

A shade of red blushed over her. "Fine." She tossed the ball at my feet instead of my hands. "But let me say that there's nothing wrong with wanting to be close with our future roommates. We've got a long life ahead of us."

I spun around in my towel, sobering up quickly as she headed for the door. "Sister…you're in this with me, aren't you?"

Macie looked hurt. "Of course I am." She nodded at the letter. "But it's apparent you don't trust me."

I studied her for a moment too long. Desperate to convince her otherwise, I kicked the wadded note off the patio and into the yard with my foot.

"I do," I giggled a little before saying it. "You're the only *'I do'* that matters."

She crossed her arms and gave me a half-smile. I followed her inside, leaving the secrets between James and Macie untouched.

3.4: JANE'S TEXTS

DAKOTA

Wait, wait, wait. What happened?

JANE

A man showed up and attacked a party guest then the house started shaking. I can't find Sillian. The police are coming now.

DAKOTA

I'm certain that Sill is OK. Do u need me to come out there?

JANE

Thx. Let's see what the cops say. People are acting weird tonight. It feels like something bad might happen. Hopefully Sill turns up and it's NBD. I'll update you tomorrow at the latest. Xoxo

DAKOTA

Be safe.

3.5: WAYNE COUNTY POLICE REPORT

WAYNE COUNTY POLICE REPORT

CASE NUMBER:	OFFICER:	DATE:
2023-555	B. Stephens	3-4-2023

INCIDENT   Young woman, Jane Parks, calls the police on behalf of a party group. A man with a machete appeared at the party. Her sister has since not been seen. She appears drunk and in distress..

EVENT DETAIL   A masked man entered the rental home. Behavior was not thought to be unusual as the party has a costume theme.. Masked man announces his intention for revenge then swings the dull side of axe at a young man. He then throws two live snakes into the room. Party members hide. The house is said to have shaken.

ACTION TAKEN   An officer team is sent out to the property immediately. The entire house is searched. The mask is found, but the man is not. The two snakes were located and identified as harmless garden snakes. Each party guest is interviewed by the police. The majority of the guests believe that the host, Sillian Parks, set up the axe stunt for a theatrical party element. Jane Parks believes that her sister is in danger, but fails to give valid explanation. The team decides to keep a security guard on the premise for the rest of the night without further investigation. The rental company that manages the house was contacted about the events.. No response returned.

SUMMARY   Danger not suspected. The events suggest that a well-intended party became disorderly. A security guard has been assigned to the premise. A follow-up call to property manager will be placed tomorrow. Frightened attendees offered a sober ride home.

SIGNED BY: Officer Brett R. Stephens

3.6: MARY'S DIARY

1944

JOSH SENT me flowers on the morning of the wedding. The same kind I'd thrown out the window on our first date. A note was wrapped around the bouquet that said:

> *"We must take care of our families where we find them. Welcome to mine, Mary."*

Relief flooded me as I put them into a vase. While Josh and I hadn't talked in weeks, he was proving again and again to be the stand-up guy I knew him to be. I could trust myself with this decision. This was a good thing. I'd made the right call.

So, just like that, we were married. Macie and I had walked each other on stage, married a pair of brothers, and executed our plan just as intended. And the crowd had gone *wild*. Our lives had just begun.

It wasn't until I saw the New York Times splashed with photos of the wedding that I realized something was wrong. Since James and Josh had kissed their brides simultaneously on a dual-platform stage, Macie and I had never watched each other's "moment." As a business arrangement formality, it hadn't bothered either of us.

Of course, the photos would go down as some of the most famous in history. We'd known they would by design. Our publicists had planned them that way: *double vision* she'd called it.

Yet, it became an image that haunted me. My gut flopped the first time I'd seen it: There I was on stage in an all-white dress, matching head to toe with Macie. Red and pink roses surrounded us. Tea-light candles had lined the stage. The scene had dripped with radiance, amplified further by Macie and me—a mirror image, symmetrically pleasing.

On my half of the stage and wedding kiss, I appeared beautiful but stoic. There was nothing wrong with that. It was proper to have such a modest kiss on your wedding day. Josh was at my face, kissing me while my arms were limp next to my side, the tips of my fingers pressing at his hips to show some form of crowd-approved association between us. We weren't pressed against one another, but we were touching. I hadn't planned it this way. We'd never even rehearsed the kiss, but it was hard not to be slightly reserved when you were kissing someone for the first time at your own wedding. All in all, my rigid posture hadn't bothered me. That was until I'd seen Macie's.

There she was, a foot beside me on stage, a carbon copy image right down to the veil. Yet James was dipping her back into the kiss, holding her steady with one open palm gripped at the small of her back. Their hips were pressed against each other at an angle. Her heel was a skywriter in the air—the word *'yes'* written all over. With two hands, she held James by the face.

My gut churned as I forced the thought out of my head. My sister had always been a great actress. Maybe my mind played tricks on me…but I could've sworn if you looked close enough at the photo, you could make out the slightest slip of tongue.

3.7: JANE'S RECOUNT

AFTER THE POLICE LEFT, everyone went back to partying. I went into a panic. It could've been the booze, my spiraling career path, or even my rocky relationship. But somehow, it felt like more than that. Something about that night felt like life or death, and I couldn't put my finger on why.

With the event now well-oiled by alcohol, I found a seat in the main corridor to take a moment for myself. Despite not having any service, I pulled out my phone and was met by the lock screen photo of Dakota and me. *Drinking always makes me a bit more emotional*, I reminded myself, wiping a tear away from my eyes.

Surely, he'd called the girl in the pink coat by now. I feared a campfire wasn't enough to keep a boy like Dakota warm.

The bass from the music pounded against my chest. I couldn't believe people were still celebrating after all that had just happened. But there was no sense in trying to stop them.

Alex appeared across the main room, his hands in his pockets. Girls surrounded him, and he looked disinterested in all of them. When we locked eyes across the party, he shot me a half-smile before dismissing himself from the group and walking in my direction.

"How are you doing?" he asked with a look of genuine concern.

"Are we just pretending everything's fine?"

Alex cocked his head the way a dog would. "You know, I saw that axe in the back of your sister's car earlier today. I'm sure she's just pulling a prank."

I buried my face in my hands, frustrated by all of it.

"When were you in— Never mind."

Alex crouched down next to my seat, making me feel like a child.

"When was I what?"

"When did you last see Sillian?"

"We talked." Alex's expression went uneasy. "We talked outside earlier. And then again in front of the garage."

"Before the axe man?"

Alex nodded.

"What did you talk about?"

Alex huffed, his face getting red—with alcohol or embarrassment, I couldn't tell. "I'm afraid that's private."

I shook my head at him in disbelief. First, he'd had the audacity to come here. Then, he wouldn't tell me something that could help me find where my sister was. I couldn't take it anymore.

"Why can't you just leave her alone?" I bumped his shoulder as I shuffled past him and the puddle of beer beneath his feet, not giving him a chance to respond.

I pushed my way through the crowd with remorse, still in shock that everyone could just go back to partying. The smell of alcohol reeked across the first floor. After I took the first few steps up toward the bedrooms, I looked down at the party from where my sister had stood just a few hours before.

The house was taking a beating; red cups had been tossed carelessly over the Victorian carpets. People were drunkenly moving in bliss, emptied drinks and souls scattered across a makeshift dance floor. Everything looked trivial from up there. All of it is so...*useless*. I wondered if Sillian had thought the same thing.

That was when I caught sight of someone familiar by the front door, a camera and tripod next to him.

"Chief Simmons?" I called out, barely loud enough to reach him. If my boss knew I was here, then he knew I wasn't on call at the paper, which meant... *Oh no.*

He heard his name and looked through the crowd a few times before finding me on the stairs. His eyes lit up with surprise, as if he hadn't been expecting to see me.

"Jane?" He approached the staircase, getting closer to me. His oversized sweatsuit suggested he hadn't expected to go in public. "I didn't think you got my calls!"

"Oh?" I didn't know how to answer. I certainly hadn't gotten his calls. I'd forgotten about the paper altogether in the commotion.

"Once I got the tip that there was a breaking story out here, I called you immediately. When you didn't pick up, I thought I'd come out here myself. I didn't want to lose a breaker. We haven't had one in so long. But here you are!"

I couldn't fight the look of shock on my face. "Oh...*right.* About the big news. I was actually here for it."

Chief Simmons tipped his head back into a laugh. He was standing across the banister from me now. "Attagirl, Parks! Attagirl."

The police had just written off the event as dangerless disorderly conduct. Why would they have tipped a breaking story?

"What exactly did the police say happened? 'Cause there's no other reporters here."

"Not the police. AeroNews. I recently made a deal with them— it's a startup company. Getting hotter by the minute, those boys. They tip our paper stories for the local news. We pay a commission fee. They call it a win-win and all that yada-yada. I took the gamble and, damn! I knew I made the right call on that deal, Jane. Week one and we already got ourselves a breaking story *and* we're the only ones here. A historical location, too. How ya like that?"

My face went flushed. AeroNews had tipped off a story tonight to my boss. Which meant Dakota had turned his girlfriend's worried text message into a company business deal. Anger swelled in my chest. *That asshole.*

"So tell me everything, kid. How'd the attacker make the house shake? Do you know if the victim is still around?"

"I don't know." I looked away, not wanting my boss to see me cry. In some sick way, maybe Dakota thought he was helping my career by throwing a story to my boss. Either way, it was inexcusable.

"Now, what's the matter, hun? By the looks of the crowd here, the dude wasn't *that* traumatic."

I sat down on the stairs, unable to hide the tears anymore. My boss quickly sat next to me.

"I can't find my sister. She's been missing since…"

"Since when?" Chief Simmons' voice shifted into a softer tone.

"Since the intruder guy came. Everyone else thinks it's a party stunt…" I sniffled, barely able to get the words out.

"A party stunt? 'Aint no way Aero tipped me off a party stunt. That son of a—"

"Something big is happening here, boss. I know it. And my twin sister is at the center of it. But I can't find her. I'm so worried… I don't know what to do."

"What do you mean, something big?"

"I think my sister's in danger. I can't put my finger on it, but I keep finding these angry notes she wrote to other party guests. And now they're all here. Then that big diversion happened, and she's nowhere to be found. I called the police, and they didn't take me seriously."

My voice was worn and sulky. A flash of surprise crossed Chief Simmons' face as if he was surprised I hadn't just arrived at the scene. He didn't comment on it, though.

"So, it sounds to me, kid, like you've got a story to get to the bottom of."

I glared over at my boss, not sure what he was suggesting.

"Your sister's in danger?"

I nodded. "I don't know for sure, but…I think she might be."

"And the police won't help ya?"

"No. They didn't see a real cause for concern. Not yet, anyway."

Chief Simmons gave my knee a pat before leaning back on the staircase. "Ahh, kid. Were you invited to this party?"

Though I wanted to lie and give the perception that I'd been working all weekend, I confirmed.

"Yes, I was invited. My sister's the host."

"So all these people...they feel pretty comfortable with your presence here?"

"Yeah. I've met most of them before this. Sill throws a lot of parties."

Chief Simmons sighed and looked down at the surroundings. "Can I offer some advice, hun?"

"Of course."

"If you're *really* worried that something happened to her, your sister, and you're *really* at a dead end with the cops..."

He paused and waited for me to look at him in the eye. His stern gaze always sent a chill down my spine.

"If you're really worried 'bout all that...you gotta come at the situation like a reporter, hun."

"How do you mean?"

"Start asking questions, keeping logs, snooping around a little bit. Start talking to the liars and uncover the truths they tell."

I looked down at the party. Robin was chatting with a swollen and uninterested Michael. Alex had returned to his place amongst some girls, a defeated look on his face. Elle was dancing on a table like a drunken maniac. All while my sister could be missing. No, I didn't trust any of them for a second.

"And then what?"

"And then...see if you can find out what's at the bottom of all this. What makes a good reporter is his gut. And if you've got a gut feeling, Jane... Let's just say that I *know* that you're a solid reporter. That's why I hired you."

"Thank you." I sniffled, wiping away my tears again.

"Try to get to the bottom of things. Keep some logs. And then, if there's a good story at the heart of all this, you can turn it into the paper."

"You want me to write a story about it?"

"Not yet, no. But if something here's going on and you think it's this major, then yeah, maybe I do. Either way, I think acting like a journalist might help you solve some of these questions you're up here asking yourself. Whether it ends up in the papers or not is up to you."

He was right. Sitting and waiting for my sister to return wouldn't do much for me if she was really in trouble. And even though I didn't know for certain yet, I didn't want to take any chances.

"Tell ya what, kid, you stay here this weekend and do your best to put your nose into this trouble you're smelling. I'll be a call away if you need another opinion. Whether it's big, small, or nothing—I want you to solve whatever it is that you're on to. Any more breakings come through, I'll take care of it. But this call that brought me up here…that story is yours. Not mine."

I smiled through wet eyes. "Thanks, boss."

He stood up and turned toward the door with a chuckle. "I'm too old to party like you youngins."

I reached out to shake my chief's hand goodbye.

"You got this, girl. Don't you forget that I'm a call away. And try not to worry so much. If your sister's anything like the girl I've seen in you, she'll be alright."

3.8: MARY'S DIARY

1944

WHEN I MARRIED JOSH, I knew I was marrying two men. James was technically Macie's spouse, but he would always be tied to my household. Expectantly, he was a part of this wedlock between Josh and me. Josh and James sat at either head of our dining table, Macie and I somewhere in between.

When you had a twin, you got used to the idea of joint everything. Couples and doubles and twos. What I hadn't anticipated was the third man at the table.

Andrew Kelly. Or as my sister and I called him, Grifter.

Grifter wasn't a Sandy. He was greedier, slimier, and a half portion of a real professional. When Grifter began managing James and Josh, he was a nobody in the New York doghouse. But he'd had a few big names in his phonebook, people who'd passed through the underground jazz scene before they made it big time. He'd pulled a few strings for James and Josh early on when it mattered. The Sophomore name was doing enough for itself with Senior Sophomore manipulating the broadcasts, but James and Josh weren't booked full-time. They didn't have their own headlines yet, mostly opening at clip joints two or three times a week. It was a time in life when it felt like everything could slip from their hands if they weren't careful. Desperate for any elevation at all, any sense of 'making it,' that they failed to remember discretion.

The first time Grifter came into my house was a month after the wedding date. Grifter had driven down to Virginia from New York City. Macie was wrapping her first and last solo film in Los Angeles, and the boys were boarding up their New York condo. I was already on vacation.

When Grifter knocked, I'd been expecting Macie. Wrapping a week early on a project wasn't so uncommon. She was scheduled to be home in just four more days. It wasn't unlike her to forget her keys. The assumption folded up nicely.

I'd kept my night robe on and swung the door wide open without breaking my attention from the crossword I was working on. Without a look, I turned on my heels and moved back toward the seating room. Macie knew I didn't like to talk in the mornings.

"Mary!" Grifter's voice was like cold water to the face. I dropped my paper in surprise.

"Gr— *Andrew?*"

I crossed my arms over my braless chest and spun around.

"The boys are closing shop in New York this week. I haven't talked to them," I'd said.

Andrew Kelly was in a baby blue suit that I'd only seen men wear on Easter Sunday. What was left of his gray hair was scraped sparsely across a gaping bald spot on his head. A withering man still grasping at whatever was left.

"I'm not here to see James and Josh. Goodness, I've seen enough of those two. I'm here to see the lovely Mary Sophomore," Andrew said.

"And what a sight you are."

Grifter had invited himself in, not worried about my disposition. Fear crept up my spine. Had the boys fired him as their manager? With the move away from New York, it was a possibility. He could have been angry and out of a job. And at that moment, inside my house.

He'd kept his hands in his pockets as he walked around the living area with downcast eyes.

"You enjoy living here?"

"It's remote. That's why we had it bought." I chewed on my cheek. "I'm expecting Macie home any minute."

"Quite charming it is…And who bought it for you? Two ladies can't be making a transaction this big. Not without a bank account."

"Our manager handled our money. And *she* had her ways."

Grifter shrugged his shoulders and let out a chuckle, looking up at the long chintz drapes and the chandelier on the ceiling with some scornful awe.

"The boys are leaving the New York scene. To come live *here*. With *you*. I think congratulations are in order!"

I tightened the grip on my forearms crossed over my nightgown.

"That's right. The marriage has already generated enough press money for us to all take a career break. We'll do a few interviews and events. They'll make some new albums here. We'll burst onto the film scene again. Eventually."

Grifter dismissed me with a laugh. "When I'm dead, girl. You'll be back on film when I'm dead."

His words had come out like a complaint rather than a threat. I turned my back to him and grabbed a coat off the rack, just to ensure I didn't showcase my nightie to this greedy old man.

"Well." Andrew Kelly sat down in the velvet settee where I'd been doing my crossword. "I've come up with a plan for 'em. And for me too. Since nobody seemed to be worried about me. Their devoted talent agent."

"Is that what you call yourself, Andrew?"

Grifter snorted.

"They signed the contracts last night that'll keep me around in this muddle for another five years. So yes, dear, that is what I call myself."

Five more years with Andrew Kelly? They surely wouldn't have. Not without talking to us.

Grifter leaned back into the chair and comfortably laced his hands behind his head, signaling his power over mine. In my own home.

"The story is that they're coming to Virginia for the troops. They'll still be booked dizzy with gigs. They wanted to move jazz closer to the Capitol. Pay tribute to those passing through the service. Wartime tunes. Their new wives—that's you, Mary—are *ecstatic* to serve their country and their husbands."

Men always needed it to be *their* plan. Not yours. Even if they were one and the same.

I nodded cooly. "I'm afraid you drove all the way over here to tell me that?"

"They're also going to move more into the political scene. Elevate their influence that way. So close to DC and all. You will open up this very home to many promotional parties. The boys will come back to New York for weekend shows once or twice a month, and you and Macie will continue acting in your own way. The lead role of supportive wives, traveling by your husbands' side. Oh, so devoted, you two. Greeting the powerful party guests with a smile. Dressing, speaking, and *living* for the Sophomore boys. None of this horseshit you have in your head about taking a career break. Partying and sleeping 'til noon like a lazy harlot."

I had to laugh at that. "Those boys wouldn't poke us in the ribs if we had knives to their throats, Andrew."

And at the time, I'd believed it. It was all about the music for them. Fame had simply been a side effect. I trusted that. I trusted Josh.

Grifter stood up from his seat and walked toward the door, ignoring my comment altogether. Once he got his wrinkled hand around the knob, he looked back at me with a growl in his eyes.

"Once you said 'I do,' you lost this fight. I own you. Your sister too. You ought to remember it, sweetheart."

Then that blowhard winked and walked out.

3.9: JANE'S RECOUNT

THE BEDDING'S patterns clashed in a way that would make every guest uneasy. I hadn't bothered saying good night to any of the other guests; they were all still partying downstairs. They likely wouldn't even notice I was gone. That fact didn't surprise me as much as the attendees not noticing, or not caring, that Sillian wasn't here. I didn't expect them to worry about me, but I did expect them to worry about her.

I locked the door and wandered back into the bedroom's attached bath to find Sill's notepad still lying there on the counter. Rubbing the card stock between my fingers, a tightness filled my chest. I found a pen near the journal and tossed the booklet between the Victorian bedposts. I imagined my sister releasing her words into the air valiantly, out of her hands, and into the air. Maybe the balloons had been a silly idea. Or perhaps they weren't silly at all.

I tore out a page of my sister's blank paper to keep for myself. Soon enough, I found myself nestled over it, trying to write my way back into mine and Dakota's relationship. Unwanted tears formed in my eyes as I put my sister's pen to paper.

Dear Dakota,

How could you be so heartless! I've been feeling off for weeks. I saw the pink coat in your house. There's another girl in your life, isn't there? I shouldn't be surprised...Everything I touch fails. Right when I start to believe in myself...

When I woke up, the smell of ink greeted me. A haze coated my brain as I took in the oddity of my surroundings. I had fallen asleep in here while writing the letter to Dakota. My face had practically married the piece of paper underneath me.

"Dammit."

I peeled my warm face from the card stock I'd fallen asleep on, knowing an imprint of the inked letter I'd started to Dakota would remain on my cheek. I crumpled the letter and tossed it back onto the bed, moving the notebook aside. The bedroom door was still locked, which meant nobody had been in or out of the room while I'd been passed out.

I unlocked the door with some hope that Sillian might find her way back into the room tonight to check in. It was already two in the morning. Surely, if she talked to any of the party guests, they'd tell her how freaked out I was, and she'd come by to quell my fears. If she weren't back here tomorrow, I'd start that investigation Chief Simmons had suggested. It was my duty.

A cold shudder went down my spine at the events I'd uncovered that night. People were angry with my sister. And my sister was angry back. That axe stunt was too cruel for Sillian's taste. I knew it in my bones. That was an ill-meaning diversion.

The memory flashed of Sill telling me it was the last party I *needed* to attend, and I shuddered. If she knew she was walking into danger, perhaps she was prepared for it. But who was on the other side of all this precariousness?

The party noises were still pressing onward downstairs. If I wanted to have clear thoughts about tonight, I needed to rest. Now.

A lingering imprint of the inked words remained on my face from where I'd fallen asleep. I'd have to wash up, but I was fading too quickly. I tugged the blanket up to my face and drifted far, far away. It was so faint that it could've been a dream, but I swore I heard a ruffling at the bedroom door. Followed by my sister's voice:

"Jane, I've got to show you something."

In my dream, she held a bouquet of flowers toward me. Blood-red roses. With a smile on her face and tears in her eyes, she said:

"I've got to show you who did all this… They did it for me. For you."

Then she twirled and laughed across the field at me. As if this was all the funniest thing in the world.

This was real twin telepathy—I knew it in my bones.

The sounds of my bedroom door opening and closing tickled my ears. I pushed my head further into the pillow, not wanting a disruption in my room to interrupt this moment between my sister and me. Even if it was only a dream. I could feel someone over me, but I had to stay with Sill. She was in danger. She was telling me something.

Still asleep, I followed her through the flower fields and watched her twirl in delight. Her laugh poisoned me. *Would it be the last one I ever heard?*

In the dream, Sill jumped off a ledge and disappeared. I never saw what happened after that. I couldn't follow her down. That was where our telepathy ended. I fought hard, trying for more clairvoyance, but nothing notable ever came. It felt like she was gone.

That was when I heard the sound of heavy footsteps invading my bedroom. I finally forced my eyes awake to reality. I was in the bed alone, but I'd sworn I heard steady walking around the bed frame. Around me.

Someone had come into my room tonight. Someone had watched me sleep. Hadn't they? Was I their next target?

My heart was racing. Out of fear, I stayed under the covers. I'd remain in that room until there was daylight. It seemed I was alone, but my gut told me a different story. Even with a security guard on site, danger felt too close.

I fought sleep hard and failed. In my drowsiness, I heard her ghost-like voice come over me again. The telepathy was back:

"Help me, Jane. Help me."

Our transference was nothing more than that. I needed Sill to show me more, but nothing else came. Just her redundant cry for help. Even in my sleep, it broke my heart. Tears poured over me like rain.

The next morning, I tore out of bed with the sunrise. I knew something terrible had happened to my sister. My dream had shaken me to my core. It hadn't just been a night terror; it had been a cry for help.

An aggressive hangover and the events of the night before hit hard like a one-two punch. The bed next to me was still empty. Sillian had never come by. Nevertheless, footsteps had surrounded me last night. I was almost certain. My nightmares and drowsiness had me dulled. The perfect time for someone to sabotage me. *What did they want?*

Queasy feelings settled in my gut as I pushed back damp hair and threw a sweatshirt over my body. Without another moment to waste, I rushed out of the bedroom to check the other rooms. The feeling in my gut told me something evil had happened to my sister, and it was up to me to find out what.

END OF FILE THREE

Third time's the charm! Below are checkpoints to keep you on track to pinpointing the right suspect:

• **HINT:** What we learn about Sillian *after* her disappearance will only come from the perspectives of others. Remember what you *know* to be true of the victim.

• **CONSIDER:** Smooth criminals don't believe they can be caught. (Time to prove them wrong!)

• **TIP:** Some characters are going to be more helpful than others. Use your discretion wisely.

• **FUN FACT:** Zip codes weren't used until 1963, but the idea was first introduced in 1944.

All stories are possible…until they're not.

CASE FILE FOUR

<u>**Case file four contains five items to be inspected.**</u>
Files should be reviewed in numerical order

- **4.1 Jane's Recount** | March 2023
- **4.2 Sillian's Text Messages**
- **4.3 Mary Sophomore's Diary** | 1944
- **4.4 Jane's Recount** | March 2023
- **4.5 Mary Sophomore's Diary** | 1944

4.1: JANE'S RECOUNT

AFTER PEERING into every bedroom with no sign of my sister, I wanted to look for her phone. If she left it behind, I'd likely be able to use the Face ID to unlock it. Reading her messages might give me some insight as to what had happened the night before. It was the closest thing I had to looking into her mind.

When I came downstairs, Elle was in the kitchen, gathering bottles into a plastic bag. The counters already looked like they'd been scrubbed clean. While I was somewhat relieved to see the majority of the mess had disappeared, I was surprised to see her up before seven in the morning, stomaching the smell of kitchen cleaner after all she'd had to drink the night before.

"Good morning, Jane," Elle said flatly as I descended the stairs. She looked like she'd barely slept. At least she'd changed clothes. "You smell nice."

"Thanks. You're up early." The distrust in my tone was immediately noticeable.

Elle started scrubbing down the sink and her blonde ponytail bobbed back and forth with the sponge in her hand. "I can't sleep in a dirty house."

"Any sign of Sill this morning?" I asked.

"You know that girl can sleep like the dead." It was true. My sister could certainly sleep in. "I haven't seen her."

"When did you last see her?" I was walking around the kitchen, peering into the trash as unsuspecting as I could be. I wondered if Elle was hiding something. Cleaning up a piece of evidence.

"My memory's a little fuzzy, Jane. I polished off the port wine myself… I don't think I ate dinner either."

The adjacent rooms also looked more orderly than they had the night before. Elle was the only one I hadn't seen in her bedroom that morning, so she must've cleaned all of that up herself.

"How long have you been up?" I asked.

"An hour? Two? I don't know. What's with all the questions this morning?"

"I'm worried about Sillian. I haven't seen her since the Brutus thing."

"Oh…well, she's probably fine. I've lived with Sill for a few years now. She errs on the side of theatrics. She's around here some-where." Elle had her back to me, scrubbing the backsplash behind the sink. Wasn't all this cleaning a bit excessive?

"I think it stormed quite a bit last night. She wouldn't have gotten far." I looked outside through the window at the porch my sister had sat on the day before. The grass looked dewy and as green as ever. The weather might be kinder.

"Did it?" Elle asked, blatantly uninterested.

There was a silence between us now that only the white noise of Elle's cleaning could flow into. She continued tidying up for several minutes, opening drawers and cabinets and wiping down surfaces. I thought about Chief Simmons' advice. If I wanted to make progress here, I needed to act like a real journalist would. I needed people to shoot straight with me.

With bags under her eyes, Elle was knocking empty cans off the table. She looked like she didn't want to be cleaning at all.

"I think I'm going to talk to everyone privately. Kind of like an interview style. See if that helps at all."

"Helps what?"

My patience was wearing thin. Was nobody concerned at all about my twin sister's whereabouts?

"Sillian is missing. We've got to find her."

"You Parks girls are always ripping and roaring. Why don't you try at least calling her first? There's service a few miles out of here, I'm sure."

"That's not a bad idea. Just to rule it out as a possibility."

"As a possibility for what?" Elle stopped cleaning now and crossed her arms over her chest. She was staring at me defensively.

"Like, a possibility of what happened to her. Her running away with her phone is one. Though, it could still be around here, too." I looked to my side at the neatly cleaned room. If Sill's phone had been left behind downstairs, Elle certainly would've beaten me to it.

"*What happened to her?* You're acting like someone here killed her."

Elle studied my face. I didn't respond.

"Good God. You really think someone killed her or something? Jane, that's preposterous."

I forced the image out of my brain. I couldn't think like that.

"No," I finally said. "Of course not. But last night was weird. We haven't seen her. She was acting a little off leading up to this... I just want to make sure nobody knows anything I don't. Wouldn't you feel worried about your family, too?"

Elle rolled her eyes. "You don't know my family."

I took a deep breath. That conversation was going nowhere. "I'm going to go circle the yard. See if I can turn up anything."

"Okie dokie."

I grabbed my coat and started with the front. Alex had mentioned he'd talked to my sister by the garage the night before. Because the house itself was so grandiose, the lackluster garage went easily unnoticed. Its two roll-up doors were covered in ivy and looked like they hadn't been used in a long time. They didn't offer much insight as to what was inside.

After a walkabout, there was nothing that notable in the front drive-up or the surrounding yard. I turned to head back inside when something glimmered from inside the dead fountain at just the right angle to catch my eye. I took a deep breath and walked over to it.

Inside was an old beach towel that almost covered my sister's phone—one corner barely peeked out to catch the light. I reached inside and uncovered it. The protective case was cracked as if it had been tossed in like an unlucky fountain coin. Before I powered it on, I took two deep breaths and made a wish.

"Damn. No signal."

Of course there wasn't. I'd have to take it out to the trail.

I cut through the main floor of the house toward the backyard.

"Elle? I'll be right back." She wasn't in the kitchen anymore, so I called out blindly.

I didn't wait for her to respond. Something told me time was of the essence.

4.2: SILLIAN'S TEXT MESSAGES

ELLE | 3:30PM YESTERDAY

Tick tock. The lease renewal is signed by everyone BUT YOU. The way you're avoiding all of this is really stressing me out. Robin and I have been NOTHING but the best of friends to you. You're so fucking ungrateful.

CAMERON | 3:35PM YESTERDAY

Hey. Michael said my glasses might be in your car. Can you make sure to bring them? Thanks :)

ALEX | 6 MINUTES AGO

Where the hell did you go? This better not be what I think it is, Sill. You wouldn't dare. I'm serious. Come back now.

ALEX | 2 MINUTES AGO

You owe me what you promised me. Please come back and talk. I meant what I said last night. You asked for this.

ALEX | JUST NOW

Trust me…I'll do it. I'm not Mr. Nice Guy all the time. I've got the balls to finish this.

You'll see, Sill.

4.3: MARY'S DIARY

1944

THE ARRANGEMENT WAS GOING SWIMMINGLY. Macie and I had taken over the adjoined bedrooms downstairs while Josh and James each had their own upstairs, in separate wings of the home. We'd usually see them around lunchtime when they'd come downstairs for the first prepared meal of the day— before they went into the garage to record music for the rest of the daylight. Macie and I spent most of our days reading and knitting. For once, we'd actually had the time to grow bored.

Occasionally, we'd play cards with James and Josh over a bottle of wine at night. For such private men, they weren't very good at holding a poker face.

"Glad I doubled down." Macie beamed across the dining room table as she moved the poker chips closer to her.

"Don't forget we manage that money," Josh said, laughing before bringing his fourth glass to his lips.

"If only you could be as discreet with your hand as you are with your women," I said in jest about the card game. It was an untold truth that James and Josh had kept seeing other girls. There were the long nights out, the hushed footsteps upstairs, and the occasional heels lingering by the front door. The agreement was that they could do whatever they wanted as long as they didn't get caught. Four weeks in, and they hadn't. Macie and I hadn't had so much as a run-in with the other girls.

Josh laughed out loud at my remark and leaned in. "Well, if you're jealous, darling, all you'd have to do is say."

"Oh, stop it. I'm surprised you aren't with a broad tonight."

"Would be if it weren't for this damned weather."

Macie stood up from the table abruptly at that, leaving the three of us behind. James's face was red as a siren. He wasn't as comfortable talking about his extramarital affairs with Macie as I was with Josh.

Josh seemed to notice it as well.

"While we're all home, there's something we need to discuss. Macie, can you fetch your seat at the table?"

Seemingly annoyed, Macie stepped back into the dining room with her arms crossed over her chest.

"What is it?" I asked Josh.

"Lily Lake."

"What about her?" asked Macie, looking at James instead of Josh.

"It's just that... Well, we're planning a party here next month," Josh said.

"Are you now?" Macie said, a hot flush in her face.

"Yes, and..." Josh sighed and looked at James, who seemed just as confused as Macie and me. "We've got to rename the home. Lily Lake isn't going to suit our guests well."

"Absolutely not," I objected immediately, feeling defensive. My mother wasn't remembered for being honorable, but she was all I had.

Josh paused a minute and looked between Macie and me. "Your mother was not only a suffragist activist, but she was accused of *seven* violent murders."

"And women can vote now, can't they? Her cause wasn't in vain."

"You can't be serious, Mary. We cannot fraternize with political leaders under a name like that. What an abomination that would be."

"Our mother's name, you mean. My family name."

Josh brought his fist down on the table. "I'm surprised that you think so highly of a woman who killed herself on your first birthday. She abandoned you to this world."

I scoffed out loud. Macie and James sat beside Josh and me like dead fish. It was clear who this fight was between.

"She was *murdered*, Josh."

Josh took a deep breath and a long pause before responding again. "I don't want to argue about all this, Mary. You certainly understand where I'm coming from, and that it's not a personal attack toward you or your sister. It's a business decision. I've already submitted the papers for the name change. The new signage for the gate should come next week."

I swallowed hard, at a loss for words.

"And what will the new sign say?" Macie asked.

"The Sophomore Manor. To represent all four of us."

"That name does not represent all four of us," I said.

"Well..." Josh sighed before patting his mute brother on the shoulder and stood up from the table. "It does now."

It was the first time I'd regretted the marriage. And there was plenty more where that came from.

4.4: JANE'S RECOUNT

WHEN I STARTED THE TRAIL, I noticed that the rainstorm had washed away all the footprints from the day before. More brush had fallen in the rain, and I scratched my legs as I passed through. I winced in pain—I'd already gotten cut up the day before trying to navigate that trail. I wondered if whoever else had been on it had experienced the same.

On Cell Mountain, my phone buzzed with messages from Dakota, asking for more details about what was happening. My stomach was in knots at the sight of his name. He certainly only wanted more of a story to sell. I couldn't believe him.

False alarm, I texted him back. I needed to buy time to think about what I would say to him next. I didn't have the space in my brain for that at that moment. I just needed to keep him and his associates away from the damn keyboard while I searched for my sister. Was it really too much to ask?

Sillian's texts came through quickly and immediately set off my suspicion, followed by several emails of authorized Venmo transactions sent from her account. I could feel my heartbeat at the bottom of my stomach.

She'd seemed so worried that day she'd come to my apartment.

I couldn't help but wonder if that fear had been brought on by one of her party guests. Which begged the question, why invite them at all?

When I got back to the manor, everyone was miraculously awake. Someone had to have woken them all up. The idea of six people getting out of bed before eight in the morning after partying all night unsettled me. Surely, some of them would be too hungover.

"Donut?" asked the man who'd been dressed as Waldo from the night before. He was walking from the kitchen into the main living area, a white paper sack in between his hands.

"How'd you get donuts?"

"I got them yesterday on the way in!" Robin's voice called out from the seating area to answer for him. "I knew we'd be hungover today. Didn't expect this place to have a diner 'round the corner."

I turned the corner and came into the seating area. The candelabras in the middle of the room had been lit along with the fireplace. Each overnight guest was positioned in their pajamas, scattered across the many velvet seats. They looked like they'd been doing a seance. When I walked in, everyone's eyes were glued to me.

"Everyone's up awfully early…" I said as I took a donut. My heart was pounding.

"Elle said you're worried about Sill. So, we all chatted and…" Michael said. He was wearing an old band tee and tight gray sweatpants. The outfit did nothing to hide his black and blue face.

"And what?" I asked.

"Well, honey," Robin said, "none of us are really *that* concerned. Even with the events of last night. This is just classic Sill behavior. But, if *you're* worried, well…we can do our best to help you out. I mean, surely all of us put together can offer the peace of mind!"

Robin was wearing a black turtleneck sweater and a floor-length skirt. She looked like she'd already gotten ready for a red carpet appearance.

"Okay… When's the last time you guys saw her?"

"Midnight."

"Before the third round of drinks."

"Ten-thirty."

Everyone answered at the same time. I could barely hear their responses over one another. I shook my head in disapproval.

"Maybe this would go better if I talked to everyone one at a time." I crossed my arms over my chest, feeling insecure about all the attention. What would a journalist do? At that moment, I felt like anything but.

Elle sighed as if annoyed and stood from her seat next to Robin. "I'm making mimosas."

"Nice." Michael perked up. "I'll take mine stiff."

"How 'bout a pot of coffee, too?" Robin said.

Alex sat quietly in an oversized accent chair beside the fireplace, staring straight at me. The look on his face was menacing.

"Alex…can I talk to you alone? In the study."

Without a word, he stood up from his chair. I held my breath.

In the words of Sillian, *let the games begin.*

4.5: MARY'S DIARY

1944

THEY'D PUT the new sign out over the front gate the day before. I'd grit my teeth about it. They said you had to do that in marriage every now and then. So that was what I'd tried to do.

Marriage was back to business as usual. It had been two weeks since our co-marital poker night. We hadn't had one since. Josh and James were staying busy at the clubs. Macie and I were staying home. We knew this break was good for us. Necessary. But sometimes, I think she forgot.

"Does it bother you at all?" Macie said on one of the nights, aggressively filing her nail down to a snub. We were in the front study, locked away. We came in here most nights to play chess or to talk. It was one of the most noise-insulated rooms in the house.

I already knew what Macie was talking about. Earlier that night, we'd heard footsteps on the floor above us—four pairs instead of two. Various women would sneak in and out of our home, tiptoeing on our hardwood floors as they lived out their affair-filled fantasies with our husbands.

And no, it didn't bother me.

"Does what get to me?" I peered at her over the pages of my book. I had been reading *Gone With The Wind* for the first time. A beautifully-written story, if you believed in romance. Not much to my taste. The new chair, however, was luxurious.

Macie looked at me wide-eyed. She hadn't been eating enough the past few weeks. Although, I wasn't sure what she had to be nervous about. Everything was just how we'd planned it to be. The career break wasn't going to last forever. I was getting annoyed at her for not enjoying it more.

"It doesn't bother you when…*other* women come over here?"

The first time James and Josh had brought women home from the bars about ten days in, she'd claimed to have gotten food poisoning. And there the food poisoning was again. I sighed, placing my bookmark back into my novel.

"Macie, do I need to remind you that this is a *business* deal?"

"It's just… What if we're found out?" she said, staring intently out the window. "What if one of their broads starts running her mouth?"

"We'd sell out on an interview or two. Make a living off the scandal for a few months. That's the worst that could happen. We've been over this."

There was a tight tension in the air then. I knew what she was about to say.

"What if we actually tried? To be *with* them."

That was the second time she'd asked that question.

"Macie…if this is too much for you, I think we should talk to the boys and have them move out. We won't say divorce until after your movie and their album comes out. But the whole point of the arrangement was so you and I could have some downtime. Not for you to feel sick to your stomach every night. You know Sandy's husband would take us back."

I said this somewhat against my greater instincts. I wasn't ready to burst back into film.

Marriage wasn't a demanding career path, especially when it wasn't marriage at all. The four of us were colleagues who shared walls, association being our paycheck. We only kissed for the camera. We never had to screw them. They never asked. In my eyes, it was the happiest marriage imaginable.

"No. This is good. I'm just adjusting. It's barely been a month," Macie said weakly.

I nodded my reassurance at Macie before she excused herself to the adjacent restroom. The sink was running for a long time. I pretended not to hear her hurling. She'd get used to our arrangement. I'd make certain of it.

The following day was gorgeous. Macie and I decided to make the most of the day and picnic at the creek. It was the best I could come up with.

I knew I needed to take her out on the town soon and have her find a new crush to keep her up at night. But to be honest, I'd never dated at all. I didn't know how to go about the whole thing. Especially since we had to keep it under wraps. Josh made hushed affairs look easy. Maybe I could talk to him.

"Great day for a picnic, isn't it, sister?" I said as we stepped out the door and into the backyard. The creek wasn't far.

Once we made it to the creek, we had our lunch. The staff had only prepared salads for us. Nothing really interesting, so the picnic wasn't going to last as long as I'd hoped. Conversation with Macie was dragging. I'd forgotten the wine.

"This weather's so wonderful; I think I'm going to go for a swim," I finally told her.

"Did you pack a suit?"

"Well, it's just us. And I've got on my slip."

Macie's jaw dropped as if I'd just said the most scandalous thing in the world. "Why, you can't do that! Once it's wet, you'll be able to see right through."

"Oh, please. We're practically on *our* property. Who gives a damn?" The statement felt like a stretch after I said it. Technically, we are on the Sophomore property. Which, legally, was ours. But was it really? I forced the thought out of my head. I had to let that one go.

While I stripped down to my slip, Macie looked around the

area, ensuring no peepers were nearby. I found the nearest rock to jump from and went in.

The water felt good. Sooner or later, Macie finally joined me in her slip, and we swam and talked for what seemed to be hours.

Macie was the most childlike I'd ever seen her, doing trick jumps off the rocks. Attempting dives of all kinds.

The water was so peaceful and joyous that day. Unlike anything I'd ever experienced before. The creek wanted nothing from us. Nothing at all. I thought if we only had this spot, this quiet little corner to run to for the rest of our lives, then we might be the wealthiest women alive.

The sun eventually went down. Time flew right past us. I think it might've been the best day of my life.

"We ought to clean up before the boys see us," Macie said on her way out of the creek.

"Let 'em stare. They see women in less clothing every night."

We both laughed. Macie seemed unbothered. *This* was what we needed.

We walked into our home for dinner without bothering to cover our soaking wet slips. We went on to exchange pleasantries with our husbands over the meal and read our night-time books. And the next day, we did it all over again. Swimming in our slips. Except that time, I didn't forget the bottle of wine.

We started to belly laugh through the days of no responsibilities. Our childhoods had finally arrived, just a few decades late. That made everything *almost* worthwhile.

We'd finally started making a habit of getting a swim, enjoying the weather, and having fun. Macie even spoke like she was ready to try her hand at a date. Secretly, of course. There would be logistics to be dealt with, but nevertheless, it was a step in the right direction.

That was until we heard the knock on the door one Sunday morning. I couldn't believe my eyes when I opened the door.

It was our agent, Sandy. And standing next to her, Grifter.

There was something surreal about Sandy's look. I noticed it before any words had been spoken. An ethereal golden light settled on the dew around our drive-up. The falls of the fountain sang eerie sounds of peacefulness. And there she was, like a grim reaper in the midst of all of it. Grifter was a gargoyle next to her. I forced a breath. This couldn't be good.

"Sandy. *Andrew.* I didn't know you knew each other?"

They didn't bother with the hellos.

"A mistress went talking to the reporters," Sandy said, sidestepping me through the door frame. Grifter followed her, a stupid grin on his face. "We got to her early enough, but it still might make the papers. Where's the rest of you kids?"

I had answered the door alone. Macie was in the kitchen, getting our lunch basket. James and Josh we never kept tabs on, so who knew?

Nerves crept up my spine with spider legs. "Dirty harlots," I heard myself say. "We can talk to James and Josh about the women. I think they're out right now. Macie's in the kitchen."

Sandy and Grifter almost matched in their gray pantsuits, as if they were in team uniform. Sandy stormed off into the kitchen. Grifter took an up-and-down look at me before following her at a distance. I almost scoffed at the audacity.

"Gr— Andrew, how do you know Sandy?" I was on his heels.

"Small business." He shrugged casually, with that dumb look still on his face. That incident had to be worse than Sandy had let on. "Agents stick together, you know."

Macie was sitting on the countertop in her silk slip when we walked in.

"Sandy, Andrew!" Macie stood up to make herself decent, tightening her slip's shoulder strap at the invasion. Sandy had seen us in all kinds of states, but that didn't make my sister any less shy around Andrew Kelly.

Grifter circled the island with his hands in his pockets. For a small man, he knew how to make himself look big.

Sandy dropped a leather bag down on the countertop dramatically. Her cheeks were scarlet red.

"So, girls, do either of you own bathing suits? Or is it just these little...*sheets?*" Grifter let out a chuckle and went over to Macie, taking the hem of her skirted slip between his thumb and index finger.

My face went hot. If he put another finger on my sister, I'd go feral. He seemed to get the message soon enough. With a wink, he slowly stepped away.

"We had to buy back photos from a photographer who got you two nearly nude on film. Might as well have been stark naked. You could see everything through those damn slips! You two... You're both very lucky we were able to catch it in time." Sandy shook her head in disbelief. "The photos cost us a fortune."

My eyes were spring-loaded. No way someone had seen us. "How could that be?"

"Don't worry, gals, I made sure to keep a couple of those photos for us to keep. Might frame 'em. They're over the mantle material." Grifter. Fucking Grifter.

"Between the boys' tomfoolery and the girls' *liberation*, I'd be surprised if this household can afford to pay us at the end of the month," Sandy said.

"Sandy, we didn't—"

Sandy's finger went to her mouth like rubber, erasing my sister's sentence from thin air.

"It's time to set up some serious ground rules. Slip-dipping being the first thing," Sandy said, pushing up her thick-framed glasses. "You girls. Dumb, dumb, dumb."

"You might think you're retired, but you're far from it as far as money is concerned," Andrew said with a serious nod.

"Listen, I love you two. You're almost my own flesh and blood. And I understand what you need here. But if you two go out of the house at all, your husbands better be there with you. If Macie goes out, James is there. If you go, Mary, Josh is at your side. If you're both out for as much as groceries, both husbands are there. Do you copy?" Sandy brought down the gavel.

I closed my eyes, taking in the blow, praying she was done speaking. But then Grifter opened his mouth.

"The other thing. There will be no more girls in this house besides you two. That's it. No more streetwalkers in thigh-highs. The only heels in this home should belong to your own closets."

"But—" I said before Sandy put another finger in the air. "Sign here. Andrew'll tell your husbands next."

"There's got to be another way," I said, pleading.

"With all due respect, *Mrs. Sophomore*, there isn't. Sandy and I made this decision. We take good care of our clients. Even when they don't like it. This marriage is your career now."

Sandy placed what looked to be a contract on the kitchen island. Macie hadn't moved from her place in the corner. I stood in front of her like a bodyguard.

"Can you give us a minute, Andrew?" Sandy turned and asked sweetly. I'd never heard her so polite.

"Get the signatures. I'll wait in the car." Grifter waved to Macie and me, a devilish smirk still smeared across his face. I wanted to hit the old man on his way out the door.

"No way are we signing this, Sandy. That man is *horrible*." Tears were in my eyes. I was begging now, but I didn't care. We couldn't lose what we had. Not now.

"That man manages your husbands. Which means he manages you. Which means *he* pays *my* bills. We're lucky he's involving me at all. He certainly doesn't have to."

Macie grabbed my arm, still not saying anything.

"Can't you talk to him? Can't you do anything? If James and Josh can't see other girls…" I didn't want to finish the thought.

"I can get you booked on another gig if that's what you want. But you're too far into this marriage now to go on crying to me for help. You bought their last name for every penny you have. That decision was made in ink."

I didn't say anything. The kitchen was quiet. In a rare moment, Sandy seemed to soften.

"Look. Your best bet is to talk to *your husbands*. They're the only ones who can deny Andrew Kelly a paycheck. As long as they're paying him, he's running the show. And if you don't wanna be in the show anymore, you ought to ask the Sophomores to cancel it. That's your only way out of a lifetime of this."

Sandy held up the contract again before slamming it back on the table.

I looked at my sister, but Macie didn't make eye contact with me as she stared down the document.

"You know, that man said he has a five-year plan for your marriage, and it doesn't read like your idea of vacation," Sandy said. I was surprised by the frightened look she wore.

"Being your manager—it's a money grab. But as your *friend*, it's nothing to laugh about. I'm worried, girl."

"We can get out of this if we must. The boys are decent. It's an honest deal," I said, my voice quivering.

"You better hope so," Sandy said.

But it was too late. My sister was already bent over the counter, carefully signing the contract in her best cursive lettering.

END OF FILE FOUR

Awesome sleuthing. Phillip Beacons stopped by and left a sticky note on your desk:

• **HINT:** Evidence will not always look like evidence.

• **STICKY NOTE FROM PHILLIP:** *"Keep focusing on the suspects for now. The 'why' always takes longer to find than the 'how.' I'll be checking in after you complete File 6. -P.B."*

• **FUN FACT:** Several of America's first female business owners started in Virginia. Maggie Lena Walker was among them. Walker piloted the first female-owned bank in Richmond, VA—an impressive feat for a black woman in the era of Jim Crow laws.

Yes. No. Maybe so.

CASE FILE FIVE

<u>Case file five contains eight items to be inspected.</u>
Files should be reviewed in numerical order

- **5.1 A. A. Unofficial Questioning**
- **5.2 E. E. Unofficial Questioning**
- **5.3 R. R. Unofficial Questioning**
- **5.4 C. C. Unofficial Questioning**
- **5.5 M. M. Unofficial Questioning**
- **5.6 Mary Sophomore's Diary** | 1944
- **5.7 Jane's Recount** | March 2023
- **5.8 Mary Sophomore's Diary** | 1945

5.1: A. A. UNOFFICIAL QUESTIONING

RECORDED BY JANE

J: "Okay. Let's start. For the record, it appears my twin sister, Sillian Parks, is missing. My name is Jane Parks. I am interviewing Alex Ansley, Sillian's *ex-boyfriend*, in the study of the Sophomore Manor."

A: "What record are we speaking for?"

J: "I'm recording this on my phone. If you're okay with that, of course? Just so I can make sure everyone's stories align and what-not. Police might need it later."

A: "Wouldn't they do their own questioning?"

J: "Yeah, but who knows how long that'll be from now? Things are best remembered when fresh. Something I learned in journalism. I'd really like to get all the details...in case something is wrong."

A: "You're really that worried about Sill?"

J: "Yeah. I guess I am."

Heavy sighing noises

A: "Fire away then."

J: "Alright… For starters, can you explain why you came?"

A: "What?"

J: "Can you explain why you came to this event? As Sill's *ex-boyfriend*."

A: "Because I was invited? C'mon, Jane. Why do I need more reason than that? Did you bring me back here just to bait me? That's such bullshi—"

J: "You were the first to arrive at the party, right?"

Long pause

A: "Yup. I was leaving another friend's house, and driving all the way home first would've been a waste of time."

J: "And what happened when you got here?"

A: "Sill and I got in a fight. She was on the back porch with a notebook full of letters. She left one addressed to me out on the patio table. I was looking around for her when I found it."

J: "And what did that letter say?"

A: "SparkNotes version was I'm a *horrible* human being."

J: "Did that make you upset?"

A: "Of course it made me upset. The narrative was downright offensive. Sill and I broke up. And while we've been trying the whole *'friends'* thing, she has no right to tell me how— That letter was ridiculous and she *knows* it."

J: "It makes sense that you got so upset. I read the letter too. Yet, I'm wondering why you stuck around at the manor after that? If it were me, I would've been out of here at the sight of an ex…much less a *fight* with them."

A: "Well, we're different people, aren't we?"

J: "Did you and Sill speak at all last night?"

A: "Yes, we spoke in the main room in plain sight like civilized people. Near the banister."

J: "What did you two talk about?"

A: "Let's see…some small talk. Then the history of the world's greatest invention: *the airbus.* Old presidents. That kind of thing. She's a buff for the past."

J: "C'mon, Alex. I wanted to give you the opportunity to tell me what you really said to her yourself…before everyone that overheard you tells me."

A: "Nobody overheard us."

J: "Are you sure about that? The main staircase was pretty populated, as I recall."

A: "Look, I don't know what game you're playing with me here. I *am* worried about Sill. Do you think I want to be grilled like a steak? No. I'm here to help *you.* So stop treating me like I'm the villain. If you really need to know what we talked about at the party, we decided to end the friendship. The decision had me feeling nervous, so I drank…hard."

J: "Right… And why didn't you tell her that you don't want to be friends when you got in a fight earlier? Before everyone else got here?"

A: "Jesus Christ, Jane."

J: "So you had an urgent mission, seemingly out of thin air, to end your friendship with Sillian last night at the party? Hmm. Care to elaborate on your timing?"

A: "To set the record straight, I'm not some horrible guy. My, uhm…girlfriend, or whatever you'd call her— I don't know. She had said it was Sill or her. So, Sill and I talked about it. That's the truth. We came to a conclusion."

J: "Wow. So you've got a girlfriend, and she knows you're here to break ties with Sill?"

A: "Well, no. Not exactly."

J: "So you came up here and *didn't* tell your current girlfriend?"

A: "It's more complicated than that. We aren't serious. Like, I don't exactly even call her my girlfriend. Publicly. And I just… Sill and I have a lot of history. You wouldn't understand."

J: "I probably wouldn't. Just like I didn't understand your text messages to Sill this morning. Care to elaborate on those?"

A: "What the… You have Sill's phone?"

Long pause

A: "Look, I'm not going to explain my private business with your sister 'cause that would just get us both in trouble. You can be assured those messages weren't about something nefarious or whatever it is you're getting at. I'm about done with this conversation. You're getting a little too comfortable with that recorder in your hand."

J: "Fine, Alex. Any last ideas on where Sill might be?"

A: "I wish I knew."

5.2: E. E. UNOFFICIAL QUESTIONING

RECORDED BY JANE

J: "For the record, we are conducting this interview in the study of the rented manor. For your information, holding an unofficial questioning might be useful to the authorities if foul play is *officially* suspected. It appears my twin sister, Sillian Parks, is missing. My name is Jane Parks. I'm interviewing Elle Ewing, Sill's roommate of two years."

E: "The way you're acting so official is a little bit nerve-wracking. We don't even know if Sill is missing. I haven't even brushed my teeth yet. I feel bad for you breathing in my hot air."

J: "Is it okay with you that this conversation will be recorded?"

E: "Would you care if it wasn't?"

J: "I've got to ask. Legally."

E: "I've got nothing to hide, so record as much as you want."

J: "Can you recount last night's events in your own words, starting from your arrival at the manor?"

E: "Mmkay… Robin and I drove up to the manor location that Sill had rented for the Halloween party. Robin drove me and some other people."

J: "Okay. What else happened when you got here?"

E: "Hmm… We noticed that Alex's car— Oh, Alex is Sill's ex for the microphone listeners—but yeah, Alex's car was already out front when we got here. So we hung outside to give them privacy. Sill and him always had something going on. Then more people showed, including you. I helped decorate the house, took a shower, and the party began."

J: "What time would you say the party ended?"

E: "I pretty much shut it down. There were a few stragglers, but I'd say everyone was settled in for the night around two or three in the morning."

J: "Do you remember who the stragglers were?"

E: "No, but I heard them from my room when I was trying to sleep. I'm closest to the stairs. Male voices, for sure. Men are always way too loud when they're drunk. I tossed and turned for another hour, thanks to them."

J: "Is there anything noteworthy that was happening in Sill's life that you saw as her roommate these past few weeks?"

E: "That's like asking if the ocean's wet, Jane."

J: "Care to elaborate?"

E: "Well, there's always some weird shit going on with Michael. They've rarely been hanging out at our place. My friends saw them fighting in the diner the other day. Pointing this way and that at a laptop screen. Sill used to tell me about their fights, but lately, she's been holding her cards close."

J: "Did your friend say what was on the laptop screen?"

E: "A calendar or map, maybe? I can't remember. I've stopped caring too much."

J: "Have you? Last I heard, you were pretty worried about your lease renewal."

Long pause

E: "Where'd you hear that?"

J: "I don't give up my sources. Is everything okay between you two? Doesn't seem like it is."

Elle yawns

E: "Yeah…well. She's changed. We used to be close, but she's barely around anymore. I shouldn't be surprised she hasn't put her name on the lease with us for next year, but at the same time, I expect her to at least *tell me* she doesn't want to live with us anymore. She owes Robin and I that courtesy. We've been friends forever. We don't have but a few weeks to find a new roommate. At some point, we've got to just ask somebody else."

J: "And you haven't talked about it at all?"

E: "Oh, you know…I've hinted at it. Several times. But every time she's stone cold. Sill's so good at avoiding the issues I bring to her that I think she should run for office."

J: "So are you two still…friends, I guess? It sounds like things are hostile at best."

E: "They are, but I'd never do anything to, like…hurt Sill. I'm not that kinda person."

J: "Who said anything about hurting her?"

E: "Are you serious right now? I was saying that as an expression."

J: "If something happens to someone you love, you never rule out all the options."

E: "Well, that's crazy then because something might've happened to someone I love too. You *know* me."

J: "Sorry to get you worked up. We can take a break."

5.3: R. R. UNOFFICIAL QUESTIONING

RECORDED BY JANE

R: "Hi, sweetheart. Will you be recording a video as well? I did my makeup in case."

J: "We're just doing an audio recording. If you're okay with being recorded, that is?"

R: "Might as well turn that camera on, too. That security guard last night was something out of a Sylvia Day novel. I don't know if he'd ever be on this *case*—if that's what you're calling it. But, like…if he is around, he should know that I'm single. And *very* pretty."

J: "For the recording, I'm here with Robin Reed today. One of Sillian's roommates."

R: "Is the camera on?"

J: "No. Just audio."

Heavy sigh

R: "You're just no fun, are you?"

J: "What can you tell me about last night's party?"

R: "What can't I tell you? I'm a wealth of knowledge when it comes to party observation. I've got eyes and ears everywhere. With that in mind, you should start with that Waldo boy."

J: "Why's that?"

R: "Camden? Cameron? Who knows what his name is? But, oh my God. He's in *love* with your sister. Obsessed is an understatement. He's, like, some math guru who tutored her through college. I'm not sure how he's managed to stick around. But that boy was always putting a move on Sillian. And get this! Now, he's befriended Michael. Not just regular friends, either. They *golf* together. That's some B-F-F shit in boy world. He seems desperate to be in the picture of Sill's life. And crazy enough to pull it off... She's too nice to the weird ones."

J: "Hmmm... Was he acting weird last night?"

R: "He's always acting strange. I saw him rummaging around some of the bedrooms last night like a total psychopath. Probably looking for Sill's panties. Girl crazy much?"

J: "Good to know... I'll be following up there. Let's go in a different direction for a minute. How have you been feeling about the lease situation?"

R: "What's that, hon?"

J: "How has your relationship with Sill been? Given that she hasn't signed your renewal lease..."

R: "She hasn't? I thought Elle said that she did."

J: "Elle said Sill hasn't resigned your lease. And she seems quite upset about it."

R: "Well…that's the first I've heard of it. But if Sill wanted to live with other people, then so be it, I guess. I'm sure we'd still be friends."

J: "That's mature."

R: "Don't sound so surprised! Sill's been there for me through it all. I'd support her through anything in return. When things went south at my job, she helped me find a new one. Didn't she tell you?"

J: "What is it that you're doing now? I don't know that she did."

R: "Jewelry sales. Which reminds me, that gold is all wrong for your skin tone. I meant to point that out yesterday when you showed up wearing that hideous pair of earrings."

J: "Right. Well, is there anything else you want to add? Anything odd on Sillian's part that you have noticed recently?"

R: "That girl shares *everything* with me. Things in her life are always interesting, per se. But I would know if she was in danger. She's not."

J: "What makes you so certain?"

R: "I've got a sixth sense for these things. We have a bond. She'd have told me."

J: "But she didn't tell you about the lease…"

R: "Well, that's an entirely different story."

J: "How s—?"

R: "Sorry, hon. It's time for my mid-morning coffee. Let's catch up later!"

5.4: C.C UNOFFICIAL QUESTIONING

RECORDED BY JANE

J: "Alright, uh…Cameron, right? What's your last name?"

C: "Yup, that's me. Cameron Cortez. "

J: "You were in the Waldo costume last night?"

C: "Right. And I was a few beers too deep. Did we already meet?"

J: "Not officially. I'm Jane—Sillian's sister."

C: "You look just alike. Minus the hair."

J: "Do you smoke? I couldn't help but notice the smell…"

C: "No."

J: "Uhm, okay… I should let you know that this conversation will be recorded. That okay with you?"

C: "Sure."

J: "Can we start with how you actually met my sister?"

C: "I was her college math tutor. All four years. She sucked at math, so we've spent a lot of time together. Ended up staying friends."

J: "You've been friends a long time then? I'm surprised I've never seen you at one of these parties before."

C: "Maybe we've just never met."

J: "So you were assigned as her tutor through school and you both just became friends? Are you the same year?"

C: "We're the same year. But no, I wasn't assigned as a tutor to Sill. I saw her posting questions on the school website damn near every day. We'd said hello in class a few times. I thought she was real cute. And I'm pretty good at math."

J: "So you were hitting on her?"

C: "You could say that. But I also helped her with math."

J: " So…were you ever successful at hitting on Sill?"

C: "You know your sister. Such a tease. We've always been flirty. We even kissed once during junior year while studying for finals. Great kiss, but no, we're just friends right now."

J: "*Right now?* Are you holding onto hope that she will want to date you after six years of friendship?"

C: "If you changed your tone, it'd actually sound romantic."

J: "Does Sill know about this?"

C: "I assume that she assumes."

J: "I'm just… Let's move on."

C: "Let's."

J: "What can you tell me about the party last night?"

C: "Well, there was the attacker who physically assaulted Michael. And the snakes. I was way too close to both of those things."

J: "What'd he look like? The guy with the axe."

C: "He was wearing a mask. But he was tall. Not a super buff build, though. More lanky. Just like Alex, if you ask me."

J: "What about the rest of the party? Notice anything off?"

C: "Other than watching Michael and Sill trade spit the entire party? So in love. And so annoying!"

J: "I didn't see them together *that* much."

C: "Well, you probably didn't stay up late enough then. I stayed up way too late myself. Alex was the only guy I remember staying up as long as I did. Walking around with a stupid smile on his face. Looked like a politician he was grinning so much. Stuffing candy and whatnot into his pockets. I even thought I saw him put half a sandwich down the front of his pants."

J: "That's quite interesting, although you're certainly leaving something out."

C: "Am I?"

J: "I heard you were sneaking around last night. Looking into different bedrooms. For what, might I ask?"

Very long pause

C: "You caught me! I was looking for Sill's journal."

J: "Her journal? You mean her notepad?"

C: "Look...I heard about the whole Alex fight. That letter she wrote. It was the talk of the party. When I thought about it, Sill had once mentioned a secret diary where she keeps all of her notes on people. She said she *always* has it with her. So I put two and two together."

J: "And?"

C: "*And* this is going to sound bad, but I went off to find it. I thought if I could read her notes on me...well, maybe I could get some clarity on where I stand. As a potential suitor. I've been waiting all this time, you see."

J: "Wow."

C: "Wow?"

J: "I... I'm going to have to circle back. I need a minute to process. Do you have anything else you want to add to all of this?"

C: "I'm an open book, Jane. If you need anything, just ask."

5.5: M. M. UNOFFICIAL QUESTIONING

RECORDED BY JANE

J: "Alright, Michael, this conversation is going to be documented. Starting…*now.* Let's start with your consent to interview."

M: "You have my consent. I'd do anything to find Sill. Even though I'm almost positive her absence has something to do with Alex's presence."

J: "Feel free to elaborate."

M: "That petty son of a *you-know-what* put on a mask and attacked me last night. It's so obvious that it was him pulling that charade."

J: "Why's that?"

M: "Maybe he hates guys from California? I think he's like that with his politics. And physically, nobody else is tall enough to have been my attacker. Plus, who else is as passionate to win Sillian's heart?"

J: "And you're saying that as her boyfriend?"

M: "Well…I don't need to win her heart."

J: "Haven't you two broken up three or four times?"

M: "True love isn't always perfect? It's been a complicated arrangement."

J: "If that's what you call it… Moving on. Is there any reason someone would have wanted to attack *you* specifically last night?"

M: "Well, I got in trouble with Sill. Which got me into a fight with the boys. But it wasn't that serious."

J: "What was Sillian upset with you for?"

M: "I mean, it isn't relevant to the situation. I've just been trying to quit smoking for the past year. I was about two months in, mostly clean, give or take. Then Sill caught me with cigars and the boys on the patio late last night. She got really upset that I lost all of my progress. She's my accountability buddy."

J: "I've seen you drunk many times. You didn't seem *that—*"

M: "Well, anyways, I got in trouble with my girlfriend, and so the boys and I threw out the smokes. Then I got hit by that fucking lunatic, Alex. Still gotta figure out what to do about him. He's got it coming."

J: "You seem more into hating Alex than loving Sill."

M: "Can you blame me?"

J: "*Okay.* Next question: Did you see anything that might be helpful for me to know last night?"

M: "Typical party antics… But you know, at some point, Robin was frantically asking everyone if they had the key to Sill's car. Don't know what she was looking for, but she seemed in a hurry."

J: "Do you remember what time?"

M: "It had to be late. I remember my face hurting at that point."

J: "Did Robin say anything about why she needed to get into Sillian's car?"

M: "Not coherently… She seemed drunk as a skunk. Gotta be battling a massive hangover today."

J: "Okay. Well, thanks, Michael. We'll talk later."

M: "Let me know how I can help."

5.6: MARY'S DIARY

1944

THINGS WERE fine for four more days. That was about how long men could control themselves. Macie and I were still sleeping in our own beds, formulating what we thought would be our strategy for the situation. On the backside of a plywood board, we'd mapped our methodology with an approach we could not fail. We were seven minutes into rehearsal when James knocked at the bedroom door.

"We should talk. All of us," James said without breaking eye contact with my sister.

I nodded and uncrossed my arms from the corner of the bedroom, firmly putting my hand on the windowsill.

"Sure. We were actually getting some material ready to chat with you about, so if you give us thirty—"

"Now." James sharpened his tone and redirected his gaze in my direction.

There it was—the price of freedom.

The look on my sister's face told me it was time to pay for our sweet liberation. A reward that, in retrospect, had just been bait all along. Hand in hand, I followed her footsteps uneasily to where Josh was already cross-legged on the couch. He was the fiery one of the two, making him a good match for me. Not romantically, but competitively. I knew I intimidated him quite a bit. I'd never let him know the feeling was reciprocated.

Josh didn't waste much time after we found our seats in the great room.

"We've decided under new circumstances…you will start sleeping with us in our bedrooms. Like a real husband and wife would." Josh dropped his jaw into his hand and glanced at his brother, avoiding our reactions.

"Yeah…" James nodded. "If we're going to do all of this. Well… we ought to try to be together."

My heart felt as if it might fail at any moment. My sister's hand quivered inside of mine. I looked up at the boys; she looked down at her toes.

I fought to ignore James's stare on my sister and positioned myself to face my own husband.

"No." I established my stance immediately for their appeal. "That was the goal of this arrangement. To avoid the relationship upkeep and live our free lives separately. We came up with another plan that—"

"It was a fathead mistake," Josh said. "Our profits are up from the soap opera operation we've been putting on. Old records are flying off the shelves. We can afford the extra peanuts it will take to keep you happy in this scenario. But we can't live disconnected lives. It isn't working." Josh held strong.

The sweat between my and my sister's palms was too thick to hold onto. I turned to face her, seeking backup, but she kept her eyes planted firmly on the floor. A silence filled the room, and I tried again.

"We'll do a divorce. Three months. Lots of money. Make another big splash and that's that."

Josh shook his head. "No. Losing you two will hurt our next album."

"How do you know?"

"Because our sales are up eight-five percent since the wedding. No new releases."

"We'll make this as pleasant as possible. By our next album, we can add to our pack. Get a nanny. Then three of four years after that, we can consider talk of divorce again." Josh poured the words as if they were sweet honey.

I couldn't believe what I'd heard. My feet found the floor in a firm stance, but the words came out in a whisper like I was already defeated.

"We will not have your children."

Josh kept his cool and leaned back onto the sofa cushion. "We'll begin trying after the Airbus release party. Until then, we can practice with protection."

Anger danced around my pupils. How foolish we were to have played games with these men. I knew it as I watched James hold a sorrow-eyed look at my sister, whose head was in her hands. A single tear fell down his face.

"No..." I said as more of a question than a statement, weak with resentment. Everything inside me was sick. "We will not sleep with you. I won't. Josh...*please.*"

"We'll bring your things up to our rooms," Josh said, stone-cold, and motioned toward a silent James to stand. It was clear he had made up his mind.

"I'm sorry it had to unfold this way, but there's no other option. You'll feel much better after we've familiarized ourselves. We'll start tonight, Mary. Like a beautiful woman with a handsome man, you have nothing to fear. I'm going to be awfully sweet to you. I promise."

He had the audacity to take my limp hand and kiss it. "Please draw a bath for yourself and be ready upstairs by nine."

James stood over the place where my sister was sitting and offered his arms out to her. She willingly leaned into him and let herself be held.

As for me, I couldn't feel my body. My legs floated toward the backdoor. A cigarette found itself between my fingers. Sweat coated my dress heavy, so I took it off right there on the porch. In only my undergarments, I caressed the sweat into my skin like lotion, massaging the body that belonged to only me for the last time.

The smoke filled my lungs to lift the weight out of my system. The stick burned in between my fingers; then I gave the cigarette two taps to drop the cinders.

Ashes, ashes. We all fall down.

5.7: JANE'S RECOUNT

AFTER I'D CONCLUDED the questioning, I felt like the party's antagonist. Most of the guests were already playing morning rounds of beer pong in the kitchen's rental or gossiping in the sitting room.

Judgmental eyes glared at me when I exited the study. It felt like the others were holding their breath at the sight of me, as if I might suck all the fun right out of the air as I walked past. I decided to take a walk and give my boss at the paper a call.

The air was cold and the bramble of the forest was thick, catching my sweater and skin as I pushed past. My heartbeat was working overtime, perhaps for Sill and me both. If I was to think logically, I needed to find a way to calm down. At that moment, I was on information overload.

When I got to Cell Mountain, new texts from Dakota came through:

DAKOTA | 38 MINUTES AGO

Hi, doll. I'm worried about you. And I'm quite bored. Should I come over?

Dakota was the last person I wanted to deal with right now, given he'd tipped off the prospect of *my* danger to *my* boss. Not to mention the anxiety that still bubbled under my chest about the girl in the pink coat. I'd have to reserve my energy and have those conversations with him later. I quickly shot off a reply, telling him I was fine and that he didn't need to come here. I worried that if he did, I'd not only be trying to find my sister, but I'd be fighting off a swarm of bloodthirsty journalists.

My boss picked up on the first ring.

"This is Chief Simmons."

"Hi."

"Jane? How'ya doing, kid?"

I exhaled sharply at the question. "Not great. I just interviewed everyone. I don't think it helped me—I'm even more confused. Nobody seems to think Sillian is missing but me."

"What's your gut saying?"

"That my sister is in trouble. Without a doubt."

I kicked the twigs under my feet. I was losing confidence in my role at the party. Perhaps it was better to go home and wait it out.

"Then you gotta keep going, hun. The reporter I know would be diggin' into every angle with an insatiable appetite. She'd be mapping possibilities, taking notes, making plans…"

"I just… Sillian doesn't exactly have the best group of friends. All of them made me more suspicious that they might have a reason to harm her. Every single one. How am I supposed to work with that? It's, like…impossible. Especially without any idea of *what* actually happened."

My boss went quiet on the other end of the line. I heard the scribbling of paper.

"You're worrying too much about all the other people who could be involved. You're not asking yourself the right questions."

"What do you mean?"

"Look, kid. You've got to figure out why your sister wanted to spend her weekend at this rental. You said it was a historical place, right?"

I paused to consider what he was saying before responding.

"Right, so...you're saying I need to do more research on the house?"

"You just need to look for information in different places. Talking to the party guests will certainly give you plenty of angles to choose from, but start looking around the house itself. It might reveal to you the story that your sister was after. A reporter doesn't just trust their sources, Jane. A reporter goes out and finds their own account, too."

I felt like I should have known that already. If my sister weren't at potential risk, I'd be embarrassed to ask for so much help.

"And kid?" Chief Simmons said. "You need to be writing all this down. It might not be a story for the papers, but if it is, I have a feeling you'll want to be the one to break it."

"Alright, Chief. I will."

"And I'm more than happy to review anything you put together and need second eyes on. Just send it over to my personal email. You've got that one?"

"Thanks. That would be an incredible help."

"Don't mention it, kid. I gotta run. You keep following that gut."

"Thanks, boss."

When I hung up the phone, I heard the sound of distant footsteps. There were a million possibilities about who else could be on the trail, but the hope that it might be Sillian swelled in me.

"Sill? Is that you?" My heart was pounding.

In the distance, I heard the sound of cracking twigs and crunching leaves. Mutters of cursing followed. Someone else was struggling with this trail.

I looked around the top of the hill for some kind of defense. The masked man from the night before could've found his way out there. And I was totally defenseless. In a state of panic, I grabbed a large stick off the ground and poised myself to take a swing.

The footsteps got closer. Then, the sound of another large branch breaking rang out.

"Dammit," I heard a voice say. A voice I knew.

"Dakota?"

Dakota appeared at the bottom of the hill with enough hiking equipment strapped to his back to scale Mount Everest. Still, his hands and face carried traces of blood-red scrapes he picked up from the trail's brush.

"Hi, doll. God, it's great to see you. I was starting to fret!" He shot up a relieved smile at me. "Were you planning to hit me with that?" He nodded toward the stick in my hands. Even with all the scratches on his face, he looked devastatingly handsome.

I did not want to talk to him. Not after everything that had happened the night before. I threw the stick back into the woods before turning back to my boyfriend. He had a spell over me in person. And I needed to be mad at him. I *had* to be.

"What are you doing here?"

"Checking on you, of course! Google Trails gave me this godfor-saken route to the manor you mentioned yesterday. Like a bloody warpath out here! But don't worry about that. It sounds like there's been a lot going on. I felt like I needed to show my girlfriend some support."

"Or you needed a new story?"

Dakota furrowed his brow. "What are you talking about?"

"Never mind," I muttered as I walked toward the base of the hill. As twisted as it was, I was happy to see Dakota. Even after all he'd done. Like the comfort of an addictive drug, I wasn't going to turn it down. Not when it had magically appeared.

"For a damsel in distress, you look fresh as ever." Dakota beamed, taking me into a hug. "You smell great as well. Like peonies."

I didn't know what to say to that, so I didn't say anything at all.

"Tell me then, what's been going on? Is your sister okay? Are you?"

"I think something bad has happened. Walk with me back to the manor."

As we headed back to the rental, I proceeded to fill Dakota in on everything that had happened. While I was angry at him for selling my personal life as a journalism tip, I figured there wasn't enough story yet to actually produce anything. And besides, Dakota was a good journalist. I could use his perspective. I thought if I could bury my disapproval for what he'd done, I might get some help from another professional.

Dakota put his arm around me as we walked. I felt shameless leaning into him after all that's happened. The police. The pink coat. I guess I was desperate for comfort.

"Well, you've got me on your team now." Dakota's smile offset the scratches on his face. "Campsite got boring anyway."

When we came up on the backside of the manor, I got another premonition. The first step up to the back entry felt like the start of a new chapter. A darker one with higher stakes.

With Dakota at my side, I turned the doorknob. The aura of the room confirmed my bad feelings. Every party guest was huddled in the sitting room in a U-shaped formation. Nobody was speaking. You could've heard a pin drop. The entire guest list looked like they'd just seen a ghost.

A swollen Michael was the first to break the silence. "Another tall guy. Just what we needed."

Cameron scoffed at him from across the room. All eyes were now on Dakota and me.

"What's going on?" I asked no one in particular.

Robin sighed dramatically and stole a sideways glance at Elle before speaking up for the group.

"Who is your little friend you brought with you?"

"Dakota," he said, reaching out his hand. I fought the urge to roll my eyes.

"Why's everyone crowded around the room like this?" I tried again.

Robin spoke up. "Because we were voting on if we should tell you something that will make you freak out."

"And?" Dakota followed before I could get to it.

"And..." Robin sighed loudly as if the whole effort was pointless. "We decided we should tell you. Even if you're going to be, like, super annoying about it."

I was losing my patience, irritable with the constant dismissal of my well-intended efforts. My face was hot and my fists were clenched. I wanted to let Robin have it, but I needed her to show me whatever *it* was first.

"Okay, okay. Follow me, Jane. And Dakota." She perked up at my boyfriend's name.

Robin stood up from the couch to lead us down the corridor toward the front door. Everyone else remained seated.

Robin's body bobbed down the hallways and outside the front porch. Dakota was behind me. It was a perfect single-file line you only saw in the second grade. When Robin led us outside, I shoved my fingers inside my sleeves and braced for impact.

Robin's wiry hands found the garage side door and twisted. The door opened. I couldn't believe I hadn't thought to look there.

"Michael ran out here to see if there were any more solo cups hidden away somewhere..." Robin said casually.

She hit the light switch, and the room illuminated.

The garage itself was freezing and uninsulated. It was also completely empty, and the room's shell had no smooth lines. There were sections of the walls that protruded in. Some protruded out, making the entry space a weird, unidentifiable shape. Like the walls had a secret language of their own. I immediately suspected there was more to this room than meets the eye.

"This is...a *weird* garage," Dakota said, echoing my thoughts out loud. He was still wearing his backpack, looking rugged from the hike.

"Right," Robin said with a nod.

I felt an ache in my stomach. Call it a gut feeling. This felt like an important place. My sister's memory whispered through the air in the room.

Come closer.

Goosebumps covered my arms as I looked around the room. I almost missed it. It was so small and delicate. A band-aid in the middle of the garage, with a small pool of blood circling it. It wasn't a large enough puddle to be lethal, but it also wasn't from a paper cut. There was no trail around it. No indication of the blood going anywhere, which made it that much more confusing.

"What the hell?" I walked over to the blood and bent down to examine it up close, the cold air piercing my face. "Where did this come from?"

Robin stayed by the door while Dakota came to stand next to me.

"If I knew, I'd probably save you from a panic attack."

I bent down on my knees, wanting to touch the pile of crimson. The blood hadn't fully dried yet as it remained bright red with a damp apple shine on the top layer.

Dakota grabbed my arms before I got to it.

"Blood has DNA in it. It could be your sister's. You don't want to contaminate it," he said.

"Pretty sure your sister's idiot boyfriend already slid his fingers through it," Robin said. "He said he didn't know what it was."

It appeared she was right. Two tracings slid through the puddle in a swirl.

"Why would he do that?" I asked under my breath.

My breath was going shallow. I needed to get out of there and think.

I was about to motion for the group to leave the garage when I noticed a tiny twinkle catching light on the ground in the corner of the garage. It was unnecessary to run, but I did anyway, going full speed toward anything that might uncover the secrets of my sister.

It was obnoxiously large. A gold-plated ring that my sister

never would've worn. I picked it up and rubbed it against my finger. A faint gray line appeared—it was a real gold ring.

"Oooh, *honeypot*," Robin said, delighted, making her way across the room. "A golden ring."

I slid it over my finger to see if it fit. It would've if it were Sill's, but it was far too big.

"Can you find out whose it is, Robin? Since you work in jewelry sales."

"By asking around? I do know how to work a crowd." She took the ring from my hand and held it up to the garage's overhead light. It was plain. Gold. No engravings were personalized into it. It was the most simple ring I'd ever seen.

Dakota was fixated on Robin as she examined the ring. She did look pretty today. I swallowed my jealousy and kept the conversation.

"No. That would be too easy for someone to lie about. Don't you know how to call the companies and find out who purchased what?"

Robin took a closer look at the jewelry, bringing it up to her face. "You want me to track it down by the serial number? Oh, honey…I don't even have cellphone service."

Dakota looked at me with a willful expression. "We could take her to the tent? Or I could. So you could stay here and keep searching."

The images of the pink coat played in my mind all over again. I desperately wanted him to take the suggestions back. The anxiety ballooned in my stomach so much that I thought I might float away.

"What tent?" Robin flipped her hair over her shoulder and looked at Dakota.

"*No*," I said firmly.

"But—" Dakota said.

"I said *no*. I'll figure this out myself." I snatched the ring from Robin's hand. The gesture was a little rude, but I didn't care. I wasn't about to have another girl to worry about. Sill and the pink-coated woman were enough on my plate. I put the ring into my pocket.

Dakota sent me a puzzling look, but I ignored him.

"Let's go try the police one more time," I said to Dakota and only Dakota.

"*Girl*," Robin said, "it's a band-aid."

I shot her a menacing look. She put her hands up in defense before turning toward the door. "I'll leave you two alone. Let me know if you need help with the ring," she said before slamming the garage's metal side door.

Everything started to become a little too much at that point. My brain thwarted me with a laundry list of facts:

- *My sister is missing.*
- *People are lying to me.*
- *There is blood on the floor.*
- *My life is falling apart.*

"Are you alright, doll?"

I had my arms crossed over my chest. It was somehow colder in the garage than it was outside.

"There's blood. Sill's gone. We need to call the cops."

Dakota glared at the puddle on the floor, then back at me. "Jane, that's about as much blood as a nosebleed."

"What's the difference? If it has DNA, it could help us find Sill."

"Well, it's certainly going to have Michael's."

I sighed and covered my eyes with my hands. I could feel a migraine coming on.

"Jane, I feel like you haven't eaten or slept well since you got here. Why don't you let me handle things for a few hours while you catch up on rest? I can keep an eye on everyone. I can keep an eye on *you*."

"You don't take breaks when your sister is missing."

I tried to hide my face from twisting. I didn't know if I could trust him alone with the situation, but he was right. My head was pounding. I needed to nourish myself. Yet, it felt selfish to even consider sitting down as long as my sister might be missing.

"You're going to," Dakota said firmly. "You have to."

Dakota led me upstairs to my room, where I went limp with exhaustion. I didn't protest when he cuddled my body or poured Benadryl into my mouth. I let myself drift, leaving the emergencies of my sister and the affairs of the household completely *unmonitored*.

5.8: MARY'S DIARY

1945

I LEANED against the base of the toilet, staring at my sister's puffed scarlet lips. I could smell the sex on her and I wanted to take a moment to be infuriated, but I knew better than to cause an argument about the man inside her body while so many people were inside our home.

A year had passed since our fate had been sealed that day in the living room. Our marriage had grown more spoiled by the second. The war was over. Celebrations were high. Josh and James were playing all their live shows at homecoming events. While I was elated by the prospect of widespread freedom from destruction, I was devastated by the lack of my own deliverance.

Emancipation was a cause many had honorably died for. Not just in the war but at home. As violent as she had been, my mother was one such person. And soon, I could be too. The thought was with me at all times. It kept me raw.

Airbus to Seventh Ave. was the title of the newest Sophomore Brothers album. It had come out that day. The release party was set at the manor. Their fame had reached new heights, as had ours. But not as film stars. Just as wives.

The boys knew of our dissatisfaction and had us on lockdown.

We could not leave the house alone, even to get fresh air in the yard. When alone, we had to be monitored at all times. I hadn't even showered without James watching in months.

Macie and I had started formulating an escape plan. A way out of the dreadful marriage. But she was more patient than I was. Things were beginning to feel indefinite. I was losing my marbles, hanging on to threads. I couldn't charade through it anymore. In the middle of the party and all of its important guests, I brought up the escape to Macie again. She dragged me to the upstairs bathroom.

The bathroom was the best chance at privacy from any gossip-seeking parasites who might have been crawling around the house.

"Mary, we *have* to wait a bit longer," my twin sister whispered quietly with a look I didn't recognize in her eyes. "We're not prepared to leave yet."

"If we wait any longer, you'll be knocked up and carrying," I shouted with my head against the front of the closed toilet, knees crossed on the floor. My upstanding class, my old, unbothered identity—all of that had died over the past year. I was a desperate character becoming deranged.

"Keep your voice low. God Almighty. This is not the time or the place for one of your episodes."

"We'd be fools to wait any longer, Macie. You must open your eyes and *close your legs*," I said, failing to keep my voice down yet again. I was practically yelling at my sister. "You know, Macie, if you get pregnant, they won't even let you pick the name."

Macie stood up from the bathroom floor. With hands on her hips, she towered over me. A soft look overtook her face. A look of pity. Not for our doomed situation. The pity was reserved only for me.

Macie wasn't supposed to fall in love with him. When we'd married the boys, I trusted she'd keep it platonic between all four of us. But I worried I was losing her to James. The boys we'd wedded had already robbed us of our money. I would not let them take away the only love I'd ever had.

But I was running out of time.

"Macie…" I uncrossed my knees and tried to stand up. Defeated was the only thing I could feel. I wanted to shout. I failed to lower my voice another time. "Rightfully…I'm concerned. Our plan to escape doesn't work if you're in love with him."

"Don't you dare start like that. Like I'm going to choose him over you. Like *I'm* the bad guy." Macie's face looked hot as she stood over me in a way that made me feel like a child, placing two fingers on my cheek. "I am not letting my emotions get the best of me. *You* are. *You* need to be patient."

Macie pushed down on my cheekbones before turning toward the door. Her violent fingers found the knob where she would re-enter into the socialite circles floating across the floors of our home. We'd never been at odds like this, and I had a very grave feeling about it. Clearly, there could not be two drivers at the head of our sinking ship.

"Enjoy the party!" I called out sarcastically before fully rising to dust off my dress and carry myself back to the performative social setting.

The cold air hit my face as I emerged from the bathroom back into the party. I never felt as emotional as I looked, but the chill of the air upstairs forced my eyes to tear. I blinked the water back a few times before turning the corner to keep my composure.

There were famous people scattered across the house. Actresses, Academy Award winners, novelists, and designers. And almost all of them wanted a piece of my husband. I guess that was what you got when you married a famous musician. But that wasn't the worst of it. The men my sister and I married had a strange habit of inviting high-profile reporters to the parties. Our husbands never drank at parties, keeping themselves out of the drunken hearsay that would likely ensue. But these events were diseased breeding grounds for dramatic events and headline splashes of the unhinged renown. There was no privacy. The Sophomore brothers liked it that way. They liked having their name in the controlled piece of the headliners, fueling their status further. It was a power they'd tasted for the first time on our wedding night. They'd grown addicted.

As I descended downstairs, Janice Kroy, an infamously snooping reporter, stopped me.

"Why the glum look, Mary? Are you feeling a little jealous? There's a lot of beautiful women circling your husband."

"It's chilly in here. Strains my eyes."

She shifted her legs underneath her over-cinched waistline.

"I heard you and your sister. Going to make a great story, you two."

My heartbeat quickened. Macie was right; I hadn't been controlling my volume.

"Pardon, Janice?"

As unsettling as it was, I couldn't show my hand. Even if she'd already seen it. If this woman knew about the state of our marriages and our plan to escape, I wouldn't risk her mouth running. If James and Josh caught on, we'd be forever trapped. Or dead. And I didn't know which was worse.

"You two girls were talking about your husbands. *You* seemed upset in particular. Any word on all that anger, by the way? I've got what I need, but I'll give you the chance to explain. For the record."

My nerves gave way, and the blood rushed quickly through my body. Janice's face was caked with vanilla powder, barely covering her poker face. I kept mine under control, distancing my expression from my emotions.

The airplane-shaped broach pinned into my sweater, right on my breast, poked at my skin. The needle was long and kept scratching me until blood showed. Josh had thought it would be sexy to sharpen it before putting it on me. He had insisted I wear the broach in provocative places on my body to promote his music. My sister and I had practically been forced to wear the sheerest clothing as the marketing pawns of their career. Cameras would catch us so that men might stumble on our ostracizing clothing and think, *The Sophomore Brothers are doing something right.*

Just another indication that it wasn't about the music anymore.

It was about the power. But those pins *hurt.* Razor-sharp and thick as steel.

"I seemed upset?" I snorted, keeping my hand over the pin. My eyes fluttered underneath the flash of a nearby camera. Someone was taking a photo of us speaking.

"I'm not ruffled over anything my husband does. We're a team." I forced my composure against a smile.

Janice sneered and clutched her notebook with a free hand. "Sure, Mrs. Sophomore."

How could this happen? Will she expose our escape plan before we've taken the first step?

If she did, I'd surely be dead by morning. I hadn't been quiet enough in the bathroom, but Janice still would've had to eavesdrop with her ear against the door to make out our conversation. Looking at her, though, I wouldn't put it past her. Janice was known as a nosy parker.

Think fast. Think faster.

The broach pin itched on my skin and I tugged my dress.

"I've always liked you, Janice. You've always treated me with respect and honor." The words seethed through my teeth. Janice had backstabbed Macie and me since the marriage had begun. She doted on *The Sophomore Brothers* while undercutting us, the wives, every chance she got. "You've always done your best work for my husband. That is most important to me."

Janice blushed and unclenched her grip on the stairwell, resting her backside on the handrail. One line and she was fully relaxed. A dumb ox was so easy to trick.

"Of course, Mrs. Sophomore. It would be ludicrous not to give your husbands a spotlight on their success."

I nodded toward Janice through seething emotions, keeping my fingers on the broach. "Would you like a sample of their radio exclusive song? It won't be released until next week, but I have an early copy on record. Maybe you could publish something about it? Get people excited. It's to be a special edition promotion for the album."

Janice's eyes lit up with eagerness. I faked a mile-wide smile.

The images were already flashing in my mind. I saw them in storyboard, as if they'd already become a movie picture. Another performance. That was all that was.

"Follow me." A pre-scripted line.

Her click-clacked footsteps rang behind me as I led Janice into the garage.

"The new car is in the garage as well. Would you care to sit in it while we're back here? It's incredibly rare." I twisted the broach upside down, ballooned with stage fright.

"We keep the top-secret records stashed in the Delahaye trunk, but don't print that," I lied as I motioned toward the bright yellow vehicle. My fingers found the miniature handle, and I switched it open with a flick of the wrist.

"After you." I motioned for her to get comfortable.

"What a beautiful car." Janice's eyes gawked at the truck. I closed the door back into place as she fixated on the passenger seat. Carefully, I crossed over to the driver's seat around the front hood. Pulling in a single motion, I tore the broach from its holder like a sword from a stone.

"What's it called?" she asked me eagerly while I opened my side carefully. "The new song."

A deep breath filled my lungs with courage. I stole a side glance at the journal in her lap and pressed my eyelids together tightly. The last thing I remembered was the doe-look on her face as the broach slid into the center of her neck. *Showtime.*

I felt her struggle against her skin breaking. Muffled cries pressed against my manicured hands.

She kicked up at me as the warm feeling of blood reminded me of what I was doing. I dragged the broach up and down the runway of her throat with depth, twisting in and out.

I fought hard to keep her down. She was getting weak.

Her hands flung into action, but I quickly caught them by straddling her with my knees in the same position Josh called his favorite.

My hands grew warm and damp, and I applied the pressure further, flying the airplane across her windpipe again and again.

The gesture could've lasted minutes. I lost track of time and morality, blurred by evil and blood.

Finally, the breathing against my hand went rapid until there was no more.

"Oh no." A gasp escaped me as I surveyed the scene around me. That part hadn't been in the storyboard. I tried not to attach a conscious meaning to the far-away look in Janice's eyes, but it was impossible.

The act that had never been done before was done. No longer a virgin angel; I'd fallen from grace. And while the moment thrilled me, it was rather disappointing now that it was over.

Janice's notebook had fallen to the floorboard. I lunged for it, still gasping for air. Squinting to make it out, I read the lines over and over.

Mary and Macie complain about the party guests on their way into the bathroom to take a powder. "I want to kick them all to the curb," Mary says. Perfect headline. "Make our husbands do it. Make them do something useful for once," says Macie.

Big drama between the couple?

I almost fainted. This was what I'd killed a woman over? Good God.

When I looked down at Janice's bloody face, I tried to convince myself that this wasn't me. A woman with an agenda for killing. This was a character I was playing—one who would kill a journalist for merely prying. A clapperboard would soon appear and dismiss me of my sins.

I wasn't sure how long I sat on top of Janice Kroy, envisioning what ought to be done to my character. The party noise in the house was pressing forward despite my actions. And while that should've made me tremble, I felt surprisingly calm. My sister and I would have to act now. Fast. There could be no more waiting to escape.

When the garage door opened, it was Macie who was looking for me. I'd been absent from the party for a while now. She said nothing at the sight of my crimes. In a wordless sprint, she ran over to me. Her expression was enveloped by shock as she grabbed Janice's scarlet neck. Quickly, I hid the notebook underneath the seat.

"She heard us in the bathroom. She was going to publish it." I cast a desperate look into my twin's reflection. Macie nodded with an expression I'd never understand and covered her eyes from the scene. We remained there for a moment in silence.

Beads of sweat trickled from my brow. My sister and I were now bound for life in my act of murder. I guess I was my mother's daughter, after all.

"Mary, may I?" Macie finally asked, signaling at the lock of the convertible.

I unlocked it from the inside with a finger. We didn't say anything past that. Instead, Macie took Janice by the shoulders, and I got out of the car to pick up the other side of her by the legs.

And at the height of the party, we carried Janice to her eternal hiding place.

<h1 style="text-align:center">END OF FILE FIVE</h1>

You're halfway there! Below are checkpoints to keep you on track to pinpointing the right suspect:

- **HINT:** Remember that a lie is not an admittance of guilt.

- **CONSIDER:** The advice of Jane's elders. It can only help!

- **TIP:** Seasoned detectives work together. Are any friends/family members reading along with you? Put your heads together!

- **FUN FACT:** Twins were more broadly accepted in 20th-century silent films before they later moved into traditional movie roles.

Keep your eyes peeled.

CASE FILE SIX

<u>Case file six contains nine items to be reviewed.</u>
Files should be reviewed in numerical order

- **6.1 Police Questioning**
- **6.2 Mary Sophomore's Diary** | 1945
- **6.3 Jane's Recount** | March 2023
- **6.4 Notepad Scrap**
- **6.5 Mary Sophomore's Diary** | 1945
- **6.6 Jane's Recount** | March 2023
- **6.7 List From Cameron's File**
- **6.8 Mary Sophomore's Diary** | 1945
- **6.9 Police Questioning**

6.1: POLICE QUESTIONING

DB: "Jane, why didn't you call the police immediately after you found the blood?"

JP: "Everything was happening so fast. It's not like I didn't want to. I did. Dakota just said he would take care of it and...I guess I trusted him to do it. He said he wanted me to rest. If it was a larger amount of blood, maybe I would've followed up and made sure I called myself."

DB: "What about calling your parents?"

JP: "That's a bit more complicated. As I said, it's just my dad. He's elderly, you know? *Super old*. Frets over everything. Ever since Mom died, he's been worried sick over anything Sillian and I do. I thought it best to wait to call him until there was certain trouble. For his health."

DB: "Do you know how much time passed between when you found the blood and when you woke up from your nap?"

JP: "Like, two hours, I think. Something around there."

DB: "And can you describe the house's condition when you woke back up?"

JP: "The house was empty except for Dakota. He told me everyone had left in a car to get food about fifteen minutes before I'd woke up. The nearest food place was a long way out. There were bottles around the house. Solo cups. Obvious signs of partiers. But no real damage or anything like that."

DB: "And the garage?"

JP: "Someone cleaned the garage floors while I was asleep. No trace of blood was left in there. That was the first sign of malicious intent."

DB: "And when did you notice that?"

JP: "After I searched the rooms. That's when I went back into the garage. Everyone got back from the food run around that time as well."

DB: "Did Dakota know you were searching through the other guests' things?"

JP: "Yes. It was his idea."

6.2: MARY'S DIARY

1945

THERE WAS blood on my hands. Nothing made you more committed than that.

We stood over Janice Kroy's body in the woods behind our home, in shock at our actions. My actions. My dress had torn in the woods, leaving a slit up to my black and blue exposed leg.

My body hadn't been my own for over a month. Macie and I didn't speak of our private affairs, which bothered me more than it should have. I couldn't help but notice our twin bodies did not match anymore. James didn't have to buy her new jewels weekly to cover up a fresh bruise.

I'd always thought I was above the battered women who liked to be gifted jewelry. And while I was still resilient, I took what little Josh gave me: an Egyptian-style gold bangle to cover up the grip marks; a silk scarf for the scrapes on my neck. He loved to keep me decorated in blacks, blues, and plated diamonds. I let it happen and even sometimes provoked the cycle because it was the only form of savings I could hold on to without a bank account for Macie and me.

With what we were about to do, we'd need it.

"Mary..." My sister was startled by the sight of my bruised and discolored skin, now foul to her. All I could manage was a mere nod. There wasn't shame in it, just a reluctant union under the weight of our circumstances.

"We need to take action. We have about three hours until the party is flushed." Macie grabbed my hand and let out a desperate choking sound. "What will we do?"

Janice's blood was splattered all over my chest. The public eye would be too risky, even with one reporter down. I needed to slow down and think, but all I wanted to do was *move*.

"We could say she assaulted us." Macie's fear cloaked the normal sound of her voice. "Self-defense."

I crouched on my hands and knees, letting the twigs on the ground poke into my bruises.

"No. We've got to bring *her* into this…" I told my sister. "It's got to be her. She's the only one who could get us out of this."

Macie shook her head. "No… That wasn't the plan. The plan was that she would be the decoy for our escape. Nothing more. She's our *best friend*. Our only friend."

My stomach flipped at my lack of compassion. "Well, she got a promotion."

The fear in my sister's eyes was almost enough to reconsider. But Macie and I were more than family. We were twins. For me, that always came first.

"What do you want her to do?"

I paused momentarily, knowing the four-word answer but not wanting to say it.

"Sleep with my husband."

6.3: JANE'S RECOUNT

I MOVED my bare feet slowly down the wooden stairs. It was one of those naps where you woke up feeling worse. The sleep had been too deep for me to sleepwalk. In fact, the sleep had been too deep to restore me at all. I detected cracks in my brain, failure in my organs, and emptiness in my stomach. Everything inside my body felt worse, with my adrenaline rush now faded.

The house had an eerie silence, apart from the sound of rain outside hitting the windows. I looked down at the base of the stairs from the top floor, seeing a leather glove half emerged from a crack in the staircase. It looked like the stairs had been built on top of its fingers, leaving the fabric to peek through to the living area. It was in a prominent spot, which surprised me since I hadn't noticed it before.

"Good morning, doll."

Dakota's voice was like cold water to the face.

"How long was I out for?"

"Coupla hours." Dakota was chewing an apple on a couch at the bottom of the stairs. He tossed it in the air as I walked down. Nothing subtle about his appearance. I ground my teeth in preparation for whatever wheels were turning behind his mind.

I hopped off the last stair with a thud, still thinking about that glove peeking out of the staircase.

"It's quiet. Where is everyone?"

"Getting pizza. They left a few minutes ago. The closest place is fifty miles out, so...they probably won't be back for at least two hours. They'll grab us a few slices."

"Two hours? Jesus."

Dakota shot me a feline glare, taking another bite of his apple. It annoyed me momentarily that he kept his shoes on the vintage furniture, but I dismissed the thought quickly. I had more important things to focus on.

"We're *alone*," he said.

"Not now. My sister is missing, for crying out loud."

Dakota smirked. "I'm not that scampy, Jane. I'm almost offended you could think so lowly of me."

I rolled my eyes.

"We're alone. Nobody is guarding their rooms."

"So, you're suggesting we look through them?" It wasn't a bad idea. Even if I wanted to pretend it was.

"That's right."

My head was aching more and more with each passing moment. I wouldn't get far on the investigation without Dakota. I was too physically weak.

"I suppose it isn't the worst idea I've ever heard."

Dakota stood up from his place on the couch, tossing his apple behind him carelessly. It was obvious he wasn't used to cleaning up his own messes.

I was still at the base of the staircase, where he met me face to face. He put two fingers under my chin and kissed me. The smell of alcohol on his lips made me gag. When he put his fingers around my hips, I turned my head.

"C'mon. We've only got two hours."

Michael's room was first. His bed was unmade. That I could've bet my life on. An imprint of two bodies was pressed into the mattress. My heart ached thinking of Sill sleeping next to a man like this.

The room had an array of sleeping bags on the floor where his nondescript friends had likely slept. Next to the sleeping bags were handles of half-drunk liquor and white Styrofoam cups. An explosion of fraternal clothing had erupted in the room; Polo socks and shirts hanging from every corner as if they were on a giant collegiate Kappa-Fucking-Something Christmas tree. The place was a wreck of unkempt young men. I shook my head and bent toward the bag, cringing as my hands ran through the neon-blue nylon.

"Class act, this one is," Dakota said, taking a swig from a nearby bottle of vodka.

I went for his wallet that he—of course—hadn't taken to grab takeout with the group—that con.

There was no money in the slip. Only a student debit card that looked as if it had survived several rough years. I was about to put the wallet down when I noticed a rolled-up scrap of paper sticking out of a zipper pocket.

It wasn't more than a page, but it immediately felt essential to this situation.

6.4: NOTEPAD SCRAP

PROPERY OF MICHAEL MULLINS

DEPOSITS TO C

DATE: SILL

ATB: $550.00
BB: $800.00
COJCH: meine liebe + $240.00
UB: $50.00
23Me: $450.00
DinoLSept: $370.00
MarHall: $240.00

6.5: MARY'S DIARY

1945

MACIE and I snuck back into our secret house corridors to wash up. A tortured silence lingered between us. Sounds of the party going strong pumped through the air ducts. I took my sister's trembling hand. She didn't know what I was about to do.

"We can't put Corrine in this situation. She's only supposed to distract the boys on escape day." Macie spat when she spoke.

Macie was hunched over near the ground, looking like she might throw up. I needed to assert confidence to keep her calm.

"Tonight, she will lay with Josh. And you with James. We'll tell the police we heard them get up in the middle of the night but state it's a common occurrence. Act nonchalant. Our alibis will be covered, and I'll light the body on fire and get rid of the evidence. After I take Janice's panties."

Macie shook her head. "I don't know. Taking things from a dead woman feels…"

"Just her undergarments. Then I'll put them in Josh and James' office. It'll be enough evidence for the police to link them."

Macie shook her head again. "It feels too dirty, Mary. They'll go to prison. There are so many ways it could go wrong…"

"They deserve prison. Look at my legs, Macie." I lifted my skirt once more to show my bruises.

"*Josh* deserves prison," she said, forgetting herself a captive once again.

Macie and I walked toward the door that held the phone. Before we opened it, before we involved Corrine, I needed Macie to agree with me. I turned to face my sister.

"Are you with me? Are you really with me in getting out of here? I need to know." I searched her face for the answer I couldn't find in her words.

My sister's eyes watered over. I looked down to see both hands covering her small torso protectively. "I don't... I don't want to be a single mother. James would make a good father, and...we haven't been careful. I think...that I'm carrying."

The news made me dizzy. All of our plans had flipped in a single sentence. We were supposed to leave before the protection stopped. "Macie...are you certain?"

My sister wouldn't look at me. The knife twisted deeper in my gut. She kept her stare on the ground, fiercely focused on the tips of her shoes. She eventually nodded. "Please, Mary. We've got to think of another way."

In an unspeakable surrender, we walked away from each other and back into the party in silence, with only our judgments whispering to one another below earshot. Our eyes carefully joined each other across the room with every few moments that passed. Each time I caught my sister's stare, I felt the distant tick of a countdown. How many more times could I look at this woman, who was a reflection of me, and feel *safe*?

My days of trusting Macie were numbered. In the midst of party music, we caught each other's glance again. The rug slipped from underneath me. And in the room full of people, I knew I was truly alone.

6.6: JANE'S RECOUNT

"WOW." I exhaled in a moment of shock, still holding the note from Michael's wallet. I had to take a second to process what it meant and look it over again.

"What's that say?" Dakota reached for the note. It quickly found my pocket.

"Receipt from a meal. Thought maybe I'd check in with the restaurant if Sill doesn't turn up. Michael probably went with Sill. They might've seen something."

Dakota seemed to accept the lie. To divert his attention, I got on my knees and searched through the frat explosion on the floor again before announcing nothing was valuable in that room.

Usually, I wouldn't keep things from Dakota, but given all the circumstances, keeping a few cards close to my chest felt safer. At that point, I didn't know what to believe.

Dakota motioned toward the door. "Shall we move on then?"

Thanks to his monogrammed luggage, Cameron's room quickly identified itself. If it weren't for his things, the room wouldn't have left a trace that anyone had been staying there at all. The bed was neatly made. There wasn't as much as a napkin out of place.

"Doesn't leave a trace behind, does he?" I muttered with my arms crossed as I took the room into account.

"Would be a nice trait for a criminal to have, wouldn't it?"

Despite his very alarming interview, I had no concrete context of Cameron's life or connection to my sister. Going through his things reminded me of that. Everything he owned was neatly stacked inside an open suitcase where all the items looked like they'd been curated for a Samsonite photo ad. His belongings looked like an overly hygienic version of normalcy. There were nice clothes, tons of printed-out 'side gig' advertisements, and beautifully pressed scarves. Nothing alarming, though.

I knew he was *fanatic* about my sister. I had to find something in there.

I almost lost my suspicion when I found a folder tucked into the deepest compartment of his suitcase.

A pen marked the face of the folder with the words: *Sillian's Work.*

Dakota kneeled next to me. "What's this?"

"He was her tutor in college."

"And he is still holding onto her college study materials?"

"Let's see."

I gathered up my bullshit tolerance in a deep cycle of breathing before I opened the yellow file. I already knew this guy was nuts.

A series of math quizzes appeared first, filed neatly inside a paperclip. There was no doubt that my kin was poor at math. I held back an inappropriate snicker when I saw my sister's name over a quiz that had scored 27 percent. I undid the paper clip and laid the quizzes out on the bed. Each score had progressively gotten higher. In the back of the file were papers labeled 'Strategies' in a neat, left-brained font. Cameron had written strategies to bring up my sister's grades. There were flirtatious thank you post-it notes stuck between the pages in Sillian's handwriting.

What was maybe a sweet gesture turned foul by the fact that this had been years before. *Why is Cameron still carrying these around?*

"It's a bit odd to hold on to something like this, isn't it? He certainly isn't tutoring her anymore," Dakota said as if he'd read my mind.

Under the next paperclip was a stack of receipts that trickled across years.

Cup of Joe's Coffeehouse, ten dollars. *Italica Tapas Bar*, fifteen dollars. *Buzzy's Brewery*, forty dollars. There was even a receipt for a new coat in there. All the stores' fonts were familiar favorites of my sister. My heartbeat quickened as I flipped to the next item: a list titled: *'Deposits.'* This behavior was well beyond a simple crush. He was documenting every moment he'd ever had with my sister... *but why?*

6.7: LIST FROM CAMERON'S FILE

FOUND BY JANE AND DAKOTA

DEPOSITS

Math Final - Cup of Joe's Java House	$60.00
Calc Quiz - Italica Tapas Bar	$65.00
Calc Series Part 2 - Mina's Brunch	$80.00
End Of The Year Pizza Party	$100.00
Buzzys - Cal 3 Summer Class	$90.00

6.8: MARY'S DIARY

1945

THE PARTY WAS BEGINNING to slow down, which meant I only had a little time before Josh would be watching my every move again.

Macie was known to give the last words of a party, which had finally proved to my advantage. I'd excused myself back into the phone booth, weaving carefully like a thread through needle-sized pockets in the crowd.

Macie had always been more emotionally connected to the idea of motherhood than I had. When we'd been transferred between foster homes, her dolls had always found a way to come with us. I'd never had dolls. I'd had lemonade stands and hand-woven baskets. Business had been my idea of entertainment. Even back then.

My experience guiding us through life as sisters was undeniable. Sure, I made bad judgments, but I also got us out of them. If Macie delivered a baby, she would play the part of a mother, and I would tend to the business matters as a father might. While misaligned from her ideal fairy-tale household, it would have to work.

Luckily, Corrine picked up on the first ring.

"This is Corrine Mercier."

"It's Mary."

I made sure to talk in a hushed tone. If someone were on the party line, we'd be screwed anyways. But it was best to minimize overall risks.

"Mary Sophomore?"

"Yes."

"Are you calling to tell me you're coming back to Hollywood? 'Cause I've been out of work since you left. My bills are about as tall as a Christmas tree."

I bit my lip. Corrine was a stunt double. One who looked just like Macie and I. But I guess she hadn't built up her film rapport doubling for anyone else. We hadn't filmed in over a year. Her money must be running dry. I felt ignorant for not thinking about it before.

"No. I need your help with something else."

"Does it pay?" she asked immediately.

My heart started beating quickly. Of course, she'd need something in it for her.

"Yes. It does."

"How much?"

"Well…name your price," I said in a whisper.

"A million."

I shook my head the moment she said it. I already didn't want to do it despite knowing I'd have to. These were desperate times.

"Corrine, you haven't even heard what the job is. You can't say—"

"A million or I'm not doing it. I know you're sitting on piles of cash in that boys' club of a home you got there, Mary. Your men are *hot*. Every sign I see downtown has their faces on it."

"Look, it's more complicated than that. I can't pay you that much for this."

Corrine let out an exaggerated sigh. "Well then. How's the weather in Virginia?"

"Fine. A million. But I can't front it."

"You're in troubling waters, aren't you, girl?"

"Yes." I replied with one word, afraid anything more would lose me more money that I didn't have.

"What is it? What do you need me to do?"

I looked back at the booth door to ensure it was closed. I was stunned by my own silence. I didn't want to say what I needed to.

"What are you up to, Mary? What is it?" Concern started to creep into Corrine's voice.

"I, uhm…"

"Yes? You sound like someone's got a pistol to your head. Are you alright?"

"I need you to come live with me. Tomorrow. Tonight. As soon as possible."

Corrine laughed. "You're going to pay me a million to come vacation in that fancy house of yours? Are you serious, Mary?"

"That's not all. You might have to sleep with Josh."

She laughed harder on the other end of the line. "Oh, good Lord! You're a real hoot, aren't you? You'll pay me to have rendezvous with your handsome celebrity husband in a giant mansion? What did I do to get on God's good side today?"

My hands trembled around the phone. They hadn't stopped trembling since that morning.

"There's more Corrine."

"This ought to be good," she said with a laugh still in her voice.

And it was.

"There's a body to burn."

6.9: POLICE QUESTIONING

DB: "Walk me through your thought process while you're in the manor alone with Dakota. What are you feeling as you go to search the rooms?"

JP: "Uneasy."

DB: "Uneasy about your relationship with Dakota?"

JP: "That, and the idea of going through people's things. Given one of them might've harmed my sister."

DB: "Are you sharing everything you found in the manor with Dakota at this point?"

JP: "Most things. Not everything. I didn't shy away from sharing highlights with him because he's a smart guy who can come up with several angles for a situation. That seemed helpful to me. Besides, he had no real reason to hurt my sister."

DB: "You said not everything. What is it that you're keeping to yourself?"

JP: "The glove I saw under the staircase. And we didn't discuss the blood cleanup either. I was too worried to think that…"

DB: "That it was him who cleaned it up?"

Inaudible

DB: "Can you walk me through when you decided to look for the house's history? What made you decide that learning more about the location might help you find your sister?"

JP: "After the call with my boss, I started thinking of it. But when I went back into the garage the second time…that's when I learned that place had secrets. Buried secrets."

File six complete. Phillip Beacons has left the following note on your desk with new information:

It's safe to say that this is quite the case, detective. From what I've gathered, you should be able to use the prior files to piece together the suspect's motive. While there are likely a few details that still need to be ironed out relating to the culprit's motivation, the past six files should give you most of the evidence you'll need when it's time to make the case. Right now, there should still be many suspects at large.

The truth always turns up. And when it does, you'll know where to look.

At this point in the case, I find it necessary to focus on the history of Mary and Macie Sophomore and their husbands, James and Josh. See what you can get from Jane about her findings around the history of the house. Our victim, Sillian Parks, seemed to know much more about this 1940s family than we might've guessed. The more we uncover, the more links we see.

There's something else that's curious to me. If we are to treat every person as a murder suspect, we need to know the timing of the crime. The hospital technician said that our victim, Sillian Parks, was likely left stranded in extreme temperatures for 18-22 hours before her body was found.

You will gain access to the priorly restrained information in the following case files. Our intern found it important to verify the information with the police force before including it in the files. Please pay close attention to not only the files themselves but the path the criminal must've taken to get through the manor.

While our sketch artist is slow as molasses, he is working up a drawing of the victim's condition upon discovery. I won't spoil his work, but I can tell you that Sillian's attacker likely came from behind. In the meantime, keep looking. You're doing well for a first-timer.

I'm eager to see your findings.

Phillip Beacons | CEO of PI Inc.

CASE FILE SEVEN

Case file seven contains nine items to be inspected.
Files should be reviewed in numerical order

- **7.1 Mary Sophomore's Diary** | 1945
- **7.2 Jane's Recount** | March 2023
- **7.3 Mary Sophomore's Diary** | 1945
- **7.4 Jane's Recount** | March 2023
- **7.5 Letter Found Underneath Staircase**
- **7.6 Guest Book Found Underneath Staircase**
- **7.7 Engineer Notes from PJ-Structures**
- **7.8 Mary Sophomore's Diary** | 1945
- **7.9 Police Questioning**

7.1: MARY'S DIARY

1945

"WOMEN like you two are a danger to the rest of us." Corrine shook her head and laid back on the bed with a sigh. We were underneath the house in the basement, where she'd be staying until the task was completed. If she agreed, that was. She drove down there to talk to me about the proposition face to face. During the party, I didn't have time to spare the details.

"Every time you walk into a room, I can feel my judgment day inch nearer," she said.

I sat cross-legged and quietly in the chair across from the bed. The underground room was small, not quaint. Staying the night down there at all was a favor in itself. I could only hope she'd have one more in her.

"Burn a body, then?" she repeated into the air. "Talk about a stunt…"

"Well, you're here, aren't you? You don't have to do the burn if you don't want to. You can *distract* Josh and James. Macie and I can do the dirty work."

"Both sound pretty dirty to me, hun."

Corrine was an interesting 'best friend' to have. Mainly because we weren't close friends at all. It wasn't an oxymoron; it's just the way it was.

She was about ten pounds heavier than I was, but it was the pure muscle a stunt double carried. Not noticeable until up close, we had an eerily similar profile. Despite our physical reflections, our relationship had not followed suit. Out of all the movies we'd shot together, we'd never grabbed a shake on release day or exchanged gossip about our co-stars. We did respect one another, though. And that respect would carry us into this situation. No matter how bad things got, I knew Corrine meant business. She understood the wear and tear women experienced in the industry. When Corrine saw me, she damn near saw herself. Which would be the only reason she might've agreed to help me out of this situation. The payment would serve as nothing more than a bonus.

Corrine let out a hearty sigh and pulled up from her position to look at me. "Let's burn Janice Kroy ourselves. Leave Macie out of it."

"But...why was that so easy to decide?"

"Well, do you want me to take it back?"

"No! No, dear, of course not. I wasn't expecting you to—"

"Your sister called me on her own a few days ago. Told me not to answer your phone calls. That she needed me for a plan."

"What are you talking about?" I asked.

"I figured you sisters were fighting. She told me not to tell you. Said she'd pay me off. Something was certainly in the works. It felt *peculiar*. Maybe sinister."

"What?" My heart pumped faster.

"Then you called not even two days later. And I decided that if I'm taking anyone's side on this, I'm going with you. I don't trust your sister with my life in her hands. And I need the money. I need it real bad. The minute you called, I knew this was gonna be ugly. I didn't think I'd be burning a body, but I *know* you're good on your word. And you know I'm good on mine. That's why I'm down here with you, innit?"

My knees fell to the floor next to hers at the realization of my sister. "My naivety..."

"Macie's going to betray you, Mary. For that smooth brute of a jazz player. I can *feel* it. This operation needs to stay between you and me."

A gloss coated my eyes. I knew she was right.

"When is this body burning? What is the plan? How are you going to protect my name?"

I tried to shield my sadness from Corrine's urgency, draping a hand over my eyes.

"Tomorrow night. And I'm going with you. I need you to do the lighting itself. I'm not as quick as I used to be. Not right now." I looked at Corrine, who was staring at my beaten and battered legs. "Then I'm getting us the hell out of here…and Macie too. She says that she's *carrying*."

"Lord help us," Corrine muttered under her breath, shaking her head.

My head was spinning with the thoughts of my sister. Years— no, a *lifetime*—of looking for a way out of the puppet-mastery that was show business. We'd been in this together. Since day one. We had an escape plan. And now…to throw it all away. To throw *me* away. I wouldn't let her. No, no, no. She'd come back to her senses. She just needed to get out of that place.

Corrine took a deep breath. "Mary, I will do this for you. And then nothing, ever again. But you must do something in return."

"Anything, Corrine."

"Macie's going to be a real problem. Even if we get away from your husbands. Especially if we get away from your husbands. She's gonna squirm. I don't want to go to jail. I don't want her to talk. To *anyone*."

I nodded. "Me neither."

"You can make sure she never writes about it. I feel like that's a task you can manage, given the proximity of your relationship. But I'm worried she'll go nuts for this boy. If he's the father of her baby and we take that away, she'll go off talking to anyone who'll listen. Vultures like Janice Kroy. You and I'll be done for."

"What do you think we do?"

"If you really want to get her out. If you don't want to just leave her, *which I would*, by the way. But if she's coming down with us… you need to cut Macie's tongue so that she may never speak of this. That boy's got her cross-eyed. I need proof that she won't speak. As hard as that may be for you."

I felt the pain in my eyes first, untreated grief already pouring over my body. *My sister is going to betray me.* I needed to hurt her to survive. I knew I couldn't do that to Macie. And I knew I wouldn't. But I had to say it.

"Deal."

7.2: JANE'S RECOUNT

IN THIRTY MINUTES, give or take, the rest of the housemates would be returning from their dinner quest. Smiles would be selfishly plastered across their face. It was the same look that stockbrokers gave. Confident, triumphant, and completely ignorant to any trauma around them because *fuck-it-I've-got-a-gold-watch*. The similarities made me snort. Sillian had a tendency to surround herself with these types. Wanna-be-somethings. None of them were actually making strides toward anything, which I was beginning to realize was the ironic glue that held them together. Talking about their moves, rather than making them, made these friends into a unit.

I hated myself for taking part in it for so long.

Dakota finished searching the rooms with me. The only other thing noteworthy found was a jewelry box packed to the brim in what seemed to be a shared room between Robin and Elle. I'd returned to the garage to inspect the area once more. I didn't know what I expected to find, just that I needed to look in here again.

When you had a twin, you occasionally had a sixth sense. It wasn't telepathy. It was more primal than that.

You could feel their presence in an area, conversation, or relationship before they ever even told you. When Sillian and I were younger, I'd always know when she was going to ask to borrow my clothes, request my advice, or need my wallet. Like having a dog that could sense your anticipation from the pheromones that only they could smell. And in turn, we always knew where the other was. When I was in third grade, I had run away. I'd failed my history exam and thought I'd never hear the end of it. My parents had taken it lightheartedly at first.

"Oh, how cute. She's running away."

Until I'd actually done it.

They'd looped the neighborhood streets for hours. Three circles around the neighborhood and it wasn't cute anymore. My parents asked Sillian if she knew where I might've gone.

"Probably the Hawkins' backyard."

Sillian and I had never even been inside the short-fenced yard behind the Hawkins house. An exchange had never occurred between us about hopping their fence or knocking on their front door like Girl Scouts. The Hawkins family was structured, much more than our family, and Sillian had watched me in the car, gazing at their backyard setup longingly. They'd had a Victorian playhouse for their children installed in the branches of an oak tree, only accessible by ladder.

Their kids were older, as were their parents, so every time we'd passed the house, I'd imagined myself in there. A little structure all to myself. Four walls of solitude. I'd never told Sill that I'd dreamed of living on my own, even at such a young age. As my best friend, she wouldn't have agreed. So, I'd kept it to myself. And like all things, she'd somehow still known.

I'd been grounded for a month. While the Hawkins family had thought it was endearing and had gregariously invited me to their treehouse anytime I wanted on my way out the door, my parents hadn't been nearly as charmed. The grounding wasn't very effective because Sill wasn't grounded, and she would sneak into our bedroom with mountains of banned books, magazines, or handheld games. Grounding me was grounding her. We'd played, read, and listened to everything together. There was nothing we hadn't shared. Except for my ideas about the Hawkins treehouse. That had been something I'd wanted to discover on my own. When I'd asked her how she'd known where I was, she'd shrugged, and said, "I know everything about you. Even when you don't want me to."

Despite my attempts later in life, I couldn't deny that Sill had been and always would be the more perceptive one. She had a gift for reading people. Especially me. She knew things that would happen to me well before they ever did. Good and bad. When we'd lived with our parents, I was always on edge about her behavior. If I noticed her making me breakfast or helping with chores, I'd begin to get nervous. Something terrible must have been heading my way. Sillian could sense it. Without fail, she was always right. "That's how twins work," she'd remind me. I nodded as if I understood. Yet, I couldn't read her quite the same way she could read me.

Her links to me were stronger than my links to her. But I still had the links. I could tell something significant had happened to her there in the garage. It had been her blood. I was convinced.

And it was gone. Someone had mopped it right up. A small pink ring was the only trace left behind.

A small dark powder was still left in a ring where the jewelry used to be. I trailed my finger through it and brought my finger to my lips. I'd expected the taste of coffee, but instead got a profoundly bitter and smoked flavor.

Intense panic crept back over me. Someone had been in here covering a trail.

Criss-crossed like a child, I sat on the floor. I scanned the floor and empty walls with silver wire crossing over them like a hatch. Some of them protruded out, while others found themselves back in the wall, flat. As if the walls were holding something.

The faintest line of spray paint traced the metal wall trim. At first, it appeared to be builder's paint. The letter 'A' in a creamed color that barely stood out from the white baseboard.

I walked over and traced my finger over the cursive lettering. *A-I-R-B-U-S.*

Airbus? *Where have I heard that?*

I squatted toward the floor, barely able to make it out. The print was so small. My eyes trailed up and around the ceiling in a deep search for meaning.

Was it Alex who'd mentioned an Airbus? The word was jagged enough to flag when it came up. But as for who'd said it, I couldn't remember.

I searched the empty room unsuccessfully, finding nothing of any use. I let myself outside into the driveway again and began to pace in the misted air. The Victorian brick was sooty with reds and maroons. I ran my hands on it as I paced to ground myself.

I started to get dizzy as I walked and remembered that I needed to eat. Nothing felt real. Food wasn't real. This wasn't real. The sound of an engine wasn't real. I heard the noise of a vehicle approaching. The reality of the sight caught me so off-guard that I was overwhelmed with the sense to hide and observe. I ducked around the back wall of the garage and kept my eyes on the drive-way. The suspects had arrived.

I watched them one by one as they trailed into the manor single-file, each with laughter and takeout boxes. All of them were accounted for, to my surprise.

I wasn't sure they'd all come back. Robin was the last to get out of the car. She took a moment to look inside the vehicle before running back in to follow the group.

A drop of water fell on me as I regained solitude in the yard. It was about to rain again. My eyes trailed up to the sky, and I noticed I was under a silent wind chime…an airplane-themed wind chime. The word *'pull'* was carved into one of the metal pieces.

My curiosity overtook me as I reached toward the chime's strings. My fingers found the beaded strand and instinctively tugged down. I don't know what I thought would happen, but it wasn't what followed. A loud structural rumble came from inside the garage. Something had moved.

I sprinted back inside the garage to see a jukebox magically extracted from the nearest wall, just left of the pink smudge where the blood had been. It was ancient and lived inside the walls there, turn-tabling out upon what seemed to be a lever system. A secret compartment. But why did a false wall in the garage need to cover an old jukebox?

Something told me the garage might have been built on some puzzle system. I'd read about houses like that when I first got into reporting. A popular concept for the wealthy. But, I thought they didn't take off until the sixties? This house was undoubtedly a few decades older. Either way, the idea of dealing with a puzzle right now made me shudder.

The walls did looked spring-loaded. Nothing was shaped ordinarily. Wind chimes had prompted a magic jukebox to come out of the garage wall. There had to be some logical explanation.

I glanced at the jukebox, then peered over at the word 'AIRBUS' still intact with spray paint on the base of the wall.

I ran my hand over the old machine. There were a few buttons intact. Instinctively, I pressed the arrow button under the red rainbow arch of the glass screen. The folders inside the screen moved, and four records suddenly appeared to face me behind the case.

- *The Early Years - Frank Yankovic and Orchestra*
- *Over The Rainbow - Judy Garland*
- *All Of Me - Billie Holiday*
- *Bird Blows the Blues - Charlie Parker*

I stepped away from the machine and the burning question branded into my skull. I wasn't sure why, but I knew I needed to get this right the first time. This was some kind of…test. It had to be. *Which one do I pick? What could happen?*

I was about to make a selection when I heard the garage side door open. Dakota came running in with a pizza slice on a napkin. Then he noticed the jukebox and went cold.

"Jane, what have you done?"

I'd need to deal with him later. At that moment, my sister needed me to play an album on this jukebox. And she needed me to *choose wisely*.

7.3: MARY'S DIARY

1945

WE'D AGREED on four in the morning. I was to drive us out to the tree line in the blood-soaked car. Corrine would start by lighting the car's body and trunk until it engulfed the surrounding trees. I'd be half a mile deeper, soaking the nearby trees in what gasoline we could carry. Corrine had pre-soaked the trunk for an extra boost.

Our idea had been to make the scene appear like a forest fire. Yet, the challenge was only having four gallons of gasoline stored in the garage. The dryness of summer would allow a slight boost for the fire, but would it be enough? We had a case of the boy's cigarettes on us to scatter across the edges of the scene, just out of the fire's probable reach. I'd climb a tree further out when Corrine dropped that match, to keep a lookout.

And the cords between our marriages could be miraculously cut.

Josh remained the best person to frame with the panties, which would give me a way out. My husband was the most dangerous between the two. Not just because of his brutality. Josh was clever enough to piece together the clues here. And I needed him locked up before he had the chance.

I would go into hiding with Macie after the operation. In hiding, we would spoof some threats from Josh and James to be found during the investigation process. That would give us a clean getaway while giving Janice's murder a real motive.

Her panties were in Josh's desk drawer. Nobody would suspect me. Not for a second. With bruises like mine, why would they?

This was my best chance at getting us free. As long as the fire carried on and Macie *didn't* talk.

I met Corrine in the garage fifteen minutes early. We'd slipped Josh a sleeping tonic. Macie was fast asleep at James' side. I'd checked. I nodded to Corrine as I entered. The idea of her being the one to show up for me, a person with the lowest obligation to be ready for the frontline, still left me perplexed. Life surprised you that way. It was never the people you expect to have your back who did, was it?

The smell of gasoline already perfumed the room with hazes of anticipation and grief. Corrine's hair matched mine now, a low knot we'd learned to do in show business when we had a scene with a lot of movement. It was a safe choice, given the circumstances of our plans. We were both wearing all-black pants that weren't widely accepted in modern women's fashion. Despite the warmth of summer, we wore wooly sweaters to match. I'd read that wool had the hardest time catching fire once before, so fitting ourselves that way made me feel as if we had some element of planning on our side. Corrine and I didn't waste a moment. In silence, I got into the blood-stained vehicle and started the engine while she manually rolled up the garage door with calculated patience.

The drive carried a ceremonial undertone. Five lives were riding on a few moments. Or if Macie was really carrying, *six*. My hands were clammy around the wheel. Peripherally, I took sight of Corrine. Her hands were folded in her lap stoically, her gaze flat. She was a soldier. Brave and ready for a cause she knew she'd never quite understood. A zealot anyway, I took a moment to revere her guts.

We approached the tree line in minutes. I wanted to offer some grandiose gesture to Corrine, something like a blood bond. But I knew there was no time. Instead, as I placed the car into the park next to the abandoned body the ants had already found, I turned to face her and spoke in a hushed tone. "I'm forever in debt. Thank you."

She placed her hand on the car's door handle. "Yes, you are."

With a singular deep breath, she opened her side. "Let's finish this, Mary."

Maybe Corrine was in her own trap back at home. Jobless. With no stunts to carry out without Macie and me. Maybe she felt like a caged animal, too. The idea of becoming someone's ransom note was a thrill to her. Maybe all it took for someone to become a fool was a box small enough.

7.4: JANE'S RECOUNT

MY HAND TREMBLED over Billie's name. But my sister's voice was so clear as it rang between my ears. Whispering confidently:

"All of me."

"All of me."

"All of me."

I'd always given my sister all of me. Every day, I gave a bit more of myself. I didn't know what I'd be left with. For Sillian, it was all or nothing. There was no going back now.

I pressed down the jukebox key.

You could've heard the noises from a mile away. They were coming from inside the manor. Tires screeching, birds screaming, furniture dragging; the sound was an odd blend of all of them.

"Did you hear that?" Dakota's voice came as a surprise. I'd forgotten that he'd followed me. He was staring over my shoulder intently.

"What the hell was that?"

The garage had remained exactly as it was. Which meant the screech had to have come from inside the house. This place was now beginning to feel like a giant maze.

All the guests were back inside now. And they were likely *very* curious about the earthquake sound that had just erupted from the manor. I needed to keep them away so that I might find out first, which didn't sound as simple as another jukebox.

I sprinted toward the house to see the group of Sillian's guests still sitting casually in the living area. Each of them had a curious head cocked toward the staircase.

"Hey, Jane, there's a weird noise coming from under the banister. It's, like, *really* loud." Elle was the first to warn me. "Rats, maybe."

"It sounded like an avalanche," Cameron said.

Without a word, I shuffled past the seated group and kneeled toward the staircase. Fully aware of the audience, I examined the staircase carefully. To the untrained eye, the staircase looked relatively the same. But, after a close look, one of the wooden boards paneled under the stairs looked loose. The jukebox had somehow structurally pushed it out.

I gave it a hearty pull to find it no longer intact with the rest of them. The panel opening was just big enough for a human to crawl inside.

I faced the opening head-on, the tan glove I'd seen earlier now exposed, a bloody gauze just underneath it. I didn't look too interested. Not with everyone watching. As casually as I could, I took off my jacket and went inside. Dakota followed me in.

The room was small and musty. The overhead light flickered, as if it had been exhausted over the ages. Dakota and I both crouched in the room, looking dumbfounded.

It was bone-chilling how you could almost feel my sister in the air.

I found the open book in the room's corner first. The letter was next to it. And it might've been the most puzzling piece in this entire story.

7.5: LETTER FOUND UNDERNEATH STAIRCASE

WHAT WILL BECOME OF SOPHOMORE MANOR?

Written by : M. Sophomore

Sophomore Manor is a quiet place compared to most places in Virginia. Two young couples lived here. My mother, who killed seven men, owned this place first. My sister and I worked hard to maintain ownership before our husbands stole it from us. The violence never left.

That was why I built the passageways. M and I are twins who married the Sophomore brothers—financial and vain and controlling men. If you've found this letter, it means you've discovered a secret in our manor. There are many.

Image by: [lcodacci x Getty Images Signature] via Canva.com
Image not intended for standalone use.

SECRETS INSIDE

I'm writing to you in the hope that you can find our story. It's bound to be huge. We were married to the biggest waltz musicians in the United States. But they were horrible people. We had to hide this story inside the walls of our own home. It's our hope that you can find it and finally expose the lies. It's safe here—from all the parties and events this house holds—inside the secret rooms.

Image by: [The Everett Collection] via Canva.com
Image not intended for standalone use.

7.6: GUEST BOOK FOUND UNDERNEATH STAIRCASE

Sophomore Manor Secret Room
Guest Book

SIGN & DATE HERE:

Bryce B.   02-11-2001

I couldn't do it. Only had a short time at an event. Good luck to whoever finds this secret next

---

Raymond J.   11-13-2007

Didn't find it. Got close and plan on coming back next time it's open for tours

---

ZACHAry P.   02-22-2021

WHErE tHE HELL DiD tHEy HiDE it?

Jillian P.   3-4-2023
I'm going to find it if it kills me. Tonight.

7.7: ENGINEER NOTES FROM PJ-STRUCTURES

REGARDING S. MANOR

Structural Engineer's Analysis

Analysis & Sketch by Joanna Haley | Senior Engineer at PJ-Structures

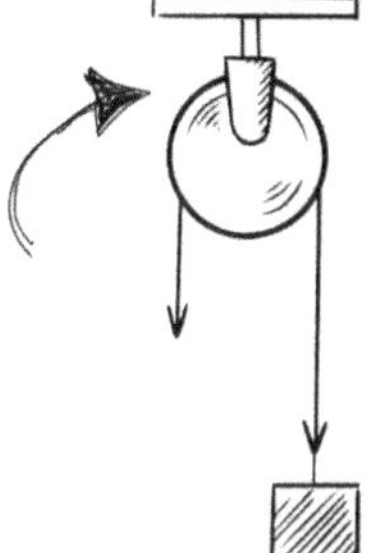

- Pulley System Outside Garage
- Disguised As Windchimes

*Pushes False Wall In Garage Forward to Room Center

System too modern for the forties. Could've been installed in the late fifties....Chimes themselves appear to have fifty or sixty years of wearing/rust.

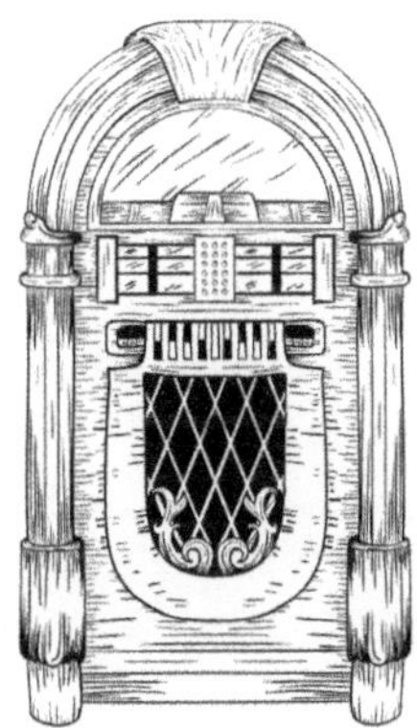

- Jukebox button triggers staircase step to pop out and expose a small crawl space underneath

Too modern for the forties. Earliest structure similar to this appeared in 1965.

Jukebox has a maintenance tag underneath from <u>1964</u>. Surprised it still works.

- Staircase with crawl space underneath.

Not a new revelation. Could've been established in any time period.

The glove in question has a tag from 2020. It certainly got stuck in the loose stair recently. Not apart of the structure.

Secret rooms like this sky-rocked in popularity around prohibition. This was likely a stash for alcoholic beverages before it was repurposed and attached to newer technology.

7.8: MARY'S DIARY

1945

THIS WAS REAL; this was happening. We were burning Janice's body.

For a brief second, I admired Corrine as she ran in total commitment toward the tree line.

Then I felt my hand on the door, finding its way to the trunk. With two gallons of gasoline in my hands, I heard my footsteps thud against the forest dirt. Even with a bad leg, Jesse Owens couldn't have outpaced me.

We didn't have time to rehearse the distance beforehand. I had to go with what felt right before I poured the oil. Knowing nerves probably made me much quicker, I fought not to second guess the distance and poured it on heavy. There wasn't a methodology in my actions. Something greater than I had taken over my motor functions as I spun like a carousel, dropping gasoline in circles around tree trunks.

With no calculations, I weaved between trees in the woods until I was out. And then I climbed a sycamore.

From what I could see, Corrine had a small glow working in front of her that would be the reporter's burning body. I couldn't see the details, but I noticed that she'd already removed the garments, based on the amount of skin showing. The smell drifting my way was smokey and rancid. The scent of hair disintegrating.

I watched carefully between the spaces of trees to see the fire start with tiny embers. My difficulty seeing was great as I forced my eyes between small dark alleyways between trees. As the glow of the fire grew, more and more was revealed to me. Corrine was about to complete the task and carry out her final sprint.

The bark on the tree scratched against my bruises and I let out a wince. I watched Corrine from the tree intently as she carried out the fate of my future.

Suddenly, a hooded figure moved closer to her. At first, I was sure my eyes were playing tricks on me. But then it became obvious to me that it was more than Corrine's shadow. Another person had followed us out there.

"Behind you, Corrine!" My lungs throbbed at the magnitude of the shriek.

"Behind you!"

My pant legs caught on the bark of the tree as I slid down. They ripped, but I didn't have time to react.

Pain stung my knees. I dropped from the heights onto the ground and I ran.

Sounds of a struggle echoed ahead of me. My legs throbbed, but I kept going. Twigs crunched between my feet. The battle got louder.

"Corrine!" I shouted.

Voices were gasping for air just ahead of me. What could only be the sounds of wrestling bodies rolled out in earshot. I couldn't make out anything but the shadows. My pace slowed as I got near the edges of the rapidly spreading fire.

The car was encapsulated in a ring of heat; the fire was a privacy fence around it.

I ran to my right to dodge the spreading edge of the ring and made my way to the front. A girlish scream erupted from the ring. Then, the sound of a skull hitting a metal structure. Over and over again.

At that moment, a roly-poly-like body rolled from the fire all the way through the flames.

Smoking, the silhouette ran quickly from the burn site before dropping to their knees again and rolling in the grass.

Still running to my best ability, I tailed the shadow. The heat behind me kept me going, with the tease of a roast taunting the back of my neck. The shadow got up in intervals, running and rolling. I wasn't supposed to be heading in that direction. It wasn't a part of the plan. I was to find the road on the backside of the woods and take it to a spot where Corrine would meet me, far away from the house. It was the most straightforward chance for each of us to beat the fire. But two shadows had been inside that ring. And only one remained. Whether I wanted to or not, I needed to find out whose blood had been added to my hands. Even if that meant dying.

"Corrine!" I called out again.

An ash-covered face turned around to face me.

"Keep running!" she shouted back, out of breath.

A trickle of relief flooded my system. Whoever had followed us, Corrine had won the fight. *We* won.

Gasping outright, we stopped running and stripped our clothes. There was no room in our lungs to speak. Corrine's face was grayed with shock. I could hear her heartbeat over mine.

"Th-the manor—" My words came out strangled. "It's yours once we jail those brutes. My payment to you."

Corrine shook her head violently as she pulled off her sweater for a night cardigan she'd left for herself in the bushes.

"Who was that back there who caught us?" I barely mustered the breath to ask. "Josh? If it was Josh, we might need to revise the whole plan toward James. That will upset Macie, but it will have to be done."

"It was..." Corrine pulled the cardigan over her left shoulder and bent down on her knees in an evident struggle. I couldn't tell if she was out of breath or avoiding the question.

"Who? Who was it?"

"Macie," Corrine said quickly, without looking up.

It was one of those impressionable moments that would stick with me forever. I didn't have many of those in my lifetime. Life never followed me around much, even in my childhood. No single moment mattered. But, in a flash, I knew I would never rid my memory of this. Even in my happiest times, this would constantly perfume my mind in the background. My sister and her *child*... I fell to my knees.

How did she wake up? I was so confident she'd stay asleep. *Didn't I make sure of it?*

Corrine made eye contact with me now. A steady look on her face.

"She came at me with a knife, Mary. She told me it was my dying day. And..." Corrine's face twisted. "And she thought I was *you*. She came for *you*."

There was a moment of silence between us that I would always be thankful for. No amount of time would allow me to process the betrayal. Pity and rage made a mixed cocktail to fog the clarity of my mind.

"I'm so sorry, Mary. I know this has got to be hard." Corrine offered a moment of sympathy before standing back up. "But, with Macie gone, we've got to frame James immediately. We need evidence in his possession before we call the department. He'll look to have enough motive for both kills, but we've got to do it *now*."

Unable to think, I moved from my trembling knees toward the manor's back door.

"I'm on it."

7.9: POLICE QUESTIONING

DB: "How did you know to select '*All of Me*' on the jukebox?"

JP: "I don't know. I just did."

DB: "Did Sill give you any information about the house that would've helped you find your way around? Did she leave behind any clues for you?"

JP: "No. None."

DB: "Did you ever try to contact the rental unit's owner?"

JP: "No. That was Sill's thing."

DB: "So you aren't aware that your group's stay didn't include the last night you were there?"

JP: "What? Yes, it did. We stayed. All the way through."

DB: "Well, you weren't supposed to."

JP: "That's impossible. We—"

DB: "Are you aware that the stay your sister booked included two nights before the attendees were invited?"

JP: "What? No, I—"

DB: "Who arrived before you at the party that night, Jane?"

JP: "Well…Michael, Robin, and Elle were already there. Alex was too. He was apparently the first one."

DB: "The glove you found under the staircase…do you remember whose costumes might have required a pair of stained beige gloves?

JP: "Oh my God, you think they left their cost—"

DB: "There's a lot of motive in this case. We're exploring all of them. But priority points to the evidence. Someone was following your sister during the secret mission she was on. We've got to place the suspect at the crime scene."

Phillip Beacons left more sticky notes at your workstation. Your desk is looking like a seasoned detective's: *messy*.

- **HINT:** Every lead will lead you…somewhere. Focus on the leads that move the investigation toward Sillian's disappearance rather than away from it.

- **STICKY NOTE FROM PHILLIP:** *"Detective Bruno finally finished questioning all the suspects. You should be getting those files soon. Stay sharp! - PB"*

- **FUN FACT:** The "homemaker" portrayal of women in classic 1940s and 1950s films is not always accurate. During WW2, more than nine million women entered the workforce to provide for their families. Women usually got paid half of a man's wage.

Trust your research!

CASE FILE EIGHT

<u>Case file eight contains seven items to be reviewed.</u>
Files should be reviewed in numerical order

- **8.1 Jane's Recount** | March 2023
- **8.2 Mary Sophomore's Diary** | 1945
- **8.3 E. E. Official Questioning**
- **8.4 Mary Sophomore's Diary** | 1945
- **8.5 R. R. Official Questioning**
- **8.6 Mary Sophomore's Diary** | 1945
- **8.7 Jane's Recount** | March 2023

8.1: JANE'S RECOUNT

THE COMMOTION that followed our exit from the room underneath the staircase was overwhelming. Dakota and I didn't have time to debrief. Questions were flying off the handle. Before we answered any of them, I made sure to slam the staircase door shut. Nobody could get back down there without knowing the ins and outs of the puzzling house.

"What the hell was that about?" Elle said, crowding the entryway staircase. "Is Sill down there? The whole house seemed to erupt like a volcano!"

"Did you find anything?" Alex asked.

"You Parks girls. Always on some scheme. I doubt she'll even tell us anything!" said Michael.

"Dakota. Won't you tell me what's going on?" Robin batted her eyelashes at my boyfriend.

Fluster found my face. The noise was overstimulating. I fought to narrow my concentration down to a single point.

"Can we talk?" I hissed under my breath at Dakota, who was already turning toward Robin, the pizza from earlier still in his hand like a football. I pulled him into the study by the sleeves of his shirt and locked the door behind us.

"She really went after something, didn't she?" Dakota said, immediately referencing Sill. I could see the journalist in his eyes, bloodthirsty for an answer. Or a story.

"What should we tell the guests?" I said, changing the topic quickly. "I need your help to distract them. I need to get a call out."

The wheels in Dakota's mind seemed to be turning. In all the turmoil, I was happy to have his sharp cunning assisting me.

"We can tell them the truth?"

I shook my head. "What if one of them wanted to harm Sillian? Or is in on it somehow? We could put ourselves in danger."

"You think one of them is *that* dangerous?"

The thought seemed ridiculous, and yet I felt there was no other option. "I have a bad feeling about the whole lot of them, to be honest with you."

My anxiety was tugging at me now. My sister had been looking for something in that house. Something several people before her had failed to find. And perhaps someone was making sure she failed, too.

Dakota waved his hand at me dismissively. "Let me handle the story. I'll stick close to the truth without giving away too much."

"What will you say?"

"That we're looking for Sillian still. We found a few things in the house that led us to believe she's run away. You're going off to call your dad and will be right back. Or something like that. Then a beer pong tournament to pass the time."

"Why would we tell them she ran away?"

"Do you want them snooping, too? I thought it might help divert attention away from the house. And whatever it is that Sillian's looking for."

He was right.

"Okay, that's a plan. Thanks, Dakota." I planted a quick kiss on his cheek.

"Don't forget this. You need to eat." Dakota handed me the pizza he'd been carrying around like a handbag. Grip marks were etched into the crust. I accepted anyway and turned toward the door. I was desperate to get out to Cell Mountain to send every photo and detail to Chief Simmons at the paper.

At that moment, he was the only one I could afford to trust.

8.2: MARY'S DIARY

1945

CORRINE and I hid underground beneath the manor for three months. Two rooms, one bed, and a barely working toilet. It was better than a jail cell, but not by much. James and Josh had been moved into offsite housing for the investigation. We never risked going up into the house. The underground was the safest place for us to hide until James and Josh were convicted.

Corrine went up for supplies on four occasions, each time in the earliest hours of morning before the sun rose. About three miles up the road, a farmer's market left its produce out overnight. We lived off their merchandise for the duration of the investigation.

On the second day following Janice's murder, we heard the investigators stomping about the floorboards. James and Josh had both been taken off the premises. According to the small box television in the basement, they were under investigation for the disappearance and possible murder of Janice Kroy, Macie, and me. It took an extra six days for the news to catch up to Corrine's vanishing, which further linked the framings. On the first and second nights, Corrine and I had cautiously gone back up to the main areas of the manor to scatter evidence that would lead the authorities to investigate James and Josh further.

Corrine, Macie, and Janice's purses were carefully stuffed in James' closet. We made sure to add type-written notes into Janice's and Corrine's bags before we crumpled them to look worn.

- That was too delightful to only do once.
- See you soon. Don't tell M.
- I wish I could shout our love from the rooftops.
- How could a man keep his hands off you?

There were moments I felt uneasy about scapegoating James because I knew he wasn't as treacherous of a human as Josh was. But, upon Macie's betrayal, it was all that could be done. I felt foul with myself, sentencing the man she loved to a crime beyond her grave.

Processing the double-cross with my sister had not been easy. Especially in the presence of my sister's executor. To make the time pass, I spent most of it writing our stories together, mine and Macie's best memories. Nothing helped me numb the pain. But for a few hours a day, my brain could escape into the past. And that was all I had left to live for.

On the other hand, Corrine was planning her way out of the underground. We'd become close friends, which I hadn't expected, given the circumstances. She spent most of her time in the living area of the basement while I was primarily glued to the desk. She never brought up payment again, as she knew I couldn't provide it yet. Instead, she'd created a way to pay herself. The week before James was arrested, she came to me with the proposal.

"I'm going to make a return to the world," Corrine said, sitting down somewhat inelegantly on the sofa.

Despite the summer months, she was as pale as I'd ever seen her. Yellow teeth and brittle hair. Her beauty was fading fast in the underground. I'm sure mine was, too; I just couldn't see it first-hand. Corrine's bones were visible now; her athletic body had withered down into a flimsy and breakable stature. Both of us had patches of hair missing. We weren't sure if it had derived from the stress or the rationing of supplies.

"Explain." I kept a hand on the typewriter while she spoke, as if our story was a fully formed third party inside the room.

"I reappear above ground. Act a bammy woman. And I'll say somewhere in the nonsense that I was one of the women James Sophomore slept with. I'll say that those brutes drugged me. Almost killed me too. But I prevailed. When they come back to search the house for evidence on the claim, I'll leave behind a few more of my things. Frame up James real nice. That'll certainly finish him."

"It won't work. James is still not in prison and they're still looking for me. Those boys have money and they could rip you to shreds in court. They could find out our plan. Find out I'm still *here*. They need to be locked up before you make claims like that. Both of them."

Corrine shook her head. "What if I say James killed you and Macie both? Saw it myself. An eye witness for the jury. On the Bible. I can lead the cops toward what's left of Macie's bones to back up the story. That should be enough to lock James up, at least. Maybe Josh too, if he was thought to be complicit. I could sell a lie that he was. In times like these, women are more believable than men."

"I don't know, Corrine. It feels flimsy at best. They're certainly armored with good lawyers right now. I think it might put us both at risk."

"If it worked, you could move toward a new identity. I could help you from above ground. I'd probably go to a shrink for a few years and slowly but surely leak news about my 'affairs' with James to some Janice-Kroy-types. I'd more than get my career back. I'll be set for life with that kind of appearance. Especially with a story this famous. They'd want my face everywhere. I'd be the heroine who locked those monsters up. In *your* honor."

She crossed her bony leg over the other, revealing ice-blue veins in her calves. I could tell she'd spent a lot of time fantasizing about this plan. It was going to be hard to talk her out of it.

"The case is just now settling." I shook my head without making eye contact with her. "They've got a dead woman's panties out of his desk and they still haven't jailed him. It's still too dangerous to go through with something like this. With him behind bars, you've got a better shot at it working."

"Mary." Corrine's voice went baritone. "You got me into this. I want to get out. *Now*."

I realized my choices were slim. She deserved her way out of this mess that Macie and I had roped her into. The anxiety settled in my gut first before it rushed toward my brain. Soon enough, I was going to be in this alone. It would be the first time I did anything completely and totally independently. I was all that was left of me. And that was a first.

"Alright." I shook my head with reluctance. Corrine was a smart woman. And she didn't deserve to suffer the way I did. "But you can never tell them where I am."

"I'll map everything out this week. Then it's time for the final act."

I could've sworn she smiled as she said it.

8.3: E. E. OFFICIAL QUESTIONING

DB: "I'm Detective Bruno, here to interview Elle Ewing at the Richmond Police Department. This is for case number 2023-555. Also present in the room is Doctor Eli Dunn of the Richmond Emergency Hospital. Elle Ewing is the roommate of the victim, Sillian Parks."

DB: "According to Jane's recorded statement, you and Sillian Parks weren't on the best terms when you arrived at the costume party?"

EE: "No...we weren't on good terms. And I know those texts looked bad, but I swear I didn't do *anything*. Like seriously, she's been my best friend for years."

DB: "We're not suggesting you did anything, Miss Ewing. Just tell us why you were so upset with her the day before her disappearance."

EE: "She hasn't been the best friend lately. Sort of distancing herself from Robin and me. It's been building up. And finding the brochure was just last my last straw."

DB: "How did finding that brochure make you feel? To find out your friend might be moving and didn't even tell you."

EE: "Hurt, obviously. Like if she's planning on moving to California, the least that she could do is tell me. Robin and I have just been waiting for her signature on the renewal. No common courtesy there at all. I felt myself a victim of her selfishness. Not to mention we're supposed to be friends. Friends share things like that."

DB: "Would you say you have a quick temper?"

EE: "I wish I wouldn't have sent those messages if that's what you're asking. I didn't ever think those could be our last…"

DB: "Did your second roommate, Robin, get involved in the situation as well? Was she angry about the brochure?"

EE: "I didn't tell her. She's just come out of unemployment. Money is tight, and she's desperate. I didn't want her stressing, thinking we might have to split our rent two ways instead of three. I thought I could handle it myself. That's why I showed the brochure to Sill's sister. I hoped to get more information, but Jane didn't know either."

DB: "Alright. Can you describe your relationship with the victim's sister, Jane Parks?"

EE: "Uh…sure. Jane's the nice girl type. Always stays out of the way. We all love her as one of us, but she's just, like…*not* one of us? If that makes sense. I've never really seen her get dramatic. That is, until this whole fiasco. She had a sixth sense something happened to Sill."

DB: "Did you think she was lying when Jane first brought it up?"

EE: "No, I just wasn't concerned. Sill's parties are run on theatrics."

DB: "Let's backtrack a bit. I understand you're a frequent attendee of the victim's events. Did you notice anything off-putting about this party apart from the others?"

EE: "Not necessarily. All of Sillian's events ride a drama high. This one didn't particularly stand out to me. Even the axe stunt was semi-typical."

DB: "Did that incident make you feel in danger?"

EE: "No, but it did make me feel like I drank too much."

DB: "Jane, Robin, and Dakota discovered a ring in the garage. It's my understanding that the ring suddenly went missing. Did you hear anything about where that ring might've gone?"

EE: "Never even heard about it."

DB: "Okay then…How about one word you'd use to describe your current relationship with the victim?"

EE: "Chilly."

8.4: MARY'S DIARY

1945

A SHARP PAIN behind my eyes woke me up. Another headache. I'd gotten used to them under the garage, a place the sun couldn't reach.

Without natural light, it was difficult to establish a circadian clock. In fact, I didn't have one at all anymore. Time didn't exist down there. Everything was void.

Corrine was better at telling time than I was. She was probably the only reason I'd remained alive. Even though I'd taken her life away from her by involving her in that insidious plot, she still kept me fed. It was Corrine who routinely raided the farmer's market. It was Corrine who encouraged me to eat at all, as my motivation to live slowly withered away.

It was apparent she was worried about leaving me. She was concerned if I could take care of myself once she was gone. I wondered about it too.

"You're growing a starvation belly," she'd remind me almost daily.

"What do you mean?"

"Your belly." Corrine stared at me with her arms crossed over her chest. "It's protruding out. Swollen. You're not getting enough protein, are you?"

I looked down at my stomach, which was beginning to round more and more by the day. "Perhaps not."

Corrine scoffed, folding a pair of trousers she'd washed the previous day in the sink. "The farmer's market carts are dreadful lately. Not near enough legumes."

We'd go about our day separately. Usually, I remained in the office area and she'd stay by the main room. Corrine had become frail, yes, but her strength was still somewhat there. Lifting arm weights every day and doing crunches made it easier for her to maintain structure. She was meant to be a soldier. A rebel without enough cause. I wondered if some part of her even enjoyed our situation.

That day, Corrine had come in with the newspaper she'd swiped above ground.

"Would you look at that!" she exclaimed.

The headlines were painfully uninteresting. I searched over the taglines again to try and understand.

"We're not on 'em anymore," she said, smiling. "Perfect timing to shake things up."

I nodded slowly. I knew Corrine was leaving that day. We'd talked about it. Even agreed. But we both still danced around the subject. Neither one of us had brought it up in days. We just knew that it was coming.

Today.

That morning, Corrine washed all her clothes in the sink and tidied up the living area. I knew the only thing she'd ever come back to this house for was the house itself. Not because she wanted it, but because days after the body burning, we'd replaced the will in the safe upstairs with a new one. One with her name on it.

That day had stuck with me in particular. Not because I didn't want to give the house to Corrine. No, I never wanted to see this house again. But some hopeful part of me, the last bit of my soul that lived on a feminine daydream, expected to see my name on that deed. I'd anticipated Josh and James to have included Macie and I in the documents after marriage. The new ones they'd ordered at the manor's name shift.

Those two brutes wanted to pass their wealth on to their business correspondent, Marc Beatty, at the time of their death. The man I'd married prejudiced women so much that he might not even trust his wife to reside in his estate beyond the grave. He'd rather I became a whore and a homeless widow. Sounded about right.

No guilt came over me as I burned that paper with Marc Beatty's name on it. Only the slight inkling of fear lingered with the ashes.

Corrine was standing in the office doorway, appearing more like a ghost than a person.

"You know the plan," she said.

"I know the plan."

Corrine was never a woman of many emotions. Her rational faculties always greeted you at the door and never invited you in. I wasn't sure anyone had ever seen the dark turmoil that lived inside of Corrine, but I was certain that disturbance had made a home out of her.

Corrine nodded and gave me one last look over.

"I wrote down a few things about the farmer's market. Where to find the morning paper. It's all on the counter."

I stood up from my seat and took a step toward her.

Grabbing her hands, I looked deep into her eyes. "With my whole heart, *thank you.*"

Corrine tore her gaze away and looked at the floor momentarily, shaking her head. "We've got to look out for one another…in this industry. In this world."

She let go of my hands and pulled me into a genuine embrace. I felt a single tear roll down my face. *How could I have done this to her?*

Corrine let go of me and nodded her head again. It felt like she was looking for the right words to say, but we already knew there were none. No exchange of them would ever be enough.

Instead, she left the room, turning back to me one last time. I knew I'd never see her again.

"May Macie rest in peace."

The wall turned to let her back into the world where she belonged. As her feet went up the stairs, a piece of my heart cracked.

Then I heard the gunshot.

8.5: R.R OFFICIAL QUESTIONING

DB: "I'm Detective Bruno, here to interview Robin Reed at the Richmond Police Department. This is for case number 2023-555. Also present in the room is Doctor Eli Dunn of the Richmond Emergency Hospital. Robin Reed is the roommate of the victim, Sillian Parks. Miss Robin, we'd like to start today by asking you a few questions about your relationship with the victim."

RR: "Go ahead."

DB: "How long have you known the victim?"

RR: "Couple years. We've lived together for the past two."

DB: "And Elle?"

RR: "Elle's lived with us for about fifteen months. She had to finish out another lease before she moved in."

DB: "What's your relationship with Sillian like?"

RR: "We don't hang out as much as we used to, but I'd still say we're close. We know so much about each other."

DB: "Like what?"

RR: "Drama. Boys. That kind of stuff. The things girls aged twenty-something build their friendships from and their lives around."

DB: "Speaking of boys, have you ever had a sexual relationship with Sillian's boyfriend, Michael?"

RR: "What? God, no."

DB: "What is your relationship with Michael, then?"

RR: "I hardly know the guy. Really. Don't know that much about him. He seems great."

DB: "So Sillian has been dating this guy on and off for a long time and you know nothing about him? Even though your friendship is said to be built on boys and drama?"

RR: "I know some stuff about him, sure. But not anything that personal."

DB: "Are you sure, Ms. Reed?"

RR: "Yes. I mean— What is this about, sir? Did Michael hurt Sillian or something?"

DB: "Have you ever hurt Michael?"

RR: "No. What kind of tactic is this? It seems a bit gaslight-y. I told you I barely even know him. Why would I hurt him? That's ludicrous!"

DB: "Just a general questioning, Miss Reed. Is it true that you've hypothetically been *borrowing* money from your roommates? Specifically, Sillian?"

RR: "What would make you think I'd ever do that?"

DB: "A couple of things. Including a laundry list of seemingly unauthorized Venmo transactions from Sillian's number. And given your unemployment, you'd think you would slow down on the shopping, but our records indicate that—"

RR: "Shopping on credit is not a crime. And if I was stealing from my roommate, she would've prosecuted me herself. Trust me, that's not what you think."

DB: "Seems like she was giving you a lengthy runway to pay her back before she did that. 'Til December.'"

RR: "I'm not sure what you mean."

DB: "What kind of job do you work now, Robin?"

RR: "I'm in jewelry sales. I help companies promote their rings, bracelets, and earrings. Things like that."

DB: "Speaking of rings, do you happen to be missing any?"

8.6: MARY'S DIARY

1945

"CORRINE!"

The gunshot at the top of the stairs set my whole body alight in goosebumps. I sat in a moment of shock before taking action.

On my feet, I scrambled to the staircase and dashed up on all fours. The door leading up to the garage was still open. A smell of wet rust tainted the air.

"Corrine?!"

My feet couldn't move fast enough. A trickle of blood rolled down the top stair.

The sight made me gasp.

"Corrine!" I cried once more.

"Don't worry, dear. She's accounted for."

I heard his voice before I saw her, my only friend left in the world, bleeding out at the top of the garage. It was James behind the gun. The man I'd estimated as the lesser of two evils. The man I thought might get me out of that mess.

A whimpering came from Corrine's body. James had shot her in the leg. She was still alive, but she was losing blood fast.

"Go inside and fetch the ambulance, James." I kneeled over her body, ignoring James and his gun altogether.

Corrine blinked at me in fear, unable to make words out of the shock.

"I'm afraid I can't do that, honey." James sighed and towered over us, still pointing his gun at Corrine.

"You promised. You swore *we* would be decent people about this." The tears were coming through now. This was my only friend. All I had left. And James wasn't going to budge. This was what I got for making a deal with the devil. A lifetime of hell to pay.

"I know." James took a step into the blood piling onto the floor. "I know I promised, but that was before you went and changed the will."

Corrine's eyes were darting between James and me, trying to piece together the conversation. Her breath came in and out in low huffs. She was in pain. Not just from the gunshot. She knew I'd made some deal with Josh. Behind her back too.

I turned my face back to James, one hand on Corrine's leg.

"You swore she'd walk away from this a free woman. Unharmed."

"*Before* you changed our will."

Corrine's eyes narrowed at me. "How dare you make a deal with him?" she whispered.

Despite everything, I needed him in that situation. I was never going to make it out of there without him. Corrine could move on. She could walk away. There could be a happily ever after for her.

"Oh my, we need to get you back to the vanity, don't we?" James looked over my appearance and laughed evilly.

"Forget the will. Burn it and write a new one. But do not kill this woman. That wasn't a part of our deal."

Shame fitfully tore at me. I was a virtueless woman. If it was all I could do, I would save her. I stood up to face James.

James shook his head and cocked the pistol in his hands. "The police found that one already. I'm afraid it's too late for a new will. As long as Corrine is alive, the estate belongs to her."

My heart sank. I knew he wasn't going to budge.

"Kill me instead! Please. Please." I put my hands in the air and begged. "Kill me, James!"

I positioned my body between James and Corrine, who was still bleeding out on the ground.

James strolled toward me; an arrogant cloud hung by his shoulders. My whole body went stiff and braced for impact. He was going to shoot me instead. Or he was going to kill us both. And I deserved to die. Oh, did I deserve to die.

He placed an unwanted kiss on my nose and laughed. "You're carrying a child. All that's left of our sad little world. I would never rid of you, darling."

Another thing I'd never told Corrine. Her eyes darkened.

He turned to Corrine and flashed a reptilian smile. "Any last words, Corrine?"

Her eyes were glossed by betrayal. Even bleeding out on the ground, she looked strong. She even looked victorious. A real woman of character. One I could never be.

Corrine sucked her lip in as she brought her head up to get a look at me. "I want *her* to kill me."

A cackle escaped James. "Well, isn't that something?"

I shook my head, crying violently.

"Believe me, Corrine, I wanted to save you. I wanted to keep you out of this. I can't kill you."

She grunted, leaning her head back against the concrete floor. "Cut the bullshit, Mary." It seemed to take all of her might, but she rolled up her body to sit up and face me with a fierce confidence that made me shake. "If you want any last respect out of me, you'll take that gun and shoot me yourself. You'll feel the treachery on your fingertips."

"No, no, no," I said through choked hiccups as James placed the gun into my hands and took a step back.

Corrine's eyes widened as if to tell me something. She darted them between the gun and James behind me in desperate communication. To the gun and then to James. Three times.

I understood her, but I understood too late.

James grabbed me from behind and coiled his hands around mine, pointing the gun straight at Corrine's head. I fought against him, but his strength persisted.

Her eyes roared with fire. Then the pop came.

Corrine was dead. I'd pulled the trigger.

James sighed and let go of my hands, leaving the smoking gun in my hands. I dropped to my knees in disbelief.

He brought his hands into my hair as if it were nothing.

"Well done, baby. I knew you were the strongest of them all."

8.7: JANE'S RECOUNT

THE BRUSH on the trail cut open an old scratch from the day before. The acute pain made me wince. I was alone on the trail in the darkness. I could barely see where I was headed. Wet and cold air danced around me, reminding me that the sun would be setting quickly.

I'd just gotten off the phone with Chief Simmons after over an hour of analysis. He had me recount every detail I could think of about Sillian's actions the night before. The pace of my heart was becoming frantic. Something told me I was running out of time.

A warm rush of heat flushed my face as I walked through the manor's back door. It could've been from the radiator or the plethora of candles someone had decided to light in the main room. The party was contained to the dining area, where a crowd played beer pong over an antique Victorian that was probably worth more than all of our belongings combined. I suspected everyone who wasn't present had finally gotten tired from the weekend and slinked off to their respective rooms. Dakota wasn't in plain sight, which peppered me with anxiety. No matter how kind it was to get the help to look for my sister, he'd still tried to sell me out for a story. And nothing could override the thoughts I had about that pink coat.

I poked my head into every room on the way up to mine, hoping my boyfriend might be tucked away in one. No luck. Our relationship shouldn't be at the top of my worries. A girl could only handle so much.

My bedroom was dark even with the curtains open. The sun was almost entirely down. I closed my eyes and placed a hand on the glass. *What would my sister do?*

I went through every detail I could think of, just like Chief Simmons had suggested. Out of nowhere, the thought dropped down to me like a heavenly gift. The keyhole table.

After finding Silian's signature underneath the staircase, I was certain the little table she'd made such a big deal about had something to do with all this.

I circled the hallways twice, looking for it. I looked in every storage closet upstairs, every nook. The table was nowhere to be found.

I was about to search the garage again out of sheer hopelessness when I heard the sound of a keyring shuffling behind the next door down the hall. If there was ever a time to get involved, it was at that moment.

I gave the adjacent door a two-finger knock. Sounds of shuffling and zippers danced behind the door. Someone was struggling for something. I knocked again.

"Just a minute," a voice that belonged to Alex Ansley cried out.

Suspicion propelled me into action. My fingers found the doorknob and twisted.

"Jane!" Alex looked frazzled in the dim light. His hair was as messy as his room. "Hi," he said as he settled onto the bedside, angling his eyes between me and his suitcase. He looked nervous. "Everything okay, Jane? You look a total mess."

"What's going on, Alex?"

He went frozen and unresponsive, which raised the skeptic in me.

Alex covered his face with his hands. I was confused, but I didn't say anything yet. My eyes circled the room once more for signs of suspicion. I hadn't found anything the first time I'd been in there with Dakota, but his room seemed to have exploded since then.

His suitcase was spilling over with the sleeves of clothes, socks, and laced straps. Wait a minute.

"I was just packing. Trying to get out of here at a decent time tomorrow." Alex crossed his arms over his chest. A move of defense. "I'm missing a piece of my costume, so I've been searching everywhere to find it. I wear the same one every year."

"Is that..." My mind didn't believe my eyes. I pointed over to the suitcase in disbelief, my heartbeat suddenly banging from the inside of my chest.

Alex's face twisted.

"My bra strap? I've been missing it. Green and lacy." The words fell out of my mouth.

"What? No. Jane, of course not."

His face turned red. He looked just as shocked as I did.

"Open the suitcase, Alex."

Slowly, he turned toward his luggage on the floor. I instinctively put my hand on the doorknob. Alex was the largest guy here. The most capable of...

"Jane," Alex said while on his knees, fumbling with his luggage. Panic painted over his poker face. "Trust me. I can explain."

He opened the suitcase on the ground slowly. Amidst enough clothes to warm an army, my lace green bra rested on top. It'd been missing for weeks, hadn't it? And just underneath it was something shiny and metal.

A ring of keys.

Only two more files to go! Below are checkpoints to keep you on track to pinpointing the right suspect:

- **HINT:** Sillian's attacker is skilled in diversion.

- **CONSIDER:** Every suspect's whereabouts during and after the party.

- **TIP:** The best detectives keep their investigations organized.

- **FUN FACT:** Post-war Hollywood was restrictive. In a film star's contracts, there were often clauses banning pregnancies, outlining approved public relationships, and forcing actors and actresses to forgo major developments in their home lives.

Look before you leap.

CASE FILE NINE

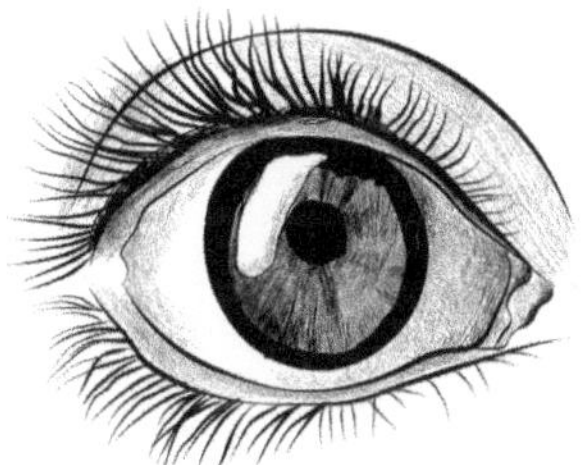

<u>**Case file nine contains seven items to be reviewed.**</u>
Files should be reviewed in numerical order

- **9.1 Mary Sophomore's Diary** | 1945
- **9.2 M. M. Official Questioning**
- **9.3 Mary Sophomore's Diary** | 1946
- **9.4 C. C. Official Questioning**
- **9.5 Jane's Recount** | March 2023
- **9.6 Torn Note From Sillian**
- **9.7 9-1-1 Call Transcript**

9.1: MARY'S DIARY

1945

"THE PAIN IS BEAUTIFUL!" I heard my husband shout at me. It was ironic, given pain was the only thing left to hold our marriage together. Through tears, I fought like hell.

My back ached with hurt, acute aching so widespread it didn't make sense. There wasn't much time to think. Hands pushed inside of me as if they were foraging through a mangled suitcase. I was going to have this baby.

I fought it for hours, sucking it up and in as much as I could. I couldn't dare bring a child into this world. Especially not a girl. Please, not a girl.

If I were to bear a boy, perhaps I could live with it. Name it in a way that he could never disappoint me. An evil name. Because this baby didn't stand a chance. With James and Josh between my legs, I fought the sensation with all my might, desperate to keep this infant away from his first breath. The warm air of Hades. Two maleficent men. One nefarious woman. A hell-damned baby it was.

"Push!" they shouted.

And boy, did I pull.

But eventually, it was too much.

The room was nearly silent. Then there was the cry. I knew by the first gasp of air that it was a boy. Furiously pissed off at the world, he took his first breath in an angry cry. A protest of life, demanding me to take him back into the unborn. As if he was aware of all the suffering in the world before ever seeing any of it.

In a language only between us, I swear I heard my child scream: *"No. No. No."*

Through flashes, I saw James and Josh smiling, cheering at the sight of another penis. Men. *Boys.* Three now. Not two.

The screaming child looked to me, his mother, draped in after-birth between the gloved hands of the two men at my feet. The fear in his eyes begged me, but I just shook my head.

I can't save you. I can't save myself.

I didn't feel the way a mother should feel. A cold detachment draped over me in a hospital gown. That boy was born to the wolves. And I was no match. Not anymore. I knew that much.

The words came up in echoes, the doctor hovering between me and the men like a bad omen.

"What will you name him?" she asked repeatedly, but nobody responded. We'd never talked about a name.

I huffed a deep breath out, fighting to stay with reality. *Had I wanted a girl? Had I wanted to see my sister's face, even just once more?* Because in the mirror, I couldn't find her anymore. She was gone. I searched my heart for her presence then, but she wasn't there.

The doctor brought him over to me. The baby with my husband's face smeared across it as if preparing for the pass-over. Smart baby, wanting to look like his dad—sparing himself the danger of looking like me.

He cried viciously at my eye contact. I felt nothing holding his unformed body. All I saw was the ferocity in his eyes. *'How dare you?'* they seemed to say. I shook my head again. *How dare I?*

The doctor asked his name again, and I just said it this time.

"Todd."

I'd named him after my father. I realize it wasn't an honorable name, but I didn't have anything honorable to pass down to the boy. I knew that child would inherit much, but I wanted him to know his history one day. His name would be a clue to the trauma that preceded him. His name would be honest.

Something I hadn't been in a long time.

9.2: M.M. OFFICIAL QUESTIONING

DB: "I'm Detective Bruno, here to interview Michael Mullins at the Richmond Police Department. This is for case number 2023-555. Also present in the room is Doctor Eli Dunn of the Richmond Emergency Hospital. Michael is the *boyfriend* of the victim, Sillian Parks."

MM: "One of the boyfriends. You met Alex yet?"

DB: "It seems you're a little bitter about Alex attending Sillian's event."

MM: "You'd be too if some other guy was flirting with your girlfriend in front of everyone and then hit you with an axe. Can I press charges for that?"

DB: "We can discuss that after we find your girlfriend, Michael. Is it true that you haven't smoked nicotine in a while?"

MM: "Who told you that?"

DB: "Can you answer the question, Michael?"

MM: "I've been trying to quit. Not perfect yet, but I'm getting close."

DB: "What is your relationship with your parents, Michael?"

MM: "Why's that relevant?"

DB: "I'm asking everyone."

Long pause

MM: "Okay... My parents think of me as the black sheep of our family. They're super into church and stuff. A little close-minded. They're really wealthy and have given me and my sisters *everything*, but, like...they hardly seem to care about who we are. Who we really are. As long as we look like the perfect family on Facebook."

DB: "Is that why you moved away from California? To get away from them?"

MM: "My mom's a big California executive. Eyes and ears every-where. Virginia seemed like the only place on Earth I could have some room to breathe without getting in trouble for skipping mass here and there. My parents still send me money, so I try to please them as best I can. But I think a little bit of space between us helps maintain the illusion."

DB: "The illusion of what, Michael?"

MM: "Oh, you know, the perfect family stuff."

DB: "And does your mom like your girlfriend? Sillian?"

MM: "Oh my God, she loves her. Thinks she's the best thing for me. We've all had dinner a few times. Couple holidays here and there. Sillian is my mom's favorite thing about me."

DB: "Would your family help your girlfriend if she needed something?"

MM: "My mom's about ready to send a private SWAT team down here to find her if that's what you mean. Sometimes it feels like Sill's more family member than I am."

DB: "Does anyone in your family know the true nature of your relationship with Sillian?"

MM: "How do you mean?"

DB: "Does anyone close to you know that you and Sillian aren't actually dating?"

MM: "What are you talking abou—"

DB: "I'm not here to tell your secrets to your family, Michael. I'm just looking for a culprit."

MM: "It was a consensual agreement, okay? Sill and I both have things we can help each other with. I may not love Sillian in the traditional sense, but she's really… I care about her a lot."

DB: "Do you really care about Cameron?"

MM: "Please leave Cameron out of this. He's innocent."

DB: "We'll see about that."

9.3: MARY'S DIARY

1946

MY SON DID NOT GROW on me. Instead, he served as a constant reminder of how numb I'd become. His laughter chilled a cold hatred deep in my bones. Sometimes, I caught him staring at the cuts on my arms as he took his milk. He didn't laugh then. Instead, he passed on the silent judgment with big brown eyes. And I hated him for it.

The jewelry was all I had now. There was the house too, my name finally on the will, but I couldn't bear to bring myself back there. Not yet. The four of us had moved to the countryside to a quaint cottage. Paranoia sickened the boys, and me like a plague. *When will we be found out? When will someone discover that we're not who we say we are?*

My husband asked me about more kids like I was nothing more than a breeder. Because maybe I wasn't. I'd tried to kill him in his sleep that night. I thought, *maybe if I stab this man, he'll stab me back. End the madness. End me.*

But he hadn't. He'd caught me sneaking into the bedroom with a knife. I'd gone for him. And he hadn't been violent. He'd just washed me down with brandy and kissed me to sleep. I think my husband thought Todd might save me from myself. Give me a reason to live. But that passed. The more he watched me, the more he realized how little I had to live for.

He began trying more. We went on a few awkward picnics, he did the dishes, and he tried to preserve my life as long as he could. I don't think either of us believes that it could be much longer. But if he could get one more baby out of me, he would.

Motherhood was killing me. The soft quietness of it all. I wasn't a loving mother; I'd accepted that, but I'd keep Todd alive.

It was what my sister would've wanted.

And I wouldn't pass down that cursed last name.

9.4: C.C OFFICIAL QUESTIONING

DB: "I'm Detective Bruno, here to interview Cameron Cortez at the Richmond Police Department. This is for case number 2023-555. Also present in the room is Doctor Eli Dunn of the Richmond Emergency Hospital. Cameron is the friend and former math tutor of the victim, Sillian Parks. We want to start with your connection to Michael."

CC: "What did he say about it?"

DB: "Trust me, Cameron, he said plenty. We'd like to hear your side."

CC: "Plenty?"

DB: "Plenty."

CC: "Well then. You already know that Michael and I have been in a private relationship for quite some time, and it's gotten very complicated."

DB: "Please elaborate. From the beginning."

CC: "Okay… Well, Michael and I started dating, and his parents do not approve of men like us. They're super traditional church people. His mom's kind of famous. I came over for dinner to meet his family for the first time. We were pretending to be friends at that point, but his mom saw through the act. She pulled me aside and threatened me. She said that if I didn't stay away from her son, she'd destroy my chances of ever working in film…which is, like, my dream."

DB: "Did you tell Michael?"

CC: "Of course, I told him. He was devastated. Wanted to get her canceled publicly. Tell the media or something. But I thought it was a bad idea at the time."

DB: "How so?"

CC: "He wasn't fully *out* yet. He grew up in one of those towns where everyone is so hateful and homophobic. A media explosion would've been a shitty thing for him to experience. He's more of a low-key guy, I guess."

DB: "So Sillian comes into the picture?"

CC: "Right. Well, Michael's mom is awful. Michael was worried about my safety, so we thought it'd be best to get a cover until he was ready to come out to the *entire* world. We thought the illusion of a girlfriend would help keep things at bay for a little bit with Michael's family. So we asked Sillian if she'd be that for Michael. I'd be able to stay close to them by pretending to be her love-struck tutor turned friend. He paid me for the hassle. The ordeal gave Michael time to get more comfortable with his orientation. We could date. Problem solved."

DB: "And why would Sillian agree to this fake relationship arrangement?"

CC: "I think she really felt for Michael and I, not feeling comfortable enough to date publicly, but it's continued on for so long because Michael has something she wants."

DB: "Which is?"

CC: "Business connections. Tons of them. His family is swimming in white-collar socials."

DB: "So Sillian wants an in with Michael's family? Even knowing how hateful they've been to you two?"

CC: "I don't think she's in love with Michael's family any more than we are, but she's definitely making the connection useful. It didn't bother us until…"

DB: "Until what?"

CC: "Sill wanted a last dinner with him and his mom next month. She said she was planning on leaving Virginia. And she was sort of icy to us about it. We agreed because she helped us out in the past…but I didn't like it. Not one bit."

DB: "And Michael?"

CC: "Michael felt like she might've been cornering him. That maybe he'd let her get too friendly with his mom. And how Sill was on some sort of ops mission for her. I knew that likely wasn't the case, but he got paranoid. It was still a strange move for Sill to pull. He had a right to be paranoid."

DB: "Does anyone else who attended the party know about your relationship with Michael?"

CC: "Robin…that gossip-fucking snoop. She overheard Sill and I talking about the arrangement a while back. Michael doesn't know that she knows. I had to protect him from it. He needed to be able to tell others at his own pace. Keeping her mouth shut is as bad as it sounds."

DB: "Is she blackmailing you?"

CC: "Something like that. I'd rather not get into it right now. I've been finding ways to pay her off."

DB: "Do you have the money to keep paying her?"

CC: "No. I've had to do some things I'm not proud of. To protect Michael from his goddamn mom."

DB: "How long has this arrangement with Sillian been going on?"

CC: "Too long. Years."

DB: "Are you getting tired of it all?"

CC: "Michael and I both are. We've been ready to go public for almost a year now, but it's Sillian we're waiting on…"

DB: "What for?"

CC: "Sill was always the one trying to buy more time in the 'relationship.' She even asked Michael and I not hang out together too much this weekend. Like *she* needed to stage-manage *us*. It's been getting too complicated. Everyone's been on edge. Michael and I are not college babies anymore. We're ready to ripcord."

DB: "Is that why you brought the files of Sillian's old tutoring and the receipts from Michael to the party? To tell everyone?"

CC: "Michael likes to feel in control. We keep the evidence of our relationship with us at all times. He wants to be the one to let the world know when the time comes. Not someone else. So we kept the files on us. At some point, we thought the files went missing. Michael panicked that Sill had stolen them. I found them in Robin's room during the party."

DB: "Did you confront Robin, then?"

CC: "Yeah. Late that night in the garage. Told her to join me for a smoke break and snuck Michael's cigs. Tried to make it look casual. I've been giving her all my jewelry to buy Michael more time to come out on his own. She's a menace—threatened to tell his mom herself. That night, I told her she could have my Burberry sunglasses, but I'd recently left them in Sillian's car. They're knock-offs, but I doubt she could tell the difference. I think she resells the stolen jewelry online."

DB: "Interesting tidbit… Was there any blood in the garage when you met Robin there?"

CC: "I didn't see any. It was dark, but…no. Don't think so."

DB: "Do you think Michael is paranoid enough to try and prevent Sillian from ever making it to that dinner with his mom?"

CC: "Our relationship dynamic hasn't been perfect, but Michael wouldn't harm Sillian in a million years. At the end of the day, he loved her like his own sister. She helped us out in a time of need."

DB: "That's not what I asked."

9.5: JANE'S RECOUNT

THERE WERE CHOICES WITH ALEX. I could run off and call the cops again and risk the possibility of Alex following me. If he was indeed dangerous, that was not the most ingenious plan. I needed another approach.

At that moment, I knew three things: Alex was rushing to leave the manor, he had a bra I'd been missing for weeks in his suitcase, and he had a ring of keys in his bag.

"You know where she is, don't you?" My voice trembled. I was still in the doorway, standing over him as he kneeled next to the suitcase.

"Not exactly." Alex's face went red. "And I swear I didn't know it was your bra. You sisters must…"

"Where is she, Alex? Please, just tell me."

"I swear, I don't know. Jane, please."

"What do you know then?" My sanity was draining away from me. This was it.

Alex's face was barely visible under the blush on his cheeks.

"I don't know where your sister is. I've been trying to find her. I'm getting worried, too." His head collapsed into his hands, and he started shaking uncontrollably.

If he wasn't genuine, he was due for an Academy Award.

"So you slept with her? That's why you have my bra in here? I knew I didn't misplace it…"

No response. Alex was crying. Or pretending to.

"Whatever you did, Alex, you can make up for it by helping me find my sister. Telling me what you know."

"I was just respecting her wishes… I didn't know that—" Alex choked.

"What is it, Alex? What do you know?"

Alex took the keyring from the suitcase and into his hands before crawling over to the foot of the bed. He bent over and pulled out the miniature table from underneath it.

He dropped the keys onto the floor before pushing his hands through his hair.

"She was messing with this right before we— I can't figure it out."

I kneeled next to Alex on the floor to get a better look at the table. For a child's table, it was obviously intentional in its design. Something that Sillian had likely caught onto when she'd seen it. We would be there for a while if we needed to unlock each of them. The ring was massive in size. So many antique keys on it.

"Have you tried any of these yet?" I asked Alex.

"Not with any rhyme or reason. I've been fiddling with it ever since you started questioning people."

The keyring was heavy with possible matches. I started with the bottom hole on the closest leg, trying each key into the hole. Some of them fit, most of them didn't.

"How many keyholes are there?"

"Twenty," said Alex. "I already counted."

"Little Tykes meets Adrain Fisher." I sighed.

Alex and I devised a system to mark off which keys we'd tried in which holes. The task seemed hopeless until one key fit the first hole perfectly. My wrist turned it clockwise.

"First one down," Alex said, his face still red from crying. I swallowed down my fear and kept going.

For what seemed like hours, we fumbled with the locks adorning the miniature table. Anticipation built as each one clicked into place. Slowly but surely, we were getting somewhere.

On the last lock, I took a deep breath. Whatever was inside could change my life or severely complicate it. Quite a fate for such a small furniture piece.

The footsteps came up the hallway next.

I rushed keys into the lock, hoping to outpace the person in the corridor.

Nothing.

Nothing.

Nothing.

Click.

A small door flapped open from the underbelly of the table, leaving a piece of dirty paper to paraglide toward the floor amongst a mist of dust.

I snatched the paper into my hands and was about to wipe the page clean when I heard an urgent knock at the door. The doorknob began to turn before I could respond.

"Dakota." I tucked the dirty paper under my arm quickly. Suddenly, I felt protective of the information.

"Jane." His eyebrows arched as he studied the scene. Was that jealousy on his face? "And...Alex?"

"What is it?" I asked him outright. My face was guilty, even though I'd done nothing wrong.

"I, uh..." He looked at me, then Alex again, the bra on the floor beside us. I knew he'd seen it hundreds of times. He shook his head before continuing. "I found this outside."

9.6: TORN NOTE FROM SILLIAN

FOUND BY DAKOTA

Be car

vicia

of a ha

toge

ful. Her

us. Like

rror now

ther soo

temper is
something out
el. We'll be
n.

-Sillian

♥

9.7: 9-1-1 CALL TRANSCRIPT

Emergency Dispatcher 4: "9-1-1, what's your emergency?"

Caller: "Well, I'm not sure it's a total emergency, but I think you guys ought to check it out again. I just got a call from Jane Parks down at the, uh…Sophomore Manor rental. Country road five hundred fifty. Your cops looked into her call last night about her sister being missing. They were having a party—some kids in their twenties. And I think something's going on down there. Worried is all."

Emergency Dispatcher 4: "Is someone in danger, sir?"

Caller: "I don't know for sure. Jane Parks called me again. I'm her boss; Chief Simmons is the name. Work at the paper, and, uh…things look like they're getting complicated for my reporter. She thinks her sister went missing. Foul play or something. She's sent me what she's onto and I think there might be more to it than the crew thought last night."

Emergency Dispatcher 4: "Is there an immediate threat of danger?"

Caller: *"Look, I'm not calling for an ambulance or anything, I just want someone looking out. She's concerned. My professional opinion is that she ought to be. Something don't seem right out there. I wanted to let your team know that."*

Emergency Dispatcher 4: *"Can you hold on one moment, sir?"*

Caller: *"Sure."*

(Caller placed on hold.)

Emergency Dispatcher 4: *"Sir?"*

Caller: *"What's that?"*

Emergency Dispatcher 4: *"We're going to send two officers out to Sophomore Manor for a checkup at the end of the night at shift end. Probably about three hours from now. If it is an emergency situation, I can request an immediate police response."*

Caller: *"End of the shift works. Thanks for checking it out again. Peace of mind for this old man."*

Emergency Dispatcher 4: *"Okay. Thank you, sir."*

Caller: *"Thanks, bye."*

(End of recording.)

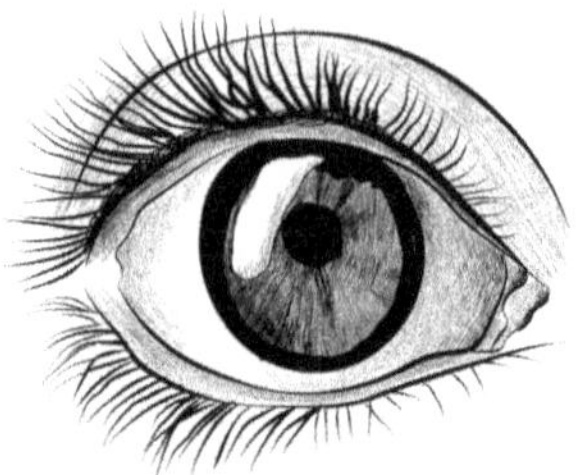

Only one more file to go, Detective! Phillip Beacons left you a very important note on your desk.

- **STICKY NOTE FROM PHILLIP:** *"The hospital estimates that our victim's attack happened around three-thirty in the morning. Hope you're close. -PB"*

- **FUN FACT:** In the decade of the 1940s, *Mary* was the most popular female baby name. *James* was the decade's favorite male name.

Last one, best one.

CASE FILE TEN

<u>Case file ten contains eight items to be reviewed.</u>
Files should be reviewed in numerical order

- **10.1 Jane's Recount** | March 2023
- **10.2 Hidden Floor Plan of S. Manor**
- **10.3 D. E. Official Questioning**
- **10.4 Jane's Recount** | March 2023
- **10.5 1966 Virginia Times**
- **10.6 A. A. Official Questioning**
- **10.7 Jane's Recount** | March 2023
- **10.8 Official Victim Profile**

10.1: JANE'S RECOUNT

"IS THERE something going on that I should know about?" Dakota asked me from the doorway of Alex's room, the bra laid out in between us.

I told Alex to give Dakota and me a minute in the hallway. At that point, Alex was my best shot at finding my sister. I needed him to stay put.

Dakota's eyes were dilated as I stepped out into the corridor with him.

"Was that your bra in Alex's room?" Dakota tilted his trail-scratched face at me. I could've freed myself of the guilt right there. He would've understood. Like any true sister, Sillian stole my clothes. Then, she seemingly happened to hook up with Alex afterward. It was the truth, but I didn't want to give it to him yet. I wanted him to squirm. I was still angry about that pink coat.

"So what if it was, Dakota?" I hissed. "It's not like you don't have girls over behind my back."

"I don't," he said with a scoff.

The last string that was holding my act together broke.

"Don't lie to me, Dakota. I saw the coat."

"What are you talking about?"

"The pink coat at your house. It belonged to another girl. And Chef Lenny working. You lied about that, too. Because you're two-timing me. You can cut the act. I was one step ahead."

"What? I'd never cheat on you. Do you think that lowly of me?"

I didn't respond.

Dakota's jaw tightened. He was shaking with fury.

"I was here to help you, Jane. Your career! But you've made a joke out of me now. I have never been anything but loyal to you."

Dakota shook his head, eyes full of disappointment.

"I'm leaving," he said as he turned his back to me, not wasting another moment. He was going back to his campsite. But what he really meant was that he was leaving me. That our relationship was over. I'd finally crossed the line.

I opened my mouth to object, but nothing came out. In an instant, I knew he was telling the truth. He hadn't cheated on me. He wasn't lying to me. I could see that. A tear rolled down my face as I watched him descend the stairs.

All this time, the character I'd made of him had been a lie. The tears were hard to fight back, but I had to find my sister. I had to focus on that. I could fix things with Dakota later. We would be okay. He knows I'm under too much pressure. *I didn't mean it.*

It took a few minutes to gather myself before returning to Alex's room. He was still sitting on the floor on his knees.

"So, what's it say? The paper." Alex's eyes were glossing over mine. He didn't ask what was wrong or if I'd been crying, a small grace that I felt entirely grateful for in the moment.

"Uh..." My voice was rocky. It took effort to bring my mind back to the search. "Let's look."

Alex tapped the paper with two fingers when I pulled it out.

"This is it. Sill's got to be there."

10.2: HIDDEN FLOOR PLAN OF S. MANOR

DISCOVERED BY JANE AND ALEX

Garage: First Floor

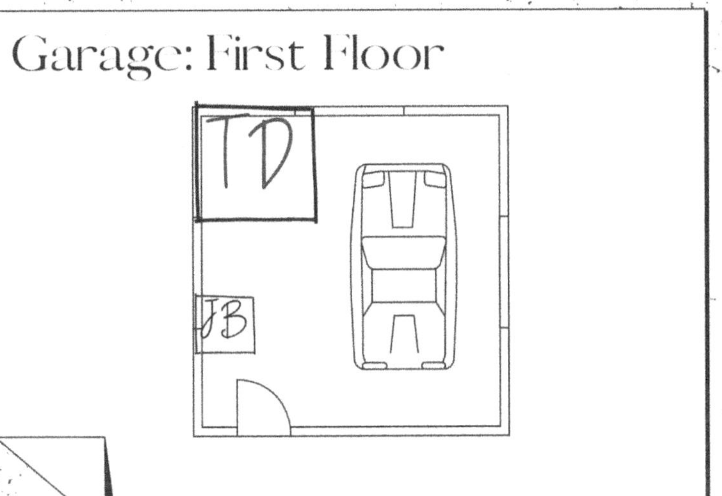

Underground Basement

10.3: D.E. OFFICIAL QUESTIONING

DB: "I'm Detective Bruno, here to interview Dakota Easton at the Richmond Police Department. This is for case number 2023-555. Also present in the room is Doctor Eli Dunn of the Richmond Emergency Hospital. Dakota is the boyfriend of the victim's sister. We'd like to start with your camping trip. When did you plan it?

DE: "I planned it when my girlfriend's sister asked me to. She wanted me to be close by."

DB: "Sillian wanted you close by to the party?"

DE: "Correct."

DB: "Why?"

DE: "I run a news company. Sill knew about the partnership my company was launching with the smaller papers. I guess she follows AeroNews on social media. Jane's career has been really slow. Sill told me we could help Jane out and position her to break a big story. She wouldn't tell me what the story was, but she said it would change Jane's life. And I thought it was a great idea."

DB: "Did Jane know about this?"

DE: "No. She wouldn't have accepted the help. She can feel a little insecure and… I don't know. Everyone gets their big start with a little help in journalism, but Jane wouldn't take the hand. It felt better to let her find it on her own. Or think that she did. She's a good writer. Deserves an audience."

DB: "Okay. How long have you known Sillian?"

DE: "Not long. Couple months? I met her at a party or two. Through Jane, obviously."

DB: "How long did it take you to form this plan with Sillian?"

DE: "No more than an hour."

DB: "Why wouldn't Sillian just invite you to the party?"

DE: "It would've been harder for me to call in a news story if I was right next to Jane all weekend. I have to go through a form-reporting process. Corporate shit. I needed Wi-Fi."

DB: "So why did you tip off Jane's boss for a story when Jane texted you that the guy with the axe came into the house?"

DE: "Since Sillian wouldn't tell me about the story she wanted Jane to break, I assumed that was it when I got the texts from Jane. All Sill said was to stay close, and that I'd know when to call in the news to the paper. I figured that had to be the story she was refer-ring to. It sounded close enough to breaking news."

DB: "I see. Did Jane ever confront you about any of this?"

DE: "No. She accused me of cheating on her, which came out of left field. I guess maybe I was acting weird about the weekend thing. I don't know. Caught me off guard."

DB: "What made you decide to come to the manor and help Jane with the search for Sillian?"

DE: "To be honest, man, I just got a bad feeling. Sillian said the news was supposed to break the night of the party. We'd tee it off for Jane, then celebrate. And when morning came and Jane said her sister was missing and no big story was out...I got a bad feeling. I never heard back from Jane after those texts. I wanted to help my girlfriend. It was instinctual."

DB: "Was cleaning up the blood in the garage instinctual?"

DE: "I don't have to answer that."

DB: "Say, Dakota, is it possible that you were trying to create a news story for Jane?"

DE: "How do you mean?"

DB: "Perhaps breaking into the party in a mask and assaulting Michael Mullins with the blunt side of an axe?"

DE: "Nope. I don't even know that guy."

DB: "How tall are you?"

DE: "Six foot six."

10.4: JANE'S RECOUNT

ALEX WAS WALKING AHEAD of me down the staircase. "I think I know where that trap door is."

Alex could've been the reason Sill disappeared, and there I was, following him around like a puppy. It wasn't ideal, but it was the best chance I had.

I observed Alex closely from this position, watching his every move. He knew where he was headed as he strolled, which fueled my vendetta further. I followed in each of his footsteps, fear and anger picking up my heels. The lack of confidence in his stature was the only thing giving me a little bit of hope. I'd swiped a knife out of the kitchen, just in case.

"How do you know where you're going?" I asked as we walked out the front door. Accusation dripped from my tone.

"Your sister found a place for, well… We're crazy about one another. We decided to…"

"Spare me the details. I already saw the bra." I rolled my eyes at the back of his head. Even though I believed he'd had relations with my sister, it wouldn't explain her disappearance. And Alex seemed to have details he was holding back. At that point, it felt like he was covering something, but what?

We found ourselves back inside the garage. Alex led us over to the protruding wall that held the jukebox. My anger quickly filled the empty space of the room.

"Have you just known about this secret spot the whole time?" I asked.

Alex grunted as he fumbled with the music player.

"I came back here with Sill. She showed me something, but it wasn't a basement. I'm just trying to figure out how she did it..."

"Why would she show you something?"

With hands and knees on the ground, Alex fumbled around the back of the ancient jukebox. The glow of the arched neon was still dimly lit despite the probable years since the last battery change.

"She asked me to come down here to the manor early. Help her look into some hunches she had about the house. She figured she'd be done by the night of the Halloween party, but she wasn't. She was looking for a story."

With the grit of a mechanic, Alex was on his back, fumbling with the nooks and crannies of the box.

I stayed at arm's length. "Why didn't you mention it beforehand?"

Alex looked up at me and scowled. "There's more to it than you think. I stayed quiet because she asked me to. *No matter what.* And I won't break that promise."

Out of nowhere, the jukebox that was plated deeply in the false wall turned back around inside the structure. In a single motion, Alex hopped out of the wake of the turning wall. I moved my body with it instinctively to save my arms from the scrape of the wood.

"It's another false wall?"

"Built like a triangle. This thing has three sides."

In a triangle fold, the wall spun again into a new base, that time nothing more than a piece of drywall with a single handle. I stood in shock for a moment at the discovery. The tri-wall had three sides. A blank. A jukebox, and now this. I shuddered for a moment, thinking of how protected the secrets inside of this house must have been. *Sill was on to a damn good story.*

"Uh…what did you just do?"

"Whatever Sill did last night," Alex said.

My will to find my sister muted my vexation with Alex momentarily. I pulled the handle on the wall down hard, expecting a secret passage to open according to the floor plan I'd found inside the dining table. Instead, a Murphy bed with makeshift rusted wheels attached to each post fell on the hard floor of the garage.

"Someone built this thing just to conceal a Murphy bed?" I was dumbfounded. It immediately felt like a dead end.

The bed itself was unmade. A hat fit for Indiana Jones rested on the top pillow. Redness blushed across Alex's face.

"She brought me back here during the party. It moves."

Alex ran his fingers through his hair, as confusion settled on his face. "Not exactly what I wanted to show you, but this is the trapdoor. I think."

"Sill didn't tell you what it was for when she found it?"

Alex shook his head. "She'd shown me so much weird shit at that point… It sounds odd, but I thought she'd explain it at the end. Once she found what she was looking for. I was just content to be…"

"In bed with my sister." I gripped the knife tighter.

Alex didn't respond. "It rolls inside the wall. Into the little area between the three false walls. There's a tiny room back there."

"And why didn't you mention this before?"

"Because Sillian asked me not to." Spit flew from his mouth.

Alex was back on the ground again, fumbling with the bed like the engineer he was, tinkering with all sorts of things.

"Sill had the instructions," he said as a clang erupted from the springs under the mattress. The veins of his arms popped through his skin while he fixated on the mechanics.

"This wall opens. And if you lie on the bed while it opens, it brings you to the other side. There's a tiny room back there. It sounds crazy because it is."

"So, post-relations, she went Inspector Gadget on you and showed you a trick? Why do I have a hard time believing that?"

The bed springs coiled in a single motion back into the wall. It didn't happen smoothly, the way it might in the movie production. The structural credibility was off-kilter at best. Alex had to give the frame an extra shove with his knee for the frame to continue receding into the wall before he hopped onto the mattress. It was the most unglamorous secret passageway imaginable.

"Quick, get on the bed," Alex said. "It's going to drag us in."

I dashed on the bed as it moved into the wall on screaming wheels. The bed was moving at minimum speed through the parting drywall. Together, we entered an unprecedented hole in the wall.

I sat on the bed dumbfounded as Alex and I went further in. I forced the thoughts about what happened on the bed out of my brain and moved my hand toward my knife. There was still business to be tended to.

The mechanical Murphy bed rolled us back into a tiny room no more than two hundred square feet. A dim overhead light was already on, revealing a single countertop, an old gas stove, and a double-door refrigerator that was so primordial it could've been a tomb. A metal toilet bowl was cornered off with a shower head faucet behind a drawn-back, raggedy curtain. A small bookshelf existed in the only corner, holding a mirage of books, a set of miniature hand weights, and a chessboard. Blankets were stacked everywhere as the air in the room was uncomfortably cold. My body immediately began to shiver.

I gasped as I took a step off the bed.

"This is where they were. The Sophomore sisters. All that time they were missing. This was it," I heard myself say aloud. "It has to be."

Alex was next to me now with arms crossed. "Your sister thought something similar. All the complex shit it took to get here. They were probably in here for years, sneaking around the manor only at night. She took me back here and we…you know… It was like a little celebration. She'd been looking for days, but at that point, she was convinced there had to be one more room. One more layer. I didn't see it through with her after we...uhm. Anyway, I promised her I would keep it a secret until she found it. Manage the party. Which I have now failed at."

"So where's Sill? She's obviously not hiding in the bunker. Why didn't you tell me about this?"

"I came down to bring her food and water last night. She said she knew how to get back up. To go upstairs and act normal. And this morning, I figured she was probably still down here. I didn't want to take her away from whatever she was working on. But after we got pizza, I went down to bring her more food...and she wasn't here. That's when I started to get worried, like you were."

I squinted my eyes with reservation. "I don't believe you."

"She wanted to keep poking around for a story. She kept saying something about a journal. I wanted to finish our relationship talk upstairs, but she kept saying she had the perfect place to chat. And we ended up back here, where we..." Alex put his hands up in defense. "I'm telling the truth, *believe me or not.*"

His story checked out. It even made sense. But at the same time, Alex was the only one I knew *for sure* had been with my sister in a basement. *How do I know he didn't harm her? How do I know he didn't kill her?*

I didn't.

"Alex, where is Sill?"

"I. Don't. Know." Spit slew from his O-shaped mouth again as he spoke.

I pulled the knife from my pocket and pointed it at him.

Alex stepped back on his heels and bumped into the age-old bed. "Jane, calm down."

"Where is my sister?"

He fell back on the bed as the grip of the knife stayed strong in my hand. The floor plan lay face-up on the sheets next to his hat.

"There are stairs on here," Alex said in a panic, showing me the paper wide eyed, like it was my sister herself. "There are stairs. This room doesn't have stairs."

The shudders of his voice got to me. I slipped it back into my pocket with my hand steady on its grip. I peered over at the paper to see if he was right. The floor plan did have stairs.

Alex immediately shot up and lunged toward the cabinets, dragging the rusted pots and pans out with a single hand.

"What are you doing?" I shouted, caught off-guard by his sudden movement.

"Finding the staircase so I don't get shanked."

I crouched down on my hands and knees to help him, metal clanging erupting with each slide of the hand. Nothing in the cabinets. Alex moved toward the bookshelf. In a single push, he moved it over to reveal just another piece of drywall behind it.

In frustration, I fumbled with the faucet and toilet unsuccessfully. The room turned into a war zone. Alex and I undid every cabinet and contraption. I was about to give up when Alex opened the fridge to reveal perfect-conditioned produce stacked inside. Supremely yellow lemons, deep red tomatoes, and vibrant purple onions.

"Wait a second." I walked over to the produce-filled drawers of the fridge. I pulled open the caddy and palmed a lemon. Cardboard. They were decorative fruits.

"Alex, these aren't real."

I removed the shelf and set it neatly on the floor. Then, I pulled out the second tray. Then, the third. Alex began to help me remove the bins until nothing was left in the fridge.

And there it was. The door with a tiny metal turn handle.

"Oh my God," Alex gasped as I went for the handle. "Are you sure?"

I took a deep breath as the handle knob gave way. This would be the last chance to find my sister. She had to be down there. The door opened inward, and a dark downward staircase was revealed. We stood dumbfounded.

On the other side of the Murphy bed wall, footsteps entered the garage. Shouting became rampant. Others knew we were in there, and they wanted to tell me something.

Robin's voice wailed from the other side. "Stop! Stop, the police are here. Stop what you're doing. Police orders."

Alex turned to look at me in fear. "You heard her." He positioned himself on the bed to go back out. "I'm going to get a cop. Are you coming out with me?" he asked.

I was too close to turn around now.

"I'm not wasting another moment."

I took a step forward onto the first stair.

10.5: 1966 VIRGINIA TIMES HEADLINES

1966

WOMAN FOUND DEAD OFF CRYERS CREEK THOUGHT TO BE MACIE SOPHOMORE OF THE INFAMOUS 'SOPHOMORE BROTHERS' CASE.

A woman was found dead on Wednesday just off the Cryers Creek, west of the Sophomore Manor. According to the release, dispatchers received a call Saturday afternoon from a passerby who saw what appeared to be a fresh body near the creek bed. At this time, there does not seem to be any signs of foul play.

The rescue crew responded and found the woman to be dead at the scene. The body was evacuated out of the creek and into a DNA-testing facility, where the woman appeared to be a DNA match to Macie Sophomore, the missing woman in the Sophomore Brothers case from 1945.

Police and investigators have made the decision not to reopen the infamous case but will be investigating the death itself. Macie Sophomore has no survivors or family alive that we are aware of. The body of Mary Sophomore remains undiscovered. If you have any information about Macie Sophomore or her whereabouts prior to her death, please contact the Richmond County police immediately.

Image by: [Deborah Fletch from Getty Images] via Canva..com | Not intended for standalone use.

10.6: A.A. OFFICIAL QUESTIONING

DB: "I'm Detective Bruno, here to interview Alex Ansley at the Richmond Police Department. This is for case number 2023-555. Also present in the room is Doctor Eli Dunn of the Richmond Emergency Hospital. Alex is the ex-boyfriend of Sillian Parks. Can you start with how Sillian invited you to this party, Alex?"

AA: "Sure. Sillian called me up about a week before the party. She said she needed help with a story and that she needed to borrow me for a weekend. Of course, I said yes. I love that girl."

DB: "Why do you think she called you?"

AA: "I think I'm the only one she trusted. Her lot of friends…*not the greatest*. Seemed like she was starting to figure that out herself. And I care about her deeply. She knew I'd help her with anything she asked. Which is why all of this is…such a mess. I was trying to protect her by not saying anything. Not kill her."

DB: "Your texts to her seemed to indicate otherwise. You told her she owed you what she promised and that you aren't always Mr. Nice Guy?"

AA: "I know they sounded bad. It's just... We had a wonderful time planning this manor search stuff together. It felt like old times. Then she asked me if I'd consider moving to California with her. As a couple. I was over the moon and started doing research, but I'd kinda been seeing this girl. Not seriously, but serious enough to not just run away with Sill. I told Sill I had to tell Khloe it wasn't working after the weekend was over. When I sent those texts to Sill, I thought she might've gone off to tell Khloe for me. I thought she didn't trust me to take care of it."

DB: "Did you and Sill get to the Sophomore Manor a night early?"

AA: "Two nights early. We went through most of the tunnels and stuff the night before. She told me everything. It was *fun.* Being with her is a thrill. And with me there, an engineer, it helped. I was able to see which structures seemed a bit...off."

DB: "And what was the purpose of inviting all these other people to the party? Why not just have the two of you go to the manor for a weekend?"

AA: "It was supposed to be a surprise going away party. She wanted her sister to break the Sophomore Sisters story, and say bye to her friends in an *interesting* way. Like I said, she decided to move to California and pursue a career in publishing. She said she had enough connections to get started. I was already planning the move myself."

DB: "What do you mean by saying farewell in an *interesting* way?"

AA: "Sillian had written goodbye letters to everyone she was friends with. Some were nice, some were not. She scattered them around the yard. Called it her final *farewell*. She thought that if she found this Sophomore story, a major publication would take her on and we could leave Virginia. She thought it would be clever to spread some breadcrumbs around to let people know they might not see her again."

DB: "And your letter?"

AA: "Was to encourage people to look for what she'd written about them. Once they heard talk of it, they'd get curious. Even though mine was supposedly fake, there was some strong truth in it. Wasn't the nicest letter."

DB: "Sounds like she orchestrated quite the production?"

AA: "She did. She always does. She's a genius, really."

DB: "And you played a part in it. Attacking another party member and throwing snakes into the crowd. That could be considered a crime..."

AA: "The garden snakes were Sill's idea. Hitting Michael was never part of the plan. He got too close, and I was trying to play my part and 'fake swing' the axe. I even used the wrong end to make sure I didn't hurt anyone. I planned to go right over Michael's head, but that shit was heavier than I thought. I made contact, but I didn't mean to. I felt so bad. Well, kind of bad."

DB: "Just kind of?"

AA: "Sillian and him are technically dating. I don't like the guy. She tells me it's complicated. That they're more friends than anything, but she never explains more. It makes me a bit suspicious of him and her.

DB: "And what was the purpose of the snake-axe stunt?"

AA: "Sill needed more time under that garage. When the party rolled around, she wasn't as far as she wanted to be. She knew people would believe her if she went fake-missing for the sake of the party. A planned mystery or something. And then if she reappeared later, it would've still made sense. Like a party stunt that no one caught on to? I don't know. It just seemed like something she'd put together. Which is why we went for it. It bought her a reason to be removed for a few more hours."

DB: "When did you last see Sillian?"

AA: "I went underground to check on her before bed. Brought her food and water when everyone seemed to be asleep. She told me she'd sleep down there if she had to, that she needed to be there until she had that story in her hands. She was so close. Of course, I let her work. That story was *our* ticket to California."

DB: "Why not just tell people she was under the garage when they started to worry? What was the harm in letting her friends know she was on to a big story?"

AA: "I figured she'd slept a little and went back down there to work. It wasn't until I went back down the next day that I started to worry. I was going to bring her pizza, but she wasn't there anymore. She had specifically asked me not to tell anyone what was going on. I think Sill was scared of them. Some of them."

DB: "Who was she scared of?"

AA: "To be honest…I think Sill was scared of *Jane*."

10.7: JANE'S RECOUNT

I COULDN'T SEE *anything* in the darkness. I heard the Murphy bed turning in and out above me. Alex had left me to find out for myself.

My sister was down here. I knew she was.

Dust was thick in the air. A fog of dirt danced around the light that edged the doorway. There was a glow in the basement that beckoned me forward, drawing me in. A horrid smell overtook me with each step downward.

Will she be tied up? Will she be dead? Will she be smiling?

It was freezing cold. The further I descended, the chillier I became.

And then I opened the door at the base of the stairs.

It was a study-like room with photos of the Sophomore sisters everywhere on every wall. Dust covered them thickly. Fit with smiling young girls, framed awards, and rotting wallpaper. An old Williston Forge typewriter was at the desk, a folding metal chair tucked underneath. Across from it was an ancient couch, the colors fading into brown.

Then I saw it. The dark lump on the hard ground. Shaped like a stone-pale girl in a Nancy Drew Halloween costume. A bright yellow coat was nestled around her body, which contrasted her skin that had turned a soft blue.

"Sill!"

The air was ice-sharp. I ran to my sister's side as the screaming above me got louder.

"Sill," I said again, knowing she wasn't conscious. I put my fingers near her chest for a pulse. I couldn't tell if I felt anything or not, the faintness of any heartbeat playing tricks on my mind. I pulled her closer to me in an attempt to warm her body.

"Help!" I screamed in excruciating fear. "Down here!"

I grabbed Sillian's gray-tinted wrist and cried for help once more. Her body was limp in my arms. Life wasn't running through her veins.

"Who did this to you? Still, please."

Helplessly, I wept.

10.8: OFFICIAL VICTIM PROFILE

PROPERTY OF PI INC.

Victim Profile: Sillian Parks

Age: 26	Weight: 126 lbs
Hair: Blonde	HEIGHT: 5ft 7inch
Eyes: Blue	shoe size: 8.5

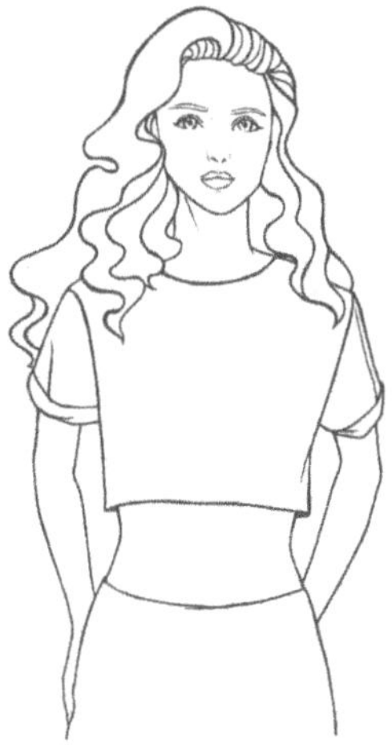

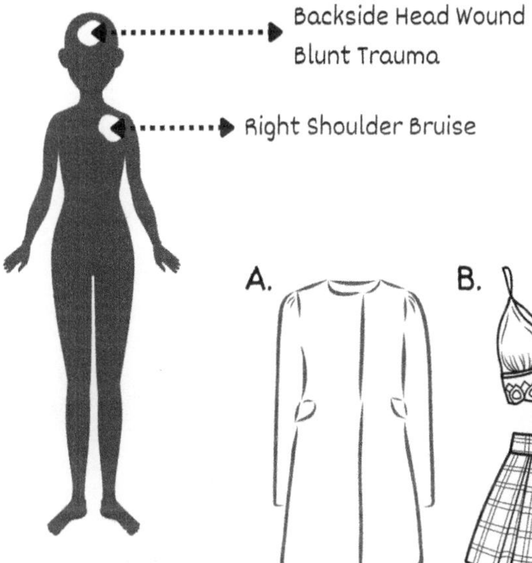
Backside Head Wound
Blunt Trauma
Right Shoulder Bruise

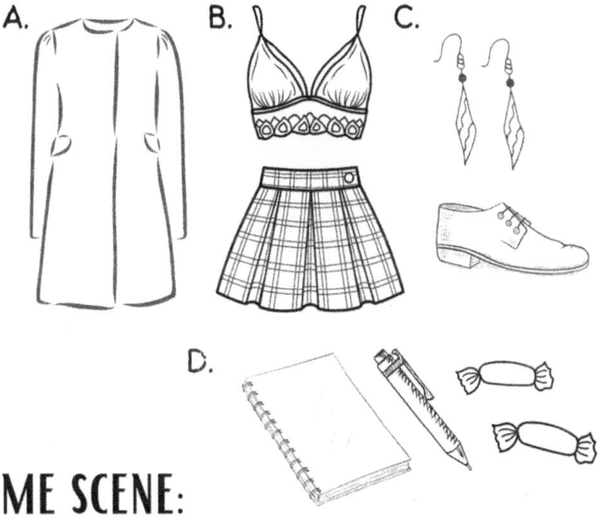
A.
B.
C.
D.

ITEMS AT CRIME SCENE:

A: Women's Top Coat, Size Small, Color #FFC1CC
B1: Women's Crop Top, Size Small, Color #D8B863
B2: Women's Skirt, Size Medium, Color #DAC17C
C1: Earrings, One Size, Silver and Gold
C2: Women's Leather Shoe's, Size 8.5
D1-3: Notebook, Pen, Party Candy

TOP SECRET

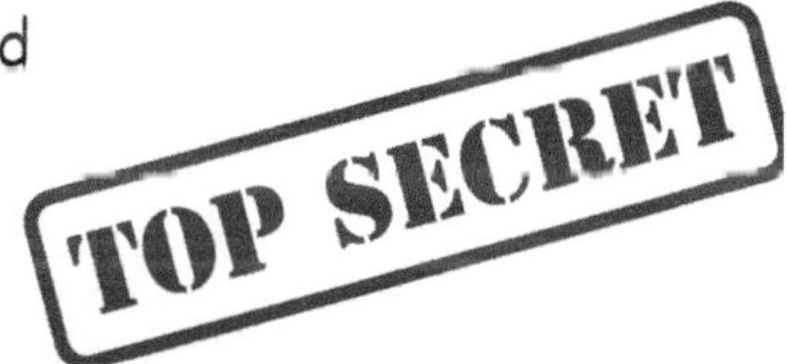

TIME'S UP, DETECTIVE!

It's time to submit PI Inc.'s recommendations to Detective Bruno. Remember that we are paid to offer a plausible recommendation for the case. I've set up a structured form for you to fill out for Detective Bruno on the next page.

PLEASE WRITE IN A LIGHT-COLORED INK.
OFFICIAL FORM ON NEXT PAGE.

Write below in ink.

PI INC. RECOMMENDS THE ARREST OF:

____

FOR THE ATTEMPTED MURDER OF SILLIAN PARKS WITH THE FOLLOWING REASONING:

MEANS:

____

____

MOTIVE:

____

____

____

____

OPPORTUNITY:

____

____

SUPPORTING EVIDENCE (Case File Numbers):

____

____

____

____

CASE DETECTIVE'S SIGNATURE (You):

____

DETECTIVE DIRECTOR'S SIGNATURE:

Phillip Beacons

THANK YOU FOR PARTNERING WITH PI INC.

Congratulations on your first recommendation! No matter how accurate, it is an accomplishment to have gotten this far. For training purposes, Detective Bruno will follow up with us about what happened in Sillian Parks' case. Although, I have a feeling you might already know.

Additionally, Bruno would like to disclose the rest of Mary Sophomore's diary to help us further understand the secondary mystery at play: *What happened to Mary Sophomore?* Your ability to seek out answers for side missions is crucial to becoming a great detective. Stories like Mary's and Sill's are often linked. If you find enough evidence as to what happened, you can ask the police to reopen the case of Macie and Mary's disappearance.

Let me know what you find.

From the desk of:
PHILLIP BEACONS

WARNING: EVIDENCE FILE

The contents of the evidence file are only for the eyes of detectives who have completed their recommendations to Detective Bruno. The evidence is filed as follows:

- **E1: Mary Sophomore's Diary** | 1966
- **E2: Culprit Accusation**
- **E3: Mary Sophomore's Diary** | 1966
- **E4: Detective's Final Reasoning**
- **E5: Mary Sophomore's Diary** | 1966
- **E6: Virginia Paper Headlines**
- **E7: Two Years Later** | 2025

E1: MARY'S DIARY

1966

WARNING: EVIDENCE AHEAD

THERE'S much for me to confess. Sorry if I'm getting ahead of myself. It's been twenty-one years without my sister, and I think it's time I come clean with my sins and clear myself with the Lord. Maybe then I will stop paying for them.

The truth is, or was, that I, Mary Sophomore, am not actually alive. You see, it is no secret that Mary wanted to leave our husbands and I didn't. And it's true that Mary wanted to kill the brothers. But Mary had to die. She just had to. I knew the story wouldn't go over well with Corrine if I were the one to ask for her help. She wanted to be on the side of justice. Female unity. And I just wanted to be in love. Can I be so wrong for that?

Faking my disguise as Mary wasn't difficult. I knew it was necessary to live underground with Corrine and to tell James my plan straightaway. He agreed to help me, like the devoted man he'd always been up to that point.

I had anticipated Mary would run after us that night to try and help us with the fire—the burning of Janice Kroy. But she was always going to be a problem for James and me. She would've done anything in her power to get us out of that house and marriage. It never would've stopped. I knew the night we burned Janice that she would be stirring in bed over the thought that I might betray her after all and that she would see the smoke go up from her bedroom's window. I could see the mistrust in her eyes when I said I was pregnant. I knew Corrine would be the woman to end the fight that I couldn't. Both women dead at my hands. Good, good women.

Mary wasn't ever going to turn her back on me, which is why I wanted to write our story as her. I thought people might read it one day if they could hear the honorable character rather than the sinister one. She deserved to be remembered.

I'm sorry that I had to lie to you all this time.

Macie

E2: CULPRIT ACCUSATION

WARNING: EVIDENCE AHEAD

DB: "Sorry for the impromptu questioning. After getting access to all the evidence, we still have a few more things to ask you, Jane Parks."

JP: "Ask away."

DB: "Do you remember sleepwalking the night your sister went missing?"

JP: "No. I was dead asleep. I'd be surprised if I even rolled over."

DB: "Do you have a history of sleepwalking?"

JP: "When I was a kid, sure."

DB: "What about the night Sillian went missing? In **File 3.9,** could that have been your sister really talking to you? Perhaps she wanted to show you what she'd found?"

JP: "I would've been excited for her to find that story. I wouldn't have hurt her."

DB: "You claimed to have fallen asleep with pen ink on your face in **File 3.9.** You also said that you slept heavily, woke up, and went straight into the investigation the next morning. You would've smelled horrible from the rain and blood you picked up walking on the trail, no?"

JP: "So I went to bed without showering. Is that a crime?"

DB: "Well, it is strange that you woke up with damp hair in **File 3.9** and that Elle made a comment about you smelling nice in **File 4.1.** While you never mentioned a shower, you'd think someone would've at least told you about the pen ink on your face."

JP: "With my sister missing, that's hardly a detail I could pull off the top of my head."

DB: In **File 7.4,** you found a bloodied gauze under the staircase. In **File 2.6,** your boyfriend offered you gauze, didn't he? For all those scratches you picked up on the trail?"

JP: "Okay, but that's hardly incriminating. It could've been anyone's bandage."

DB: "Perhaps, but in **File 10.4,** you knew to move your arm instinctively from the scrape of the wood on the turning false wall. Perhaps it felt like 'instinct' because you'd already gotten a cut scraped open the night before, leaving a small pool of blood behind in the garage."

JP: "What are you getting at? If you think—"

DB: "Then that boyfriend of yours picked up on the possibility and tried to clean up your mess for you, didn't he?"

JP: "This is ridiculous. Dakota wouldn't do that."

DB: "Perhaps not. Maybe if he'd pieced together the note in **File 9.6** earlier, he would've walked away. He got that warning about your temper a little too late, didn't he?"

JP: "This is crazy. You're crazy!"

DB: "Alex told me that Sillian was a bit scared of you. Her body language in **File 1.2** suggested he was right."

JP: "I want a lawyer."

DB: "You will need one, Jane. What was it that made you lose it with your sister? Were you jealous that she'd discovered a big story? I mean, a *huge* story, wow. She discovered history! Your career isn't moving very fast. You had to be a little envious. Especially since you didn't know that she was planning on letting you break the news after all."

JP: "I said I want a lawyer!"

DB: "Or was it because you found out in **File 2.9** that she was planning on moving to California and didn't tell you? **File 1.4** told us you certainly were looking to move there yourself. How could Sill have kept that from you? The grudge you must've held..."

JP: "I was never mad about that, Elle was! Did you see those texts?"

DB: "Or maybe, and this is my best theory, you pushed your sister down that staircase because she was wearing the pink coat. The one that caused you all of that grief with Dakota in **File 1.3.** Of course, you had no idea Sillian had actually met with Dakota to *help you.* So, you pushed Sill down that staircase, half asleep maybe, then showered away your sins and returned to bed. All because of misplaced jealousy and a silly pink garment."

JP: "Sill's coat was yellow! I swear it."

DB: "**File 10.8** suggests otherwise. Lying to the police is not good, Jane. You know, the people we suspect the most in a criminal investigation are usually the ones who disclose too much information. It didn't help that you talked about your *comatose* sister in the past tense. Between all your recounts, we have enough evidence to prosecute. While we don't know whether you intended to murder your sister or not—"

JP: "Of course I didn't mean to!"

DB: "There's the confession! *Jane Parks*, you're under arrest."

E3: MARY'S DIARY

1966

WARNING: EVIDENCE AHEAD

IN THE WEEKS after Mary's death, James and I devised a plan; a plan that Mary would've loved after all. We pinned up the Sophomore brothers as potential murder suspects, just like Corrine and I had agreed to. Then, we would get away under disguise quietly. Without bodies, there was no crime.

But, of course, there was speculation about one.

Josh and James spoke with their friend in the industry: Andrew Kelly. And what Grifter did for us was continue to pay our royalties for our contribution to the industry: James and Josh's music and mine and Mary's films. Grifter signed an under-wraps contract with the brothers that as long as the three of us could keep our names attached to the conspiracy and our faces out of the public eye, we would get paid. And with the deliciousness of the unsolved case, the sales from our past projects soared to record-breaking heights.

We moved into a countryside cottage where James and I quickly bore the child. We only raised Todd to age three before we passed him to a confidant inside the industry. Paranoia was running our parenthood, and we wanted what was best for our son. Or James did. I went crazy those months after his birth. Downright bammy. And James always loved me, didn't he?

Letting Todd go was the one good thing I ever did. I tried to become a decent person after Mary's passing, but it never quite came.

Josh eventually found a quiet woman to settle down with—a woman who eerily resembled my sister—and we all led a quiet life away from the noise of pop culture. He mishandled her on occasion, which hurt me deeply. I saw Mary's bruises on a new woman's body, and I couldn't help but think of how much she must have hated me from beneath the grave.

My last piece of Mary was her box of jewelry. It became like a tombstone to me, a place I visited often to touch the things she touched, and to cry my apologies. I know the jewels would be worth millions when the story came out. Which was why I hid them in the cottage basement. I wouldn't pay my debts with the last remnants of my sister. I knew I couldn't betray her in that way any longer.

Ten years ago, Josh and his wife were brutally killed in a car accident where Josh appeared to be driving drunk and had collided with a tree. James and I had burned the crash evidence, afraid that getting the police or news involved would blow our cover. This strained my marriage greatly.

James stopped touching me altogether. He told me often that I was the devil and that everything I touched would go up in flames. He worried himself into sickness. Three years later, James died a month after Grifter—both of typhoid. I buried him myself out by the crash spot, where James' ashes rest.

A month after my husband's death, I also fell ill.

Since I couldn't see a doctor with my fake identity, I spent the family's wealth on something else. Down to the last hundred.

I'd put out an ad for a structural engineer under an alias. Initially, I'd just wanted to seal off the basement. Leave this story down under.

But the man I found had worked on the Hoover Damn and wanted a challenge. A lethal ex-con named Owen, with dark secrets of his own. He fell obsessed with the trickery of mazes and my dead husband. It would've only taken him a week to seal off the bottom, but to create a labyrinth would take much longer. I'd pay him a lot more money. He needed stable work, he'd said.

I became his lover during those five months he worked on the manor, mostly out of boredom. He was a possessive man in my late and sick age. Nothing I wasn't used to. But Owen designed the puzzle that became today's Sophomore Manor. Some of me thought he might've made it too difficult on purpose, wanting to keep the last bits of me all for himself. Because none of my stories ever belonged to me anyway.

Eventually, my wallet ran dry, and he disappeared. I thought it was over for me then. My secrets would be his tell. Yet nothing ever happened. No one ever came for me.

I'm sick and I've got no money left to me. My judgment day is near. So, I wrote to Todd for the first time in my life. I told him that I was his birth mother, that I was very sick, and that I was leaving him a countryside cottage. I did not tell him who I am. *What* I am.

I simply signed it: '*Mom*'

E4: DETECTIVE'S FINAL REASONING

WARNING: EVIDENCE AHEAD

"HOW'S SHE DOING, Doc? The girl..." Detective Bruno sat dumbfounded at the questioning table. While no one was across from him, he couldn't stand up yet. Standing up would mean solidifying the interview he'd just had with Jane. A girl who seemed to believe she was innocent. *Did he get it wrong?*

Doctor Eli Dunn stood up from the chair behind the table. "Fighting for her life. She was in very low temperatures for a long time. Far too long for a girl wearing nothing but a mini-skirt. Hypothermia kicked in quick."

Detective Bruno took a deep breath, trying to accept that the girl, Sillian, might not make it. Although he'd never met her, he felt like he knew her through all those people and their stories. It was hard to see her face through all the drama she'd created around her life.

But Alex's story checked out. He was just helpless for that girl. She planted letters for her party and left them upstairs for her sister to find. **File 5.4** validated Alex's story about bringing Sillian food and checking on her often. Despite his dumb theatrics, he was just an irrational boy in love.

He'd known Michael's mother had something to do with all of this once she came up in **File 2.3** and Elle found the brochure in **File 2.9.** Michael had mentioned he was from California in **File 5.5** after he likely assumed a hate crime was committed against him. (Even though that wasn't the case, Detective Bruno still wanted to smack Alex for him.) In **File 9.4**, it became evident that Sill was using her relationship with Michael's mom to publish her findings at Sophomore Manor. No matter the nature of their relationship, Bruno couldn't help but find that a bit tasteless.

Bruno had seen guys like Michael before. Michael's parents seemed to be the real villains in his story, forcing his true identity under the rug and making Michael pay for his private relationship. In **File 5.2,** Elle hinted at Michael and Sillian's final approach to his family, looking at calendars and maps for when Sill was to move away. Whether Michael knew it or not, the man deserved to be able to be himself all the time. To have a real relationship out in the open. Away from girls who just want to know his judgmental mother. Michael, a sufferer of his family's harsh prejudices, was perhaps the most unworthy victim in this mess.

And then there was Robin. Bruno's first impression of Robin had been wrong. It hadn't been harsh enough. Robin Reed was about as evil as they came, blackmailing others for her own dime. At first, he thought she was stealing from Sillian, given the note in **File 3.3.** Sillian seemed to think so too—their "secret shared" was certainly about Cameron and Michael. But Robin ended up being more of a bigot and a blackmailer than a thief, leaving Cameron the one with sticky fingers. **File 9.4** said enough to figure that one out. While Detective Bruno did not approve of the theft, he did understand that Cameron had been trying to protect Michael. Yet, he thought Cameron would do a lot more good by trying to support his partner rather than protect him from everything. That was the father in Bruno, though. It wasn't his place to say.

Detective Bruno had enough interview evidence to go after both

Robin and Cameron for their crimes. But Robin, whose intentions seemed much more selfish and malicious, felt better suited for a prosecution. He made a note to follow up on that later in the month.

Elle was a lead for a short time, given the brochure and the angry text messages to Sill. Elle appeared a bit possessive. Given the turmoil around Sillian, it started to seem she was more of a protective friend than anything. Part of the business was being able to tell drama from ice-cold revenge.

Dakota threw off Detective Bruno when he wasn't an original member of the party, yet he had somehow gotten involved. While Bruno could never put his finger on it, he always felt suspicious of Dakota. Perhaps it was Jane's anxiety about unfaithfulness or his obvious signs of wealth. But as it turned out, Dakota was only around to help out his girlfriend at her sister's request. Even though Bruno had a hunch that Dakota had cleaned up that blood once he saw his girlfriend's old gauze in **File 7.4** and he *could* prosecute him for that, he decided not to. Overall, he seemed caught up in all of this for trying to be a decent guy.

What took the longest for Bruno to understand was why Sillian picked the Sophomore Manor for all of these events to unfold. Sure, there was the party and the undiscovered history, but he couldn't figure out what else. Until he remembered **File 1.1** - the mention of Sill's 23andMe kit. Sillian's DNA tested and found that she was related to Mary and Macie Sophomore. She wanted to share the discovery of their story with her sister, who, because of her outfit, had nearly gotten her killed.

Detective Bruno didn't feel the victory he usually did when solving a case. It was a damn shame, really. A bunch of twenty-somethings caught up in drama like this… He hoped Sillian Parks would recover, but he also hoped that she'd learn her lesson about honesty. There were better ways to achieve things in life. Using your friends and lying to your family was more costly than one might have believed.

Jane Parks, being at the bottom of all of this, was dumbfounding to Bruno. Throughout the entire investigation, he hadn't seen it. Not a mean streak visible in that girl. Especially one who was working so hard to find her sister. If Sill lived, Jane would likely get ten years in prison. Bruno hoped that she could find mercy within her family in due course. The kid had made some horrible mistakes, but he held on to hope that there might be a new beginning for her again someday.

Bruno signed the last of the papers. With the necessary help of PI Inc., he had found the truth. It was now time to release it. Bruno bowed his head and prayed that the Parks family, that those young girls, might eventually be able to heal.

E5: MARY'S DIARY

1966

TO MY SURPRISE, my son, Todd, wrote me back. I believe it was my final gift on Earth. Todd told me he understood my situation when I was younger, that I'd been too poor to raise him, and that I found his adopted parents. Another lie he'd been told. I reminded myself that this one was for his benefit. Keeping him far away from this family curse might be the only thing to save him.

My son revealed in the letter that he had married a beautiful and good woman named Madelyn. They lived about an hour from me and that they'd been trying for children for years, but had suspicions that they were barren. They had dreams of two daughters and already had their names picked out: *Jane and Sillian*. The last line in the only letter I ever got from my son:

We're going to keep trying to conceive naturally. I know with confidence that the Lord will give us these girls. Even if it's when we're fifty!

The day I got the words from Todd, I fell to my knees and cried. I knew it was time to write the last page of this journal. For I was about to expire, and my son had given me a permission slip to be *done*.

I let myself through the window of Sophomore Manor, the abandoned crime scene and hallowed halls I'd once called home. In the dusted sitting room, I said one last prayer to a God I wasn't sure existed.

"If you're out there...take my life away and give my son his girls. Right my generational wrongs. Let children complete the cycle of lies and live like *sisters*. Turn them into what Mary and I should've been. What we still should be. Even if my son is fifty. Even if I cannot live another day."

Then I went into the underground once more to type the words you are reading now.

I dream of a world where Mary will forgive me and a world where I can be worthy of her love again, even if in another life. I would give my last breath to see our sisterhood, friendship, and purity again. It is my wish to spend tonight at the creek, where Mary and I had our best day. And there, I will drift to sleep with a heart full of longing for my sister's presence again.

I have a feeling that God will not wake me up.

E6: VIRGINIA PAPER HEADLINES

2023

WARNING: EVIDENCE AHEAD

The Virginia Times

ARTICLE BY: CHIEF STUART SIMMONS

DARK HISTORY
SHOULD IT BE REMEMBERED?

SOPHOMORE MANOR TO BE RESTORED TO ORIGINAL NAME: LILY LAKE ESTATE

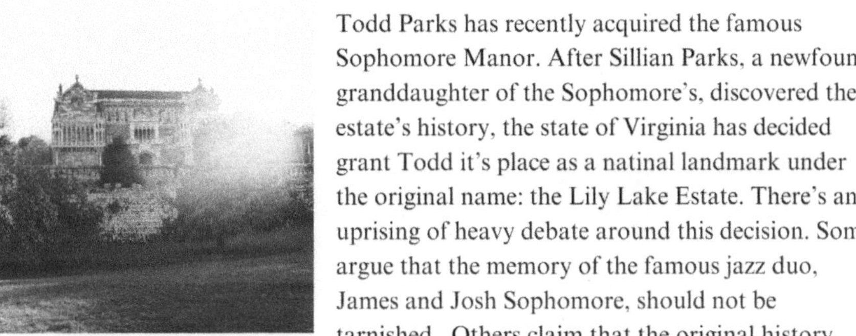

Todd Parks has recently acquired the famous Sophomore Manor. After Sillian Parks, a newfound granddaughter of the Sophomore's, discovered the estate's history, the state of Virginia has decided grant Todd it's place as a natinal landmark under the original name: the Lily Lake Estate. There's an uprising of heavy debate around this decision. Some argue that the memory of the famous jazz duo, James and Josh Sophomore, should not be tarnished. Others claim that the original history of the estate should be remembered. Lily Lake was a women's rights activist and the mother of twins Macie and Mary Sophomore before she died in the 1920's. On the day of her death, she was accused of seven violent murders in the pursuit of her cause. In 1945, the manor was renamed 'The Sophomore Manor' when Macie and Mary Sophomore moved into their departed mother's home with their husbands. This was said to be a political move to cover up the dark history that came with the estate. With the discovery of the property's longstanding history, many citizens of Virginia are at odds with the name. Some say that Todd Parks should come up with a new name entirely; dark history shouldn't be commemorated. Others claim that the name 'Lily Lake Estate' showcases a more evil past than the name 'The Sophomore Manor.' The Lily Lake Estate, which will open as a museum in 2025, is not new to controversy. But I've got to ask the readers: what do you think? Should history, even the darkest of history, set out to be remembered?

E7: TWO YEARS LATER

WARNING: EVIDENCE AHEAD

SEVEN HUNDRED AND THIRTY DAYS. No one came to see me. No one wrote to me. *Jane Parks versus the State of Virginia* was two years ago. There wasn't a single familiar face at my trial. My favorite person in the world hated me, and the person she trusted most tried to kill her. I am alive, but the shame and guilt have made a skeleton of my body and a ghost out of my soul.

I knew I did it when I saw the coat, but I couldn't say if I ever meant to. I wanted to be the hero and became my worst enemy in the process.

I paced the first few days. Those were the good times. Pacing is a level of stress reserved for those who still think they can figure it out. Between those steps, a solution path could be revealed. Blood is still moving, thoughts still churning, and hope is still hanging there in the front of the brain like a carrot. Eventually, that light goes out between your eyes and you realize maybe it never was there at all.

But now I sit here in my cell and rot. I don't pace or move or think. My spirit has crushed my bones.

A year ago, one of the guards slipped me a magazine. My sister's beautiful face was on the front page, on top of a body that sat in a wheelchair. Up until then, I had no idea what fate met Sillian with. I knew she was at least alive because my prison sentence had remained ten years. If she'd died, they'd undoubtedly transition my charges to outright murder. Twenty more years at a minimum. But she didn't. Reading the newspaper interview and confirming she was alive… It was the last thing I had left to care about.

The article said Sillian spent six months in the hospital fighting for her life. After being exposed to extreme temperatures for such a long time, she lost almost all the blood flow to her brain. She'd never walk again. She has a lisp now. I can't bear to think about it for more than a few moments.

Sillian said in the magazine that she was writing a story about her findings from Sophomore Manor. The magazine article talked about me some. Not much, but enough. I deserved what it said. In fact, I reread the article out loud every night like some sort of confessional. A masochistic release.

My prison sentence is set to last eight more years. I'll be thirty-six at my release, but I don't know if I can make it any further. Sharing a small prison cell with a lethal amount of guilt is smothering me. My life is now nothing more than a family tragedy, a story of caution, and a Virginia inmate number. I'm no one's friend. No one's daughter. No one's sister. A blemish of a past life.

That's what I thought anyway, until the guard came to get me this morning.

"Jane Parks. Visitor."

His voice washes over my body like waves at the beach. It takes me a few moments to understand what he's saying.

"Jane Parks, you have a visitor."

"Wh-what?" My voice is raspy and choked dry. I never have to use it anymore.

"Visitor. Come on, now. Get up off the ground."

It takes me over a minute to stand up on my shaking legs.

"I'm coming," I mutter.

My eyes go to her immediately. In the most mundane room in a building full of the most evil creatures in Virginia sits my pretty sister, shining as bright as daylight. Her skin glows underneath her golden hair. A bright yellow shirt drapes across her arms. I want to bask in her rays, yet I can't bear to look too long. It's too painful, like looking directly into the sun.

She brings the phone up to her ear across the glass as she sits in her wheelchair across from me. I'm already in tears. I can't meet her eye. I can't pick up the phone.

I close my eyes and succumb to the pain. The humiliating disgrace that I am, my sister shining across from me right into my ugly orange reality. If I look at her, I will see what I could've been and it will hurt too much.

Finally, she knocks on the glass. It's then that I know I have a choice. It's not a big choice. It won't change anything or right my wrongs, but it's a choice to be better. To face the past. I know I need to take it, no matter how small.

With closed eyes, I place the phone up to my ear.

"Jane." The familiarity of her sound is paralyzing, even with the lisp. The softness of her voice. How I've missed it…

My breathing begins to wheeze in and out as I search for the words. I look down to the ground.

"Jane, it's me."

"I'm so sorry. For everything." I begin to cry waves of unworthiness. "You have no idea how sorry I am."

"I know."

"You should hate me. I'm evil. I deserve to—" I'm heaving on my words, spinning them out in a state of vertigo. I want her to see all of my self-loathing. How much I despise myself for hurting her. It's all that's left of me.

"Look at me, Jane," Sillian says across the glass. I take a deep breath and force myself to look her in the eyes. They aren't teary, they're strong.

"I'm so sorry," I cry again. I don't know what else I can ever say.

"I brought you something, Jane. The guard told me he'd give it to you tonight." She's twirling the ends of her hair uneasily.

I stare back at her blankly. I want her to yell at me. Scream. But she's so calm.

"It's...a file. With everything. It's all there." My sister sighs into the phone across from me.

"Did you find out what happened? With the Sophomore sisters?"

She nods, still holding my eye contact valiantly. "I did. Mary was Dad's mom. Our grandmother."

I gasped at the thought of my father. I've missed him so much. I want to ask her a million questions about him. About her. A small and simple slice of their lives. I could live off of the tiniest morsel for eight more years. What they're doing. How they're living. The most minor story would sustain me. But I hold back. My sister didn't come here to comfort me.

My sister keeps going when she realizes I'm not able to respond.

"And you and I...we almost repeated our family history," Sill says. "Macie Sophomore killed Mary."

"Wow. That's..."

"Awful," she finishes my sentence.

"Right," I say, breaking the eye contact and looking down with tears.

"How did you find out? About them being our ancestors?"

"Remember the 23AndMe kit party?"

"Wow. That's why you rented it out? The Sophomore Manor. You knew."

"They actually call it Lily Lake Estate now actually. It's going to be a museum. It opens in September. Tickets are sold out. Dad even owns it..."

"And your book? The magazine said you were writing a book."

"It's canceled." Her eyes are wet.

"What? Why?"

"Michael's mom. Michael finally publicly outed her. She's a hateful woman. Lost her job. And I made a deal with her for the book beforehand. Exclusive contract. She paid me thirty thousand dollars. Now that she's fired, my book is canceled. I owe the money back. I'd already spent most of it."

"I'm so—"

"Don't be. That's what happens when you make deals with the devil. It's a lesson for me. An expensive one with interest. Michael did the right thing."

So much silence stands between us. It seems to take hours to find words. After all this time. My head is spinning. I want to keep her there across from me. I scan her face for something to say.

"I-I like your earrings." That's the best thing I can come up with? "Sorry. I don't know why I…"

My sister nods at me patiently. "They're, uh…Mary's. Our grandmother's sister. She left behind a bunch of old jewelry. For *us.*"

My heart breaks at that word. *Us.* I never thought I'd hear it from her mouth again. It hurts. I couldn't bear it any more. This is too much for me to handle. I need to go back to my cell. That's where I belong.

"Sillian, why did you come here?"

My sister shifts in the seat across from me. Sweat trickles down her forehead. It didn't occur to me that she might also be nervous to see me.

"I… I'm in trouble. I'm in debt. I wrote this story about every-thing that happened, and I can't sell the manuscript because of the exclusivity contract. But your old boss—"

"Simmons?"

She nods. "He said he'd consider doing a podcast series inter-viewing us. He's trying to modernize his news delivery. He wants the Sophomore story. But more importantly, he wants us to tell it. Both of us. And face what we've done. What *we've* lost."

I'm speechless. There are no words for me to say.

"Before you say yes…" Sill puts her hand in the air. "You should know that it wouldn't be a pretty podcast. We'd have to do it from here somehow. And we'd have to talk about our mistakes. Head on.

Me with the lying and using people and you with the…attempted murder. It wouldn't just be about the Sophomores. It would be about *us*."

"You deserve to tell the truth," I whisper brokenly.

There's a long silence between us. Sillian still knows me better than anyone. I don't have to tell her I'm confused by all this. *Why now? Why ever?*

"You know…" She sighs into the phone, looking away. "I was hoping that if we could showcase some reconciliation through the podcast…or we could at least try to talk about it more publicly— our relationship broken but not hateful. I thought that a little humanity might help get your sentence reduced. Maybe start your life over again. There's more for you beyond this, Jane."

I shake my head.

"No. I traded that possibility in a moment of selfishness."

"I think we can look ahead. Find a new spot in the world for you. Maybe not right next to me, but *somewhere*. I don't think you don't belong in here."

"Why not? I almost killed you."

She swallows hard. "I lost everything, too. I know you're in here and I'm not, but…I treated people horribly. I lied. And I lost every- thing. Everyone. That night, you almost killed me at the manor. There are days I wish you would have. But then, I always remember that you came back to help me. You came back to right your wrong. I'm alive because you came back." Her voice is breaking and I start to cry.

"I want to help move us forward. We can come back. Be better people," she says with a newfound sturdiness.

"I don't deserve that, Sill."

"You're right. You don't." She nods with tears in her eyes. "I don't either. But we have the opportunity to tell our history. To correct our mistakes. Even if it's a small one."

I don't say anything. I'm stuck in a shattered awe.

"When I found our grandmother's story that night in the manor basement, it almost killed me. And if we let it keep going, the cycle of betrayal and hate and remorse, history *will* kill *us*. We deserve to move on. We deserve to be better."

And there it is, my second chance at life. Sillian's daylight found me in my darkest hour. Broken pieces are better than none at all.

"Nothing could be more catastrophic than building a future out of our past."

"Okay," I whisper to my sister, barely audible. Gratitude swirls through my chest like a new heartbeat.

"So you'll take a look at the file then? Chief Simmons wants to start recording in a few weeks. If you decide that you want to."

"I want to."

When I return to my cell, there's a manilla file on the bed filled with family history. And next to it, a pearled vintage bracelet. Mary Sophomore's, I assume. It wouldn't be until later that I learned what the jewelry meant to Mary. A symbol of her honorable ferocity, her desire to keep pressing forward in the darkest hour, and her unconditional love for her fitfully unworthy sister.

With the heirloom wrapped around my wrist, I open the file and find a new purpose. It's finally time to move forward.

THE END

FILE FROM LINDSEY

Thank you for every word that you read. I consider our time together to be my life's greatest adventure.

Your readership was always the ambition that propelled my sophomore novel forward. However, *You've Been Summoned* was originally intended as a simple piece of poetry called *The Sophomore Letters*. I was going through a time where I felt like I'd locked half of myself away from the other half. Like I couldn't have fun with my work and still be taken seriously. So, I tried to write my split personality into union through the symbolism of twins. And then the mystery writer in me took over.

Thirty-thousand words later, I played a mystery board game with my parents around Christmas. It was then I decided that games and literature could be married into an experience. An experiment, if you will. So, I purchased some design licensing and software to toy with the idea of weaving the reader into the story as a character through formatting and visuals. I loved the idea of giving the reader some power inside a traditional whodunit. Instead of waiting to be told what happens, I wanted you to actively feel that you could solve the case. More than anything, I wanted to write a story where solving the case was 100% possible without compromising the elements of surprise and intrigue. That was my goal when I decided to undertake this project.

The twins were meant to feel at odds from the start. I chose the name Sillian because of its carefree whimsy and then the name Jane for how plain it was. Sill was meant to be an enigmatic character that contrasted Jane's pragmatism. Their split narrative was written to mildly distress the reader. The way growing into an individual might feel when you've always seen yourself as a half.

Mary and Macie came into the story almost a year later. I'd discovered postwar cinema and felt compelled to challenge myself to bring a character to life from a dated timeline. Mary's voice came through strong enough that I felt I had to do her justice and find a place for her in the novel. Her story felt necessary to Jane's and I thought the two to be beautiful parallels about what history often looks like: dark.

While this novel was created with a lighthearted intention, I hope it raised questions about history. Especially for my fellow Zillenials. As I age, I have felt the external pressure to erase the darker parts of history from memory. To overlook global injustices, colossal mistakes, and even my own shortcomings. This piece was my small looking glass for those feelings. To remember history so that we do not repeat it.

The agent I spoke with about this novel told me it was too exhaustive to bend literature into a game. I couldn't stomach that answer and decided to take the gamble on the project by myself. I designed every clue. I formatted every word. I've spent every penny it has taken to build this idea because I truly think someone out there might share the love of mystery and enjoy the experience. I hope that this book has found that person. After all, some things don't make sense until they happen. Like an interactive mystery. Or Halloween in March.

Cheers to all of that. Cheers to you.

-linds

ACKNOWLEDGMENTS

There have been many times over the last three years where this novel's transformation has left me at a loss for words. The first of these began with my family, who unknowingly nudged me toward the idea of an interactive mystery in 2021:

To my parents—Thank you for always playing every mystery game with me into adulthood and reading every word I write. Your encouragement means so much. I hope to have made you proud.

To my mom and my grandmothers—I feel lucky to know what generations of fierce women look like through your lives and stories. May they live on for years to come.

To my brother and Hannah—Like Hannah says, siblings are built-in best friends. I'm grateful for that sentiment: past, present, and future. (Lord, help me remember it during our next Spades match.)

To my family at WCP—Thank you for giving me your blessing to attempt my own publishing strategy. I'm so grateful to you, Mike and Paula, for the support that began my writing career. I need to remind you more often.

To my brilliant editors—Bella Ellwood-Clayton, your sage wisdom propelled this book into something greater every time you touched it. Maxine Myer, your keen eyes and attention to detail were a force to be reckoned with. Thank you both.

To my amazing cover designer—Jeff Miller, thank you for your excellence. The book cover you've created exceeded my greatest expectations. I'll be recommending you and Torrey Sharp for a lifetime.

To my beta and sensitivity readers—Louise, your feedback was the polish I needed on the manuscript. Max, your excitement for the novel helped me get to the finish line. I appreciate you both.

To my friends in the industry—God, I love you. It would take another book to explain the warm and fuzzy feelings I get from our writer's community.

To my friends at home—Thank you for keeping me sane for the past three years. (Or insane?) I'm thankful for our crazy journeys that seem to only make sense when we are together.

To Austin, Texas—It's only fitting that this work was finished where it started. I'm amazed by this city and its' supportive, creative community.

To everyone who enjoyed this work—Leaving a storefront review would be a blessing to my career. It's an honor to create things that you delight in. I'd like to keep it up for a long while. You really do give all of this a meaning.

& Finally, to Colin—Your unwavering belief in me is behind every sentence in this book. You've doubtlessly supported my passion from the novel's first page. I'm honored that you chose to sit beside me on the rollercoaster. May it be a constant and wondrous ride together, always holding hands.

Lindsey Lamar is an emerging author in the mystery-thriller space. She's twenty-six and lives in Austin, Texas. Her first novel, *Better Off Guilty,* was published when she was twenty-three. *You've Been Summoned* is Lindsey's sophomore novel and her first self-published work.

You can find more of her work at lindseywritesbooks.com or lindseywritesbooks.substack.com

———————

ABOUT EXPERIMENT 42

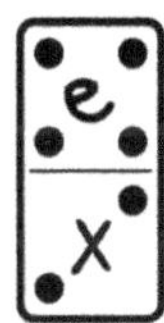

EXPERIMENT 42 is a publishing experiment conducted by Lindsey Lamar. The experiment was founded in 2023 on the hypothesis that independent authors can advocate for their own visibility by taking majority ownership over their own work.

The experiment predicts that authors can hold a majority proprietorship of their writing and still produce high-quality projects. A favorable experiment would result in ex42 assisting authors in bringing their publication dreams to fruition without compromising mass shares of their work. *You've Been Summoned* is the first trial within the ex42 experiment.

---

ex42.net

BOOKS BY LINDSEY LAMAR

- **BETTER OFF GUILTY** | 2021
- **YOU'VE BEEN SUMMONED** | 2024

BOOKS BY OTHER INDEPENDENT AUTHORS

- **DO YOU FOLLOW?** | JC Bidonde
- **GATE 76** | Andrew Diamond

-

Independent authors only have their readers to recommend them. If you enjoyed a book by an indie author, please consider leaving a review.